DEAR CHEYANNE

Copyright © 2024 by Aimee Lynn

All rights reserved. Printed in the United States of America. No part of this book may be used or reproduced in any manner whatsoever without written permission except in the case of brief quotations embodied in critical articles or reviews.

This book is a work of fiction. Names, characters, businesses, organizations, places, events and incidents either are the product of the author's imagination or are used fictitiously. Any resemblance to actual persons, living or dead, events, or locales is entirely coincidental.

For information contact :
http://www.aimeelynnauthor.com
Cover design by Shirley T.
Editor by Abby Eve Editorial
ISBN: 979-8-9888202-0-8

Second Edition: March 2024

10 9 8 7 6 5 4 3 2

Dear Cheyanne

A Tragedy with A Twist

Aimee Lynn

Songs Inspired By the Book

Scared To Be Lonely By Dua Lipa & Martin Garrix
Your Song Saved My Life by U2
Save Your Tears By The Weekend
September By Daughtry
Yellow By Coldplay
Let Me Let You Go By Violet Orlandi
Thistles & Weeds By Mumford And Sons
Faded By Alen Walker
When Your Gone By Avril Lavigne
Oath(Ft. Becky G) By Cher Lloyd
Nobody's Home By Avril Lavigne
Over My Head(Cable Car) By The Fray
Symphony(Ft Zara Larsson) By Clean Bandit
Here's To Us By Halestorm
Unconditionally By Katy Perry
Elephant By Hannah Georgas
Wide Awake By Katy Perry
A Year Without Rain By Selena Gomez
You Broke Me First By Tate McRae
All Too Well(Taylor's Version) By Taylor Swift
The Last Time By Within Temptation
How To Save a Life By The Fray
Dark Side By Kelly Clarkson
Don't Go By Hannah Georgas

Interesting in being the first to see updates, new releases and exciting news?

Sign up for my newsletter on my website: www.aimeelynnauthor.com

Just scroll to the bottom of the home page, fill out the box with your email and you have access to everything above!

This book contains references pertaining to mild language, domestic abuse, violence, topics of death and depression. Viewer discretion is advised.

For my Daughter Eryn Noelle
Mama loves you

Prologue

Dear Cheyanne,
I used to be happy.
 I would wake up in the most significant mood from the best sleep every morning. I was relaxed, rested, happy, pleasant, and lively. I had so many friends I would sit and laugh with for hours. The average laugh a normal human does a day is seventeen times. For me, that number varied from twenty to twenty-five.
 My life was full of grace and warmth. Everything seemed right. Nothing could put me in the worst possible mood. Not even my mother.
 You were taken away from us too soon. My heart ripped from my chest when I learned about the news. I was at school. I went into panic mode and practically turned into Godzilla.
 Part of me felt like no one cared that you were gone. Maybe a few people. Perhaps I may be in denial of the situation. I'm only thinking about myself and my feelings.
 Nothing felt right at that moment.
 I didn't even get to say a proper goodbye to you.

How could I have known you would be taken quicker than I assumed?
I feel empty.
Again, I used to be happy.
Now, I'm not so sure.

Dear Cheyanne—you're gone.

1

Every day, I wake up feeling like a hot curling iron has just been stuck down my throat.
I can't tell if it's from crying at night or screaming into a pillow. No matter what it is, I'm just sad.
I feel blue.
Nothing I try to do will cover up the sadness, not even a hint of makeup.
It was a cloudy day. There was no sight of sunshine in the sky.
That's how I knew that the day was going to be horrible.
That was the kind of weather you get in Hillsboro, Oregon, especially during that time of year, mid-fall.
It did not matter how the weather looked. Today was still very bleak.
I sat, my knees planted against my chest while my arms locked them into place. I felt like I'd been sitting there for days. My hair fell in a low ponytail with curly baby hairs poking out from the side of my head. I wore comfy clothes,

a large-sized sweatshirt, and plaid pajama pants. My black fuzzy socks matched the color of my sweatshirt. My chin rested gently on my knees.

I felt like a statue on a pedestal.

My ears rang from my mom's voice calling for me to get ready, reacting by slowly turning my head toward my bedroom door.

I huffed softly.

It was giving me a migraine. I did not want to get ready. I wanted to stay in my room and never leave. My room had become my sanctuary, and I was not eager to evacuate.

I got some courage to get up and went to my dresser to take Tylenol. It only helps a little but will work for an hour max.

I then proceeded to get ready.

My hair was wavy, and I barely bothered trying to look nice. I wore a black dress with a matching cardigan to hide my shoulders. I hate my shoulders. The sandals were the shoes I was thinking of wearing. My mom was calling for me over and over.

I was dreading this funeral service. I wish I could skip it.

I didn't want to hear all the sappy stories about her and how she would be missed. Because, yes, she would be deeply missed.

I hated even bringing her up in conversation now.

A few weeks ago, my best friend, Cheyanne Wrangler, was driving home from work when a drunk driver slammed into her. I didn't get the call until 3 AM from her sister, Leah. It was a bad situation from the beginning. The doctors said she was lucky to be alive when she got to the hospital.

My heart burned like it was being ripped to pieces when she told me she was in an accident.

I remember asking, "Is she okay?" But all Leah said was, "You better come quickly."

That made my heart tear more. I couldn't tell you how quickly I got out of bed and went to the hospital. I sat in the waiting room for three days; I didn't move. People brought me food, and I only nibbled on it. I did not have the stomach to eat.

I got in trouble for leaving the house that morning and didn't tell my mom where I went. She had been looking for me all morning, and when she figured out what had happened to Cheyanne, she showed up at the hospital.

For most of that morning, she was in surgery. She had a punctured lung, broken arm, and leg, and she had a lot of head trauma from hitting her head on the steering wheel. The rest of that day, she slept. I would, too, if I was in her shoes.

The next day, she woke up once but wasn't speaking, just looking around at everybody with tears.

I was there. She looked scared.

I held her hand, and she even squeezed it a little bit. That made me feel like she was going to be okay. Later that day, she had a seizure, and her brain started bleeding from all the inflammation she had from her head injury. After the seizure, they had to put her on a ventilator into a coma because she was unresponsive.

She didn't respond after two weeks, and soon enough, she was gone.

My head was still pounding—crying was not going to help this situation. I heard my mom calling me repeatedly. I couldn't help but get aggravated.

I grabbed my things and left the room, slamming the door shut behind me. I already knew it made my mom furious, and I was not even near her. I walked down the stairs to see my mother standing at the bottom of the steps. Her arms crossed her chest—as if it bothered her that she was waiting for me. She looked nice for the funeral. She had on a light purple dress with matching heels. It was like she had been waiting on me for hours, if her facial expressions were anything to go by.

As I reached the bottom of the steps, I stared at my mom—before grabbing the keys to my car.

"I'm driving myself," I murmured harshly before walking toward the door.

My mother gripped my arm and pulled me away from the door. She was worried. I get it, but it was the fact she was pushing me to talk about the situation that I was not ready for. I want to grieve on my own.

"Emma-Jean, you are riding with me!" My mother snapped while I pulled my arm out of her grip.

My best friend just had the plug pulled on her five days ago, and she expected me to talk about it already. I wished I could go back to my room and stay in bed. I needed space, but I needed to be there for Cheyanne like she was always there for me. I didn't even get to say goodbye.

"No thanks," I grumbled, walking out the door. I could hear my mother grumble under her breath while I walked out. I got inside my car quickly and pulled out of the driveway.

It didn't take me long to get to the cemetery. It was right in town. There weren't many people there, upon the family's request, which I understood. I saw Cheyanne's ex-boyfriend, Thomas, talking to her family. He was pretty devastated when he heard the news. Cheyanne and Thomas ended their relationship on good terms and remained close friends.

I sighed, my heart beating out my chest. Then, I saw one of our best friends standing and talking to Cheyanne's sister, Leah.

Vada Graham.

A beautiful blue-eyed brunette. I didn't talk to her at first unless Cheyanne was around. I met Vada through Cheyanne. It was all a crazy story. But now, we were all inseparable.

I knew Leah first before I became close to Cheyanne.

She was my best friend in kindergarten. Leah came around with us occasionally, but she also had her group of friends. But Leah and I were still close.

But that was before...

Of course, I'd been hiding away these past few days, not talking to anybody. Vada called to check in three times a day. She always knew what to say and how to make things better for you. Vada is a fantastic friend.

So was Cheyanne.

Oh, I'm getting emotional again.

I needed to sit inside the car to get myself a little more under control. That had become a little harder for me to do. I did hate these kinds of feelings, but losing your best friend was like somebody stabbing you in the heart repeatedly. I had depression a bit in the past, but not like this. Mom thought I should see a psychiatrist to be put on medication.

Right, like drugs were going to help this pain I felt.

I was ready.

I closed my eyes and inhaled the most enormous breath, opening my eyes again and exhaling. I finally stepped out of the car, and Vada immediately saw me.

My mother was pulling up to the cemetery as I got out. As I turned back toward the crowd, Vada was already in front of me with her arms out. She hugged me tighter than ever. She knew I needed a hug. Of course, I hugged her back, but not as tight. She needed one, too.

Vada always gave the sweetest and most genuine hugs. They were warm and comforting.

"Hey, how are you?" Vada asked in her sweet and soft voice. I shrugged.

I was screaming on the inside, wanting to go home— I just needed to let the scream that was built up inside me out into my pillow.

That had been a regular thing for me recently.

I looked to the side to see my mom standing in front of her car. Her eyes were burning into me with a snarl. I wished she would leave me alone about this and let me grieve on my own. Pushing someone to get over a loss wasn't the way to cope. If anything, it made more anger build up inside.

I looked back at Vada, giving her a small smile.

"Fine, thanks—" Was all I said as she locked our arms together, pulling me toward the small crowd of people standing near where Cheyanne was going to be buried. This day was grey and quiet. The weather fits perfectly with how I felt and the situation.

Gloomy and depressing.

"We'll be okay. I got you." She said, squeezing my arm in comfort. It wasn't much comfort for me. My thoughts were circling like a NASCAR race.

Cheyanne was about to be put to rest. I knew realistically if they hadn't pulled the plug, she would've been suffering for months. Even years. They said she would never bounce back. I never really asked what had happened in the accident or where the car was hit. I wanted to know. I looked back to see my mom following, but she stopped to converse with Cheyanne's parents, who hugged each other and cried into their handkerchiefs. You could tell they were old school. The ceremony was about to start. I hope it was a short one.

Cheyanne's casket was sitting still, shut, and ready to be lowered down to the ground.

My heart was pounding in rhythm with my head.

The preacher was talking for what felt like forever. It was time for Cheyanne's mom to speak; I wasn't ready. I sighed, and Vada did, too, while laying her head on my shoulder. It made me tear up. Cheyanne's mom cleared her throat before spitting a few words out.

"I don't—" She stopped abruptly with tiny breaths in her words. "I can't explain the loss all of you are feeling. We all feel the same way." She started as tears began pouring from her eyes.

Her mom was a soft and sensitive lady. I couldn't imagine how she felt losing a daughter. Her dad stood there with his hands folded before him, his head hanging low on his shoulders. Leah was silent. The whole family was in mourning. Her mother continued.

"Losing your child has to be the worst thing for a mother to go through. It's a lot of emotions all mixed into one. Sadness, anger, hopelessness—" I began to cry more. "We will not forget our precious girl. She did not deserve what had happened to her. Pulling the plug on someone you love is not an easy choice to make. But she is no longer suffering and no longer in pain— life for her would have been a living hell if we had not chosen to let her go. We will remember you forever. You will always be in our hearts. May you be laid to rest now, Cheyanne Rose."

I cried more as they instructed me to lower her casket. Vada did, too. We both just held each other and cried. It was silent. Soon enough, the casket was in the ground, and the dirt was tossed in after her.

That was the worst day of my life.

2

1 Month Later

Have you ever stopped for a minute and realized you felt like you had nothing to live for?

At least for me, I sensed that way.

It had been a month since Cheyanne's funeral, and each day seemed more complex and more challenging to wake up.

I felt drained all the time. This had become a problem, but I chose to ignore it. My room was my haven and only had a small amount of light from the open section of the curtains. It wasn't much, but I enjoyed being in the dark now. The light gave me migraines.

Mom had been making me get out of bed and go to therapy in the mornings. My family doctor had prescribed me Prozac for depression and anxiety. I was prescribed some rizatriptan for migraines since that has become an everyday thing now. Plus, Tylenol was beginning not to work. I now had two prescriptions that made me feel dead inside.

Mom said she was worried about me. I understood. I stayed in bed all day in the same clothes I wore the night before. I barely got up to take showers and eat twice a day. I've only seen Vada five times since the funeral. I'd missed so many sessions that my mom became impatient with me. She was still pushing me to be active and get over myself.

But how could I?

Mom insisted I talk to my therapist today.

She was even dragging Vada along with me. Not that I didn't want Vada to come; I didn't want her to feel pushed by my mom. I guessed today I didn't have much of a choice. I had to get out of bed. Even my legs felt done with me today. Every time I tried to stand up, my muscles felt like noodles.

I walked over to my closet to change into something else. I pulled out a light pink sweatshirt and some shorts. I changed quickly, pulling my hair into a high ponytail with baby hairs coming from the sides. I would never fail to keep those baby hairs tame. I had to look somewhat presentable, or I would get yelled at again.

As I finished getting ready, I stood in front of the mirror, checking myself out. Honestly, I looked awful.

It was the first time I had looked in a mirror in so long. My face was flushed and oily. My hair was greasy. I could see it shining in the small amount of light peeking through the window. I hadn't showered in a couple of days. I knew I needed to. I would when I came home.

Promise.

I looked like I'd been hit by a bus. Standing in front of the mirror made me realize how much I hadn't taken care of myself.

My hygiene was a disaster.

My under-eye bags were showing clear as day, heavy and swollen. I was over being sad, but at the same time, it made me feel good when I allowed myself to sit in my misery.

So many thoughts were running through my head. I wished they'd stop.

And then...

She was there.

I could see her sitting on my bed, staring right at me. What was in this medication? I must have been hallucinating.

But I wasn't.

Her same medium-length chestnut hair and her golden-brown eyes were looking right at me.

Cheyanne was sitting on my bed right now, looking at me with a disappointed expression. I must have been dreaming.

She was wearing the last thing I saw her in—her hospital gown. That made things sad. I knew I'd been a disappointment to my peers, but the fact she was watching me with that same look as everybody else didn't make it any better.

Why was she here?

"What are you doing, Emma?" Cheyanne spoke with the same voice I remembered from just a month ago.

She just spoke to me.

I gasped; my body went into shock, taken back from the scene I was playing out in front of me. I felt frozen in a way. I was slightly scared to respond to her question. Her spirit was in my room, looking right at me, seeing what I was doing. Ghosts weren't real. I finally answered after a minute. I
    stared, my eyes attached to the mirror.

"You are dead," I mumbled, turning around slowly.

I wanted to see if I was imagining this through the mirror, but I wasn't. She and I were looking at each other face to face, eye to eye.

The pain in my head began to fester more than it already was. I rubbed my eyes to see if she would go away. As my eyesight focused again, she was still there.

"What are you doing?" I asked hesitantly.

"Checking up on you. You look horrible." Cheyanne stated. I chuckled, licking my dry lips.

"I could say the same for you," I replied.

Cheyanne laughed at my reply. Her teeth showed and were as white as a piece of blank paper.

It frightened me.

Tears were starting to gather in my tear ducts.

Was I talking to my deceased friend?

"No. You aren't real." I spoke, slowly starting to back up to my wall. I was still in shock. Cheyanne stood up, causing me to jump out of terror. She walked toward me with her hand out before me, trying to clutch on.

"I am as real as it gets," Cheyanne spoke delicately. She must know I was frightened.

"This is not real." I rubbed my eyes so hard I saw stars. I needed to wake up from this dream. When I got my vision back, she stood again before me. It was like she was trying to reach out to touch me, but I refused it.

"Emma, hear me out." I felt like I could not move from my spot like I was chained in shackles.

Wake up, Emma.

"You are dead," I mumbled, covering my face with my hands again. *First, it went from losing her and slipping into my depression, and now I was seeing ghosts.*

I must be going crazy.

"I may be dead, but that doesn't mean I'm not watching over you." I heard clearly, my face still hidden.

"Go away." I pleaded, my voice cracking as I begged.

"I am still here for you."

"Wake up, Emma," I mumbled, shaking my head, still hearing her voice.

"Yes, you need to wake up and get your shit together." I heard Cheyanne's voice once again ringing through my ears. It caused my perpetual headache to somehow worsen. That sounded like something Cheyanne would tell me if she was still alive.

"You are dead," I mumbled once again. I moved my hands to cover my ears, hearing nothing but ringing from the silence. I opened my eyes, and she was still there. However, she was not as close as before I closed my eyes. I let go of my ears at a snail's pace.

"I don't believe in—"

"Ghosts? Yeah, well, believe in it." Cheyanne replied with a scoff. She sat back down on my bed, making her ghost self-comfortable. "I'm here to help."

"You can't help me by being here," I whispered. "I cannot grieve if I see and talk to you."

"I'm here always."

And then it was silent.

She was gone, and it made me jump again. I was sweating out of fear. I was, once again, alone in my room. I could hear footsteps walking around my house with how silent it was now. But the footsteps were coming right to my door. I sighed, knowing it was either my mom or Vada.

Luckily, it was Vada. I heard her voice from behind my door, asking if she could come in. I told her to. My door slowly opened, and she peered her head through the crack and smiled at me.

"Hey. Are you almost ready to go? Your mom is waiting for you." I sighed.

Of course, she was waiting for me.

She'd probably been listening through my door.

I wanted to tell Vada about what happened a few seconds ago. I wasn't crazy. I did see Cheyanne, and I heard her voice. We were standing five feet from each other in the same room. If I told Vada what I saw, she'd think I was crazy. I shook my head and came back to reality.

"Yes, I'm ready," I said before grabbing my things and walking out of my room past Vada. I got a whiff of her perfume when I slid past her. I was so frustrated with everything. My mom was already making me go to therapy. If I told anybody that I was seeing ghosts, they would think I was crazy and think I had created imaginary friends.

I began to sluggishly descend the steps to where my mom stood at the door, gathering her things to go. Vada followed me down the steps.

We all strutted to the car; I sat in the back and gave Vada the front seat. I didn't want to sit next to my mom right now. My eyes just stared out the window at my neighborhood. Children played outside on bicycles, skateboards, swing sets, and more. I wished I was a kid again; everything was so simple back then. I could laugh or cry, and people would think I was sleepy or in a bad mood. But not in this reality. If you laugh, you are crazy; if you cry, you need help.

Mom and Vada conversed in the front, but I wanted nothing to do with it.

Don't get me wrong, I did love my mother more than anything. Even after all the difficult times of not seeing Dad because of work, she still put up with my anger. I couldn't be prouder of my mother. But the one thing we all knew she was not good with was boundaries.

Cheyanne was the first person I'd experienced death with at an age I'd understand. My mom's dad died when I was younger. My mom should understand death since she went through it with Grandpa. She took her dad's death hard, but losing your best friend as your first experience losing someone wasn't the way to go mentally.

Sometimes, we needed to cope in our ways, not be pushed to talk. She should be thankful I hadn't even thought about the next steps of depression. As sad and angry I was for losing Cheyanne, suicide had never entered my mind.

I don't think I could ever put that into my mind.

"Are you ready for therapy today?" My mom asked. Her eyes stared at me from the rearview mirror. I didn't know what to say.

"Sure," I murmured, turning my head to stare at everything that was blurring past the car window.

"Maybe some progress will be made." My mom spoke. "I hope."

I wouldn't say I liked talking to my therapist. She was nosy and asked way too many questions for my liking.

Before I knew it, we had finally arrived at the one place I didn't want to be.

Therapy.

3

The room was very bright, like always. It was making my eyes burn. I could feel the excruciating but nauseating headache rising into my brain. There was a chemical smell in the office and a cruel smell. It always seemed to come before a migraine. I might say something about it today.

There was a window on almost every wall. There were posters on the wall that had positive quotes and people smiling. I didn't feel like smiling. I was aggravated to even be sitting on this red, lumpy loveseat. It started to hurt my back. I didn't even remember her name. I glanced down at the desk she was sitting at, looking for a name tag.

Jessie Dayton. Ms. Dayton to me.

She was dressed in a white blouse and a black skirt with heels. The typical outfit that a therapist would wear. Her short yet curly jet-black hair stood still with all the hairspray she had in it. You could see it clearly through the sun shining through the window. She was a pretty person. Her room smelled like the perfume that my mom wore. She was tapping her foot and writing things down in her notebook—it must have been a nervous tick for her.

I wondered what she was going to make me talk about today.

The one thing that was making me so depressed, but maybe she'd make me talk about something else. I highly doubted it. Every time I was here, it was always about Cheyanne. Don't get me wrong, I always loved discussing Cheyanne, but not how I wanted to talk about her. I wished I could talk about something else.

Looking back at Ms. Dayton, I saw she clicked her pen and threw her glasses on. It was time to talk. I sighed. Here we go.

"So, Emma, how are you today?" Ms. Dayton asked me. I looked up at her.

I could feel the smart-ass look growing on my face. I ignored the question about my feelings.

"I've been having some issues with my migraines. I have been smelling chemicals when I feel one coming."

"Yeah, that can happen with migraines. Let me know if it does not get better, and we will get your doctor to look more into this and make sure it is nothing too serious," Ms. Dayton said, writing things down. "Other than that, how are you?"

I shrugged, not making eye contact with her. I didn't respond to her second question. I didn't feel like responding.

I hated looking at Ms. Dayton. I didn't like to see the disappointed look on her face when she heard my answers. She was, if not always, almost disappointed in me for still feeling the way I did. I sincerely apologized for how I felt, but Ms. Dayton also said that I needed to stop apologizing all the time.

That was another reason I couldn't overcome death as quickly as others. Sometimes, I wished people would let me grieve on my terms. You couldn't magically get better.

I heard Ms. Dayton sigh. I looked up and saw the look I was talking about.

Disappointment.

"What?" I spoke harshly.

"You tell me about your smelling problem but will not discuss your feelings." Ms. Dayton replied.

"I don't want to," I spoke truthfully. Ms. Dayton shook her head, listening to my nonsense. I became aggravated with her reactions to me.

"These sessions are for you to discuss your problems, not hide them." Ms. Dayton assured me. My eyebrows shot up.

"What if I don't want to discuss my problems? I should not be forced to speak when I don't want to." I spoke with confidence in my voice. But I watched that same look from Ms. Dayton pop up quickly.

"Emma," She grumbled, her glasses on the bridge of her nose sticking out. Fine. I cleared my throat, making direct eye contact with her.

"I hate it here," I spoke fluently. I could see the frustration show in Ms. Dayton's eyes. She sighed, looking down to write some stuff down.

"You want me to lie?" I snapped, throwing my hands up.

"No, but you need to be serious about this." Ms. Dayton said firmly.

I could see her crossing her legs from underneath the desk she was sitting at. I was not trying to antagonize my therapist; I was again speaking the truth like she wanted. I could be a little harsh at therapy, but that was because I hated talking about my feelings now. Everybody knew that.

I rolled my eyes at my therapist's comment. "You need to be serious about this."

"You want me to be serious?" I hissed a little in a whisper tone. I didn't mean to be rude; it just happened. I was not sorry for it. Ms. Dayton started writing stuff down inside her notebook. What could she be writing down?

"What are you doing—? Stop writing." I snapped, tension rising high in the room. Ms. Dayton immediately stopped scraping the pen across the paper. Her eyes met mine as they snapped from looking down at me. My demeanor was slightly off-putting, but I clarified that I did not want to be there. Ms. Dayton knew how I felt about talking about my emotions.

"I feel like there is some anger inside you, Emma. And it shows." Ms. Dayton said, which made me even more upset, but showing that I was upset meant that she was right. She was testing my anger now. "Especially about the loss of your friend." Ms. Dayton added. "The outbursts you leash are nothing but built-up anger."

I looked up at her, biting at the inside of my cheek. I shook my head with a bit of an eye roll. I was in denial now.

"You don't know anything," I mumbled. I was arguing about the denial I knew I had.

My apologies for not wanting to talk. Then again, I shouldn't be sorry. I hated being forced to speak about something I'd rather not discuss. I wasn't calling shots on how I felt or what I wanted to talk about.

"No, I don't, but you can tell me. Clarify it to me so I can know how you feel." She spoke. I shrugged.

"It's a touchy subject," I murmured, looking down at my lap and picking the skin off my dry, crusty hands.

"This shows that this subject needs to be discussed and addressed more in our sessions." Ms. Dayton replied softly. My eyes slowly rose back up to hers. I sighed softly, breaking our eye contact.

"Ms. Dayton," I paused, looking at what I wanted to say. "I am not ready to discuss this."

"Why is that?" She asked, staring hard into my soul like she knew tension was building up in me. I was doing everything in my power not to have a meltdown.

"Because this is still fresh in my mind, and I believe pushing someone to speak is not the right way to do things." I felt the sharpness in my voice as I spoke. I was becoming angry with the pressure. I took a deep breath in through my nose to relax more.

"Let's start slow." Ms. Dayton recommended clicking her pen so the ballpoint tip would stick out. "So, let's start with the first night." She spoke.

I gulped, my head snapping up when she mentioned the first night. I wouldn't say I liked to talk about that. She meant the night I got the call from Leah about the accident. It was a sensitive topic like all the other ones. I did not want to talk at all. I also knew that Mom would ground me if I didn't at least manage to speak today. It would not be the first time she grounded me from therapy.

"No, I—"

"Tell me about that night, Emma." I gulped at my therapist's words.

Would it get her to be quiet if I talked about this? Maybe. I sighed, closed my eyes, returned to that night, and finally decided to tell my story.

***

I was sleeping.

The room was dark and quiet, and I liked it that way—a hint of light from the streetlights outside. However, the dark was the best way to sleep. My dreams were peaceful. I remember having a dream about me playing with my dog in our backyard. I was throwing her bone, and she ran to catch it. It was a positive, uplifting dream.

It suddenly all stopped, and I heard my phone ringing. I shot up from my sleep, moving my long hair from my face. I was half asleep but also wide awake from the startling ring. It was the beginning of the weekend, so all I wanted to do was sleep in and not be woken this early. It was still pitch-black outside.

I looked over with squinting eyes to see it was Cheyanne's sister, Leah. I sighed. I glanced at the alarm clock on my nightstand to see it was 3:15 in the morning.

What could Leah possibly need at this time of night? I unhooked my phone from the charger, answering it with a dark and dry voice.

"Hello?" I said, rubbing my eyes. "Leah, what do you need at 3 in the—"

She interrupted me, and all I heard was her yelling. My head could not wrap around what she was honestly saying. All I heard was "Cheyanne," "car," "drunk," and "hospital."

I needed clarification. My eyes shot open, and I shook my head.

"Wait. Leah. Slow down. I can't understand you," I said, waving my hand in the air, trying to get at least a concept of what was happening even though she could not see me. I then heard the words that I would never get out of my head for as long as I lived.

"Cheyanne was in a car accident and was hit head-on by a drunk driver. We're on our way to the hospital now." Leah finally spits out. My body froze while sitting in my bed. My mouth dropped open in shock. I threw my legs out from underneath my bed sheets to hang over the bed.

"I-is she okay?" I asked. But I didn't hear a response. I began to panic. "Leah?!" I screeched a bit. I gripped my bed sheets in panic. I needed to squeeze at something to bring my tension down. I heard her hiccup through the phone.

"You better come quick."

***

I was back in that bright white cubed office.

My eyes shot open as I replayed the whole scene in my head. Some tears trickled down my cheek when my eyes opened. I looked up to see Ms. Dayton writing stuff down. She had her glasses back on, taking some serious notes from the looks of it. I sighed a bit, slowly. I could feel the tears begin to burn up in my eyes more. I quickly wiped them away before she saw them.

Talking about that drained me.

I'd never talked about it that way. I wasn't even sure what I told her. I just played back what happened that night and went on and on. It was like I blacked out. Ms. Dayton clicked her pen and threw it down on the notepad like she was finished writing. Even she looked wiped. She took her glasses off and folded her hands together. She looked up at me and gave me the biggest smile I'd ever seen from her.

"You just made the first bit of progress since you started. Great job, Emma." She complimented. I sighed again.

"I've..." I started saying, but instead, I looked down at my hands, picking at them again—nervous habits. "I've never fully talked about that till now," I murmured, looking back at her. She nodded, pressing her lips into a thin line.

"Are you tired?" She asked me. I squinted a bit at her question. What did she mean by that? I just nodded softly, looking up at her. I was tired. Then again, I'm always tired. This isn't anything new for me.

"That's what happens when you make progress." I couldn't help but give her the softest smile. I was glad to have made some progress.

"That's good," I mumbled, letting out a shaky sigh.

Maybe it'll get my mom to shut up for once and leave me alone. She will make me keep talking more. Making progress was a good feeling.

Everything felt a little better.

I got caught off guard.

My eyes were now directed not at my therapist but at the familiar figure standing behind her, giving me a small smile and showing her pride in me.

It was Cheyanne again.

4

Therapy felt like decades before it was over.

I had one-hour sessions twice a week. I had my next session on Friday, in three days. I couldn't wrap my head around the fact that I saw Cheyanne again.

It was like she was following me everywhere. Was she trying to send me messages? Or help me cope with her loss? Whatever the case was, I did love seeing her, but it was not helping me, to be honest.

It makes me feel worse. It makes me miss her more.

So, what if I try? I didn't ask for this.

My mom was inside talking to Ms. Dayton about how my session went. She didn't tell her in-depth what we discussed but summarized how I did. I knew she didn't give my mom the full rundown because my mom hadn't asked me about the mental breakdowns I had the last few sessions. I just sat there and cried for 30 minutes, not saying a word. But that was what therapy was for. You would either feel great after a session or drained and unsuccessful.

I was sitting in the car with Vada. It was the first time she and I had been alone since Cheyanne's accident.

Vada liked keeping to herself after everything happened. She did that even before. But I didn't blame her. I kept to myself; she was just now coming out of her shell. I already knew it would take some time for me. I wanted to tell her that I had been seeing Cheyanne. I'd seen her twice today, but if I told Vada something like that, she would probably tell my mom—or not believe me. My mom would freak out and put me in a crazy house because I saw dead people.

My thoughts were circling.

I glanced over at Vada to see she was smiling at her phone. It looked like she was texting somebody. She was sitting in the back seat with me, but I couldn't determine who she was talking to as the phone screen was dark. I chuckled a bit, shaking my head.

"You going to tell me who's making you smile over there, or will you leave me out of all your secrets again?" I finally said to her, the awkward silence breaking after so long. She quickly looked up at me and locked her phone, putting it down.

"Sorry, it's just a boy I have been talking to. Nothing too serious." She said, trying to hide the pink blooming on her pale cheeks.

I didn't understand why Vada was being so secretive with me. I remembered plenty of times when she and Cheyanne would get into fights, and she would come running to me. I would be the first one to hear about it.

Vada always said, "Don't tell Cheyanne, but..." And then I'd be stuck in the middle of their fights. I swore Vada could never keep quiet when she and Cheyanne got into a fight.

I remember Vada's first heartbreak, too.

Boy, that one was a ride.

When Vada was 13, she started dating Elijah, but we all called him Eli. They were together for three years. They just recently broke up almost a year ago. Since they weren't in school, Vada and Cheyanne attended a party one night. Eli was there. They all got drunk, and Eli cheated on Vada with another girl while intoxicated. But then, a couple of days after the party, he cheated on her again with the same girl when they both were completely sober and then Vada found out about it. Cheyanne and I encouraged her to leave him, and she did.

She was highly torn up over that relationship. Though I couldn't say, I blamed her. It was her first one, and you start having trust issues when your first relationship ends with them cheating. Vada had every right to be upset over a situation like that. I knew I would have been.

She and Cheyanne disagreed because Vada did nothing but complain about him and how much she missed him. Cheyanne knew that he messed up and that she had no reason to miss him. But Vada did. Then again, it happens to everyone at some point. You may miss someone who hurt you, but don't see yourself returning to them.

Cheyanne told her, "Stop dreaming over a boy who does not want you."

It hurt Vada's feelings, but she needed to find a way to get over it. Vada always hated the ugly truth. And Cheyanne always gave it to her. I didn't, so she always came to me if she hated what Cheyanne had to say.

"So, is keeping secrets a thing you do now with me? Because you've been keeping secrets from me for weeks now." I asked in a harsh tone, giving Vada a side-eye.

I heard her sigh softly.

"No, I'm not keeping secrets. I just—" She stopped herself, hesitant to tell me something. I raised my brow at her. "I've been talking to this guy for a little while, but I didn't want to make it public until I knew it was real."

I could see that she was a little serious about this, but Vada has never been someone to keep a relationship a secret. When she was happy with someone, she expressed it as she should.

I just laughed and shook my head at the lies. I didn't care to ask why or when.

"I don't buy it," I mumbled before looking out the window. I didn't, though. I didn't understand what was so secretive about this guy. Was it someone I knew? Was it an ex of someone I knew? So many questions were running through my head again. It was giving me a headache.

It was silent in the car for a moment. Not to mention that Vada had been distant from me since Cheyanne died. I'd been wondering why. I mean, I'd been distant, too, but even before her death, she was like this with me. I asked if she even liked me as a friend anymore. Another thought passed through my mind. But then I felt a tug on my shoulder from Vada's direction. I turned toward her.

"His name is Ezra." She started saying. I was ready to listen to her since she never told me about guys. I felt excited. "He's twenty-three." She said as my eyes grew wide. I mean, yeah, sure, Vada just turned nineteen, but this boy was twenty-three years old. You'd think she would go for someone a little younger.

"Twenty-three?" was all I replied. Vada chuckled, giving me a slight nod.

"He's a good guy, Emma. You'll see it one day." Vada replied to me. I probably wouldn't. I'd never met any of Vada's boyfriends first, at least not before Cheyanne. I got it, though. Cheyanne knew Vada first and vice versa. I also understand that Vada didn't have a friend anymore she could go to and feel comfortable talking to boys with. But it did kill me a bit that she didn't tell me things like she did Cheyanne.

"Will I, though? You tend to keep secrets from me." It didn't sound polite, but it was the truth. Vada laughed softly, nodding to me.

"I know I have been keeping some distance since Cheyanne died, but I promise to stay around from now on." She replied. "I'm sorry for always keeping secrets. I just... like keeping you away from drama." She added, making me roll my eyes when she couldn't see me.

"It's been a constant thing since you and Cheyanne graduated," I replied, returning my head to her. We made eye contact. She could tell that it hurt my feelings, keeping me out of things the two used to do.

"That's our fault. We did not mean to make you feel excluded." The silence grew over the car for a moment. "But I need to add that you have been excluding me since Cheyanne died. You won't talk to or try to hang out with me or anybody. That is also not my fault." Vada said proudly.

I didn't know what she was trying to do here. I was not trying to fight; I was speaking the truth. Vada never seemed to want to hear the truth.

"I was not trying to fight with you, Vada," I spoke as she returned to staring at her phone. She was most likely texting whoever she was 'talking' to. She raised her eyebrow and shook her head softly at my comment. I decided to let it go and discuss something she was fascinated with.

"So, tell me more about Ezra," I told her. Vada looked over at me, confused. Sometimes I felt like she didn't trust me.

I saw my mom and Ms. Dayton walking out of her office and talking still. They seemed to be in happy spirits.

That was good.

That meant Ms. Dayton told my mom I did well today, though I have yet to be told what she and my therapist discussed.

"I'll tell you another time," Vada murmured as I saw my mom start walking toward the car, hopping inside when she opened the door. "I don't want to have boy talk in front of your mom." She whispered to me so my mom couldn't hear what she was talking about.

"Okay, guys, let's get home." My mom said, looking back at us and smiling at us. "Vada, would you like to stay for dinner?"

"No thanks," Vada replied, shaking her head before her eyes were glued to her phone. I could tell all she wanted to do was go home.

She did not want to be around or talk to me now that I confronted her.

"Mom, mind if I shower when we get home before dinner?" I asked softly, noticing Vada in the corner of my eye growing a smile through her phone. It must be Ezra again.

My stomach twisted at the thought of love. What even is love?

"That's fine." My mom replied. We then dropped Vada off and started making our way home. She barely said bye to me. She jumped out, thanking us, and then ran into her house.

She was ready to be home.

Vada set off that vibe when you knew she didn't want to be around you anymore. She just wanted to be at home, talking to all the boys she spoke to. Maybe I asked too many questions.

If I was being frank, since Cheyanne passed, she had been very distant and would only want to be around when she wanted to be. I heard that from Cheyanne's sister, Leah, since she and I were closer than I was with Vada; she'd been around this boy a lot since before the funeral.

I didn't know about it.

Truthfully, I think I heard it through Cheyanne. I stayed the night with her three days before her crash. I remember her telling me that they got into a fight, but I couldn't remember what about now.

"Ms. Dayton said you did a great job today." My mom said, breaking our silence. I looked up at her from the back, smiling softly.

Thanks." I replied
We rode home in silence again.

5

    The burning water hitting my body felt like little bee stings. I loved the pain of it.
    I enjoyed taking a nice hot shower. It had been a few days since my last shower.
    My mental state had been telling me no to the showers. When I did shower, I took so long. Standing there under the water was like a breath of fresh air. I could feel all the toxic feelings being washed away. I had the dimmest light on in the bathroom to help my pulsing headache.
    It indeed did work.
    When the citrus-smelling shampoo was scrubbed into my head, the headache felt like it was releasing. The only sad part was that it did not stay gone forever. When it all got washed out, it went away. The smell of conditioner on the ends of my hair made my whole- body tingle with positive vibes.
    But I knew the vibes wouldn't last. I wish I could stay here all day.

When I squeezed my loofah, the sweet smell of my Dove body wash, cucumber, and green tea flooded my senses. It was my favorite scent and always made me feel clean and refreshed. I used my hands to soak all the soap into bubbles and lather my skin.

Showering used always to be my favorite part of the evening. I used to take baths and have candles lit with bath salts sprinkled inside the tub. I could sit there for hours. Those bath salts always helped my feet after a long day. I played many sports back then, so sitting in a hot bath with those salts always took the tension off my feet and legs.

I wished I could be like that again.

Right now, I didn't care.

I rinsed off the soapy substance from my body, watching all the suds swirl down the drain. I sighed, inhaling the wondrous scent my body gave off. I wanted to wash for a second time but chose not to. I had to get out.

I then proceeded to wash the oils off my face with my face wash.

I could smell my mom's cooking through the vents from the bathroom. I smelled spaghetti sauce. She must have been making her famous spaghetti for dinner.

Being it just her and I, most of the time, she doesn't have to do too much cooking. I had an older brother named David, but he's off college doing his own thing. We rarely see him anymore, but that's because he's one of those boys who locks himself in his room to play video games. He was always that mean brother who didn't care about anything.

My dad was barely home. He is a heart surgeon and worked over 12-hour shifts six days a week.

Sometimes seven.

He worked at a hospital in Portland. I was surprised my parents were still together. They met in the same hospital since my mom was a nurse. He was more of a big boss in the cardio wing of the hospital. He made good money. My mom was a stay-at-home mom when David and I were younger, but once we returned to school, she returned to work.

After realizing I'd been in the shower for over 30 minutes, I had to leave. Sadly. I leaned down to turn the water off.

I grabbed my towel and was instantly hit with a cold blast of air. Goosebumps started forming on every inch of my body. I wrapped my towel around my body, feeling warm and comfy. The bathroom was still warm from all the steam from the blazing hot shower. You couldn't see anything through the mirror from how fogged it was.

I started drying my whole body off so I could walk without leaving a trail of water from the bathroom to my room. As I was drying my body off, my hair was next. I quickly dried that off. I opened the bathroom door, letting all the steam shoot out from that little room into the hallway.

I quickly made my way into my room so I could dress. My mom's voice from downstairs in the kitchen stopped me.

"Emma! Dinner is about to be ready. Come on down when you are done!" She yelled from the bottom of the stairs.

I responded with a quick "okay" before entering my room to put some clothes on. As I entered my room, I went through my drawers, grabbing underwear, a sports bra, grey leggings, and a black sweatshirt. I threw my clothes on quickly so I was warm and cozy. I grabbed my brush from the dresser and walked over to the mirror to brush it out.

As I brushed it out, I kept looking behind me through the mirror to see if Cheyanne could sit there like she was this morning. I sighed; she wasn't. I wished she was. I finished brushing my hair and closed my eyes for a second. The first thing that popped into my head was what she was like before she died. How good of a friend she was to me.

As I opened my eyes, she still wasn't sitting there.

I'd been wondering why suddenly I'd been seeing her, hearing her talk, and acknowledging her features. What, indeed, was she trying to tell me?
I then remembered my mom had dinner ready. Shockingly, I was hungry for once. I hadn't had the strength to eat anything for the past month. My mom would make my favorite meals, but I never wanted it. But today, I'd been hungry all day. I put my brush down and left my room, heading downstairs to eat.

When I entered my kitchen, the whole room smelled amazing. Mom had a plate ready for me sitting on the island of our counter. My dad was home for once, making me happy to see him. I never do. I gasped softly at his presence.

"Hey, Dad." I greeted him, walking to the island to sit beside him. I glanced down at both of our plates. He was halfway done. My plate had spaghetti, meatballs, a piece of garlic bread, and a water bottle. Mom had it all ready for me. I gave her a small smile, walking over and sitting down.

"Thanks, Mom. How was work?" I asked my dad, trying to converse with him since I had never seen him.

"Good." He spoke. "I did three surgeries today from 6 AM till 5 PM. All three recovered well. It was a pretty good day!"

I couldn't help but smile at how proud my dad was of his work. He should be. From what I'd been told, he was an outstanding heart surgeon. Many people came from states away to have procedures done by him.

He was the best.

"How are you, sweetheart?" He asked, looking at me, waiting for some honesty. I shrugged at his response.

"I'm fine. Just tired, is all." I replied and began eating my spaghetti. I was taking massive bites—more than what I usually ate. As I said, I was hungry.

My dad and I were having a whole conversation about our days when we were interrupted by my mom.

"Jim—" Both my dad and I looked at my mom, who looked to have a severe look on her face. My dad also got serious, like they were communicating through their minds.

In the back of my head, I kept thinking, "What's wrong?" I say this because my mom never had a plate ready for me. These past few weeks, I had been different because my mom had been trying to get me to eat something since the funeral. She never had my food decked out like this.

I finally built up the courage to ask.

"What? What's the occasion?" I asked them both, swirling my spaghetti and taking a big bite. I could hear my mom sigh as she made herself a plate. I watched her. She was moving at a slow pace like she was nervous. I raised my brow, taking a big bite of my garlic bread. I got three bites into my food until my mom started the whole talking stage.

"We'd like to talk, honey." She said in a sweetish-toned voice. Great. Here came the 'you can talk to me' speech. No matter how often she begged me, I didn't want to talk about it. What part of that did she not quite understand? I rolled my eyes at the thought of my mom wanting to 'talk,' chuckling right after.

"I could tell something was up with you two. You are making my plate all nice. Dad's home and sitting with us. I could tell that I was getting an intervention." I spoke sharply.

My dad did not look pleased with the attitude in my voice.

Mom always made a delicious meal and then ruined it with 'the talk.' She finished making her plate and stood before me, leaning against the counter to start eating.

"Not that talk." She spoke. "I am talking about... possibly getting back to school."

I scrunched my nose at the topic of getting back to school. I didn't want to go back to school. I had no friends there, really, except for Leah. But Leah and I didn't have any classes together because I was at a higher learning level than she was. It gave me anxiety thinking about going back to school.

"Why?" I asked. "I thought I was going to be homeschooled?" I added. My mom and I talked about homeschooling before, but that was before Cheyanne died. That would be nice to be homeschooled. I could do everything from my room and listen to music all day. That, to me, was life. My mom looked hesitant, eyeing my dad, trying to get him to say something. She knew that was something we were talking about doing.

"Yes, it was something you two discussed, but I think you need... human interaction," My dad said.

Human interaction? I don't need that.

Not to mention, my mom probably had a rehearsal talk with him.

"A depressed person needs people in her life." My mom added.

"Mom, I don't need anybody else. I have you, Dad, Vada, Leah, and well... that's it." I said as I took one last bite of my food. I knew this conversation wouldn't get anywhere, and just talking about things made me less hungry. I could tell what I said to my mom made her sad. I knew she was worried about me, but I wished she would give it time.

"I think that's good enough for me," I said, taking another big bite of my salad.

"Emma, returning to Glencoe High will be good for you. It's a great school." My dad said, finishing the last bit of spaghetti on his plate. I didn't say anything. I'd rather not. I just started taking small bites of my food, growing uncomfortable with this topic.

"Honey, I think you need more people to socialize with." My mom said.

"I'm good," I replied, eating more.

"Emma— "

"I said I am good, mom." I started to get infuriated. She was becoming pushy with this talk she planned.

I was starting to lose my appetite more.

"Emma Jean, don't talk to your mother like that." My dad grumbled, making me annoyed. Most of the time, my dad had my back when my mom started getting too close for comfort. But now the shifts had changed. "It is not your decision whether you go to school."

"Guys, I don't want to go back to school. It gives me lots of anxiety, and the last time I was there, I—" I was interrupted by my mom.

"Emma, you need to go too," I interrupted her as well. My anger grew quicker than I could control.

"No!" I snapped. "I don't want to go to school. I want to stay here. Is that so much to ask?" I raised my voice slightly. I could tell it was making my mom mad at me, raising my voice at her. My dad looked dumbfounded. He did not know what to say or how to react to my episode.

"I don't appreciate you to-" I know she was about to say tone.

"My tone, Mom? You've told me that too many times now. When will you realize that I want to grieve on my terms? "I jumped up, not wanting dinner anymore. I was just angry now. I wanted to be alone, but my mother never let me. "I lost my best friend, and I don't think pestering me to do the things you want me to do is going to help anything."

"Emma!" She yelled at me as I walked out of the room. I ignored it.

"I'm done having this conversation!" I yelled, running upstairs. Anger grew more, but anger started turning into anxiety.

I got to my room and shut the door. I was tired of being sad. I was just exhausted, angry, weak, and scared. I began sobbing, once again, like before. My fingers locked into my hair and began pulling the top of it; my head started hurting from how hard I was pulling. I wanted to throw something.

I could hear my parents talking downstairs. I was a disappointment to them.

"I don't know what else to do for her, Jim."

"You can't be so demanding when she is going through a rough patch in her life. Come on. Her friend just died. You need to give her a moment to breathe." Thanks, Dad.

"Well, Jim, I am here with her day and night. I don't see you doing something about her little episodes when you are here." *Bitch.* There is no need to be mad at Dad for paying the bills and saving lives.

"Well, Patricia, if you would give the kid her space, maybe she wouldn't be so overwhelmed with life." *Thanks again, Dad.* This was turning into an argument.

My chest began hurting from the bickering.

Yes, anxiety was coming.

I started throwing a tantrum like a baby would.

Everything from my dresser went flying onto the floor. I did not hear my mom yelling for me. She was used to the noise by now.

I dropped to the floor. I was tired of fighting this feeling.

What made things worse was I looked up at Cheyanne sitting on my bed again, right where she was this morning.

6

I was beginning to get frustrated with this situation.
Why was Cheyanne here?
I could see the same disappointed look she had been giving me every time I saw her. I had the sensation of growling in frustration. In the back of my head, I was so excited to see her every time she popped up. I wanted to hug her and never let go. However, it was weird. I began realizing how selfish of a friend I was.

Seeing Cheyanne was a blessing, a weird but crazy blessing. I was just frustrated.

"Why are you here?!" I yelled, walking toward my deceased friend. I finally just wanted answers. She did not say anything. She just sat there, blinking at me when I raised my voice. "Answer me!" I yelled louder.

No response.

She did not even blink from the intense echo of my voice. I felt like I was slowly turning into a crazy person. One month after her funeral, she decided to make an appearance in front of me. I just really needed to know what she wanted from me.

"Answer! Me!" My voice echoed through my whole room.

All I saw of Cheyanne was her watching me. I then heard my mom running up the stairs, yelling my name. Cheyanne eyed the door when hearing my mom's voice. Before I knew it, she was busting through my door without permission. My dad was right behind her. It was an obvious elephant in the room that I just had a mental breakdown.

A very much-needed mental breakdown I had. It'd been days.

"Emma, who are you talking to, and why are your things on the floor!?" She yelled, obviously a little annoyed with me. I turned toward where I saw Cheyanne, about to say something, but she was nowhere in sight.

I was lost.

I saw the anger in my mom's eyes. My dad whispered my mom's name, trying to calm her down, but it was not working. As I've said before, I did not want to tell my mom about me seeing Cheyanne. She would think I've jumped the bandwagon and lost it. I didn't say anything.

"I—" Was all that I got out without freezing. I never fought with my mom, not like this. I was never this way before the tragedy. I just had so much anger in me for the person that did this to Cheyanne. I couldn't bear it.

"Okay," Was all my mom got out before I started walking over to the mess I had made on the floor. You could tell she was furious, and my dad was growing annoyed with her inpatient tone with me. I get it. I was too much for her—the only way of 'getting me to talk' involved yelling at me.

"First of all, you need to clean this up. Second, you are going back a day early to see your therapist again tomorrow because this right here is you not being okay. And third, as an end to our discussion, you are returning to school next week. That is final." My mom snapped a bit at the end. It hurt me.

I just had a hysterical breakdown, and all she did was talk about the worst things to bring up instead of hugging me. My dad mouthed, "I'm sorry," before leaving the room and shutting the door behind him. If my dad were around more, he would be the parent I'd go to for anything.

I could hear my parents' voices bickering more as they returned downstairs. I started to cry again.

I felt trapped. Truthfully, I just wanted a hug. My mom didn't know how to help me grieve in a comforting manner. My dad was too busy dealing with work and her. I started rubbing my eyes and then my face in frustration.

"Wow." Was all I heard, causing me to jump out of my skin. I looked up to see Cheyanne again. I groaned. "Your mom has never changed, has she," Cheyanne said. I closed my eyes again, rubbing my eyes to see if she would go away. She didn't.

"Chey, what do you want?" I asked softly, staying as calm as I possibly could. How do you talk to someone deceased?

"I'm just checking on you." She said softly.

"You need to go. Please." I demanded, but she still stayed.

I have said this thousands of times, but how possible is it to see ghosts? I didn't believe her. She was not just checking on me. I had no time to go through this. I shook my head. I needed to get out of this house. But who should I go to?

I didn't feel like talking to Vada about these things. It didn't seem like she cared. I stood thinking while Cheyanne just sat there. Then it hit me, and I started to gather my things to head out.

"What are you doing?" Cheyanne's voice rang through my ears. I tried so hard to ignore it. It was hard, but I was doing it. I grabbed my phone and scrolled for Leah's name. It'd been a little while since I'd talked to her.

"Going to see your sister. I need a friend." I mumbled before grabbing my things.

"But I'm here." I heard Cheyanne's voice from behind me. I couldn't help but break down inside again. I shook my head.

"No, you are not," I mumbled, walking out of my bedroom and leaving Cheyanne alone.

***

It'd been forever since I'd been in Leah's home. It was so weird to say the house was just Leah's. Her family welcomed me with no questions asked. I sighed.

The Wrangler's home looked the same as the last time I'd been here. They had always been the kind of people who stayed clean, and they taught that to Cheyanne and Leah. I remember they had to clean their rooms every day and couldn't leave the house until they were spotless. Their parents taught them cleanliness when they were young.

I even learned a few things from them, but obviously, I'd gone off balance with that routine.

Leah and Cheyanne's parents were money-makers, believe it or not. They bought a beat-up house and transformed it into a marvelous place on the inside. Their mom was a teacher; she taught English at a school within our district area. Not the school we went to, but a school in a different town.

Their dad was a businessman; he owned his own business. It was a couple of fast-food franchises. One was an ice cream Parlor in town, and the other was a fancy, expensive restaurant in Portland. He had two more fancy restaurants open worldwide in California and New York.

He always told me I could get a job at the ice cream place when I was ready. It was still in the back of my mind.

I sighed at the sweet smell of their house. Candles were always lit up; scents were continuously sprayed. I told you, clean people. I was greeted by their mom, Cathy. She was a lovely lady. She always greeted me at the door, asked me about my day, and offered me a drink. I just needed to be out of the house, and this was where my thoughts were safe.

"So, Emma, how have you been doing?" Mrs. Cathy Wrangler asked me, bringing my thoughts back to reality. I sighed.

What did I say to a mom who just lost their daughter a month ago? Maybe something like, "I feel awful. I miss Cheyanne a lot. My head and eyes burn, and I am in a severe depression."

No. Don't say that to a grieving mother.

"Good. Could be better, you know?" That was all I said, giving her a small smile. "Um..." I stumbled a bit. For some reason, my words weren't gathering at all. It was a little sad. Why was I stumbling? "How are you?" I asked gently.

"Doing my best. I go back to work next week." She said, pouring some coffee for her and Leah's dad. Coffee was always their parents' guilty pleasure.

Four cups of coffee a day.

"You are brave," I spoke awkwardly to Mrs. Wrangler. She laughed, walking to the living room to give her husband his coffee.

"Yeah, well, we need the money." She replied, sitting next to her husband on the couch. "How is your mother?"

"She's good," I answered her question carefully. "She's still at home and doing her best to be there for me." Though my mom and I just got into a disagreement before coming over here, my heart hurt for the way I treated her. She was worried for me, but invading my emotions wasn't the way to go at me. Even my dad gave her an earful. I finally ended our awkward encounter and asked the question I had wanted to ask since I stepped inside the house.

"Is Leah here?" I asked, scratching the side of my head like a nervous tick. They had the evening news playing throughout the living room. Her mom nodded.

"Yes. She's in her room. She said she was expecting you." Mrs. Wrangler said. I thanked her before ducking off into the upstairs area of the house. I walked past Cheyanne's old bedroom, which made my heart sink into a big wave of depression. I just wanted to go in there and see her room.

Should I peek in? Yes. I should.

I slowly crept over and opened the door slightly. It was the same. I wanted to cry.

I sighed, shutting my eyes, remembering when I stayed the night here three days before Cheyanne's accident.

***

The room was dimmed. The ample light attached to the ceiling fan was turned off, and all the string lights that floated around Cheyanne's room were on. We were laughing. It was just the two of us. Cheyanne wanted to do my hair and braid it. God bless her because I could never braid, no matter how many times somebody showed me. It never worked.

This was a happy time in my life when I felt complete. I had my friend, and we were having the best time.

"Hey, do you want to call Vada and ask if she wants to join us?" I asked, turning toward Cheyanne, who was braiding my hair. I saw her shake her head in the corner of my eye, giving a dirty look to nowhere.

"No. She's with her new boyfriend." Cheyanne mumbled. I could feel her finishing my braid and tying my hair down. I scrunched my nose, hearing that Vada had a new boyfriend. She'd never mentioned the boys in her life, except for Eli. But that was a whole different story.

"I didn't know she had a boyfriend," I said, turning my body toward Cheyanne. She shrugged, looking down and playing with her hair.

She seemed to know the boy and didn't like him.

"Yeah, well, he's disrespectful to me, and I told her that he doesn't need to be around you or me," Cheyanne spoke. "If she wants to choose boys over a friendship, that's her doing. I won't sit around and let a grown man say things about me." Cheyanne seemed angry with this new boy Vada was seeing. Cheyanne was describing him as a grown man. I needed clarification.

Cheyanne and Vada must be in another fight.

"What did he say?" I asked kindly, being careful not to trigger Cheyanne into anger. That could quickly be done when it came to Vada's actions.

"Seems like he will do anything to get rid of anybody to have Vada all to himself," Cheyanne mumbled.

7

"Seriously, Emma?"

Leah was giving me a look like I was crazy. I finally told someone I was seeing Cheyanne. I knew she wasn't going to believe me. How would anyone feel when they heard that someone was visiting your deceased sister? I could see the judgmental look on her face. It disappointed me for a moment.

"I'm serious," I mumbled, pacing back and forth inside Leah's room.

Anxiety was getting the best of me again. I could see Leah shaking her head, resting her hand on her forehead.

"Why would I come here and make something up like that?" I asked. I stopped pacing, looking over at Leah, throwing my arms in the air. I sounded crazy. It was silent for a moment before Leah broke it.

"How much sleep have you been getting?" Leah asked. I groaned in frustration. I was depressed. I slept more than the average, but I was okay. Was I, though?

"I'm fine on sleep," I mumbled, continuing to pace. I bit my lip, not knowing what else to say to her—not knowing how to explain it and what I was seeing. "I'm being serious. I've been seeing Cheyanne, and I think she is trying to tell me something." I quickly said. Leah shook her head.

I knew it was hard to believe things like that, and I knew I sounded crazy. You know, in TV shows and movies where the dead person returns as a ghost haunting the main character? That dead person is trying to tell them something about their death or that main character's life. Call me crazy, but it happens in many shows and movies.

So, they go and tell someone before they go crazy.

For me, I was going to get worse if I didn't tell someone. Who else was I going to tell? Vada barely listens to me as it is. My mom would put me in a psych ward if I told her. Cheyanne was gone. I had nobody else. I heard a distraught Leah sigh. I think all of this was too much for her.

"I don't know. Truthfully, you sound crazy." Leah spoke. I knew I did.

"Yes, I do, but it is true," I added. I felt like ripping my hair out.

"Please sit. You are making me dizzy." Leah blurted out.

I realized I'd been pacing back and forth in her room. My legs were starting to feel like noodles from the amount of pacing I was doing. It was the most exercise I had gotten in a long time. I stopped, turned toward her, and quickly shuffled to sit on the bed. We were silent for a moment, but my mind wasn't.

What if Cheyanne was here because she was trying to help me find the person who hit her head-on? She possibly gave me clues when she showed up as to who I could turn to. Maybe she knew who hit her; she couldn't speak when she woke up. But maybe! She knew who did it.

"Maybe..." I started saying to Leah. "She is here to help me find her killer," I mumbled. I could see Leah's cheeks go from pink to flush. It cringed Leah to hear that her sister was killed. I didn't blame her. Leah rolled her eyes. "No, I'm being serious. Maybe we can figure out who hit Cheyanne in that other car together."

"Emma, do you hear yourself? You sound like you're from Law and Order." Leah looked aggravated by my conspiracies.

I wanted to know who hit Cheyanne and who the drunk driver was. I felt like this would help me cope with her loss; knowing that her killer was locked away, maybe I'd feel better.

"Come on, Leah. Wouldn't you like to know who hit your sister?" I asked, watching Leah roll her eyes at me once again. I knew she did want to know. She'd wanted to see since they closed Cheyanne's case after not finding enough evidence—they called it a drunk driver who hit her.

"Maybe that is why I'm seeing her spirit," I added.

"Okay, so tell me, is Cheyanne here right now?" Leah asked. I looked around slowly. I knew she wasn't going to be here.

Being inside her house couldn't be a clue as to who hurt her. That was unless one of her family members did it, but I couldn't see them being a part of something like that or wanting to hurt their child. I shook my head.

"No, I don't see her," I mumbled. "She's not going to be here. There are no clues in your room anyway." I spoke.

"This just sounds insane," Leah spoke, picking at the ends of her light blonde hair. "What are you trying to do here, Emma?"

"I want to know what happened," I replied, making eye contact with Leah. "Don't you?"

"Of course, I do, but her case is closed—they couldn't find anything. There is nothing on mine or your end we could do." Leah spoke softly. "We have to come to terms with that."

We were in silent mode again for a few minutes. That's when Leah's eyes grew wide, giving me a small smile.

"Maybe something in her room is a clue," Leah said before getting up and walking toward her bedroom door. I followed.

I didn't want to go back to Cheyanne's room. I didn't want to go digging through it, either. That place was full of memories.

Good memories.

I could not ruin a good memory. But I still followed.

Did I want to invade her privacy? No. But did I want to help her find peace? Yes. This may help her go to peace.

Leah opened the door to Cheyanne's room. A blast of cold air hit us as the door opened.

That wasn't spooky at all.

Goosebumps began forming on my arms. That usually happened when there was a presence of a spirit nearby. Cheyanne better pops out if I was feeling this way. The goosebumps from the cold air made me shiver a bit out loud. Leah laughed softly.

"Sorry, sometimes this room is colder than normal." She explained as she turned the light on and walked inside the room. I smiled softly. It was creepy to hear that Cheyanne's room had always been so cold since she died. How does Leah sleep in the room next to Cheyanne's, knowing how cold this room can get?

Even though I snuck inside here to see her room before I went into Leah's room, seeing and remembering the memories I had here made my heart tingle. "Let's see what we can find," Leah added, looking around at Cheyanne's stuff.

I stepped into the room to look around like Leah was doing. I smiled as I walked to Cheyanne's picture wall over her bed. I could see so many people on that wall. Of course, Leah and I were one of them. I saw a picture of her, Leah, and her parents that they took at Cheyanne's graduation party two years ago. I took that picture for them. Then, I saw photos with a few other people that same day. I saw her,

Vada, and a girl and guy from the group they were in with their grades.

Daniel and Chelsea. I'd never met them, but I heard they were always sweet. I also saw many pictures of her and me on that wall. She and Vada and so on. Some of her work friends. I never realized how many people Cheyanne was close with before.

I walked over to her dresser, or as she called it, her clutter space. I slowly opened her top drawer, seeing it was, for sure, her junk drawer. She had pictures of her ex, Thomas Avery, and a dried bouquet of roses he got for her before they split up.

Cheyanne used to dry her flowers and make crafts with them or hang them on her walls. She and Thomas broke up a couple of weeks before her accident. They stayed good friends, so she kept his things. He disappeared after hearing the news about her death. Nobody had seen him since. It is sketchy, but I last saw him at her funeral.

I saw old pictures of her and Vada in middle school. I couldn't help but laugh. They both were babies. Something also caught my attention. She had a lot of pictures of the two of them in there.

I slowly headed to the wall to see that the only pictures on her wall that Vada was in were the ones with her high school friends and the three of us. She replaced Vada's photos with those of others like Leah and me.

That was strange. Why did she take pictures of Vada off her unique wall? Vada was always on that wall. Apart from Thomas when they were together. The last time I was in her room was our previous sleepover, which came to mind, and their pictures were on her wall. She must have taken them down after I left or something.

When I turned towards Leah, I gasped softly. Cheyanne was standing next to Leah, watching her go through her things.

"Getting warmer," Cheyanne sang softly while pacing around her sister. I wanted to yell Cheyanne's name out while I was watching her. She didn't seem mad about us going through her things.

What did Cheyanne mean by getting warmer?

"Emma, over here." I heard Leah's voice coming from her make-up vanity. She was looking around at her stand, which was full of make-up. I closed her junk drawer and headed over to Leah.

"You'd probably know more than me, but did Chey and Vada get into it before she died?" Leah asked, picking up a picture frame that was sitting face down. It was a picture of her and Vada. Cheyanne was kissing Vada on the cheek. But what made it strange was the black "X" over Vada's face that said traitor at the top of the picture.

I found this strange because the answer to Leah's question was a fat yes. They got into it over Vada's boyfriend, Ezra.

"Yes." I heard Cheyanne whispering next to me. "Big fight."

"Shh, I can't think," I whispered to Cheyanne. When I turned back, Leah looked at me with a scrunched brow. That's when her eyes widened, looking behind my shoulder.

"Is she here?" She asked with a screech in her voice. I could see the tears poking through her eyes. I nodded, smiling softly at her.

"Tell her I said hey," Cheyanne whispered again in my ear. I cringed at the whispery voice in my ear, turning back to her. She had a smile planted across her face.

"Cheyanne says hey," I murmured to Leah, who lost control of her emotions. At first, she did not believe that her sister was here with us. Now, hearing this from me, she had realized I was not as crazy as she made me out to be.

If only Cheyanne would show herself to Leah.

"Not now," I heard Cheyanne's voice behind me, watching Leah attempt to control herself. After Leah had her emotional breakdown, she wiped her face from the wet tears. I got back to the question that Leah asked me earlier, not forgetting the question she asked me.

"I believe so. It was about Ezra, Vada's boyfriend. He made mean comments about Cheyanne, and Vada didn't speak up for her. That's all I know." I explained to Leah. Her face looked like she was hit with a light bulb. I asked her what was wrong and what she was thinking about. I heard her sigh, looking at the picture facing down on the vanity.

"Something tells me that she and Vada weren't on talking terms when she died," Leah said, stating what I was thinking too.

This just got a whole lot more interesting.

When I looked over at Cheyanne, she had an expression showing I was right.

8

It's Friday.
You know what that means.
Late morning therapy sessions.
I had to drive myself there today since my mom had errands to run this morning.

When I walked into this building, I felt like my heart would escape from my chest and run away. I hated speaking to my therapist. As much as the last time was progress, it did not mean I wanted that progress. My head was hurting today. It was tragic to discover that Cheyanne left this world fighting with Vada. I wondered what she thought about this. It broke my heart.

She never told me they ended on bad terms.

Vada went around like that didn't faze her. How?

Then again, those two fought like cats and dogs but were fine the next day. If I was honest, they were selfish on both ends with each other when they fought. They always came to me, told me one story, and then a different one.

I walked into the building of my therapist. I made eye contact with the ladies at the front desk.

I stopped to check-in. I started writing my name down on the clipboard in front of me.

"Emma-Jean O'Connor," I said, putting the pen of the clipboard down. I stood there, picking the skin off my nails. I was nervous, like always. The clicking from the computer mouse was frustrating, too. The woman at the front desk verified all my information about myself. Insurance, phone number, address, ext. It was all my mom's stuff.

It sucked I couldn't have my information in there, considering this was my therapy session.

"Okay, you are back in room 207 today." The front desk woman said, giving me a sincere customer smile you could tell was fake. Everybody sounded fake. I nodded.

"Thanks."

I made my long departure up to the second floor of the building. I knew where to go. It was the same room I always went to. It seemed like a long walk every time, just like my days.

I could close my eyes and walk to this room.

Walking inside my usual room, I shut the door behind me. I couldn't help but look at the always white walls between me. They were so bright; it made the mood go down. Was that what they were trying to do when designing this room? It's not a good concept, in my opinion.

What did I know?

I was a bright person. I used to be, but not anymore.

But what didn't make me feel better was that I had to sit in a white room twice a week and talk to someone I would rather not talk to. I'd rather not speak to anyone.

Ms. Jesse Dayton was a lovely lady. I also know her job was to be friendly and listen to people's needs and sad lives. Intentionally, I was not too fond of having a stranger know what was wrong with me.

It was uncomfortable.

Nothing was wrong with me.

I sat there patiently, waiting for her to enter the room. I could hear a different voice inside of the room next to me.

Thin walls.

It sounded like a little kid. He was screaming. I feel his pain from my own throat. He must know how I felt sitting here.

I sighed—that poor kid.

The door opened as Ms. Dayton entered the room, greeting me with a huge smile. I couldn't smile. She was too cheery for me. I didn't see how one person could have so much positive energy. I'd heard positive energy is contagious. Lucky for me, I didn't have any of that energy. Ms. Dayton walked over to her desk and started sorting things out. She opened her notepad like always, pulling out her black ballpoint pen so she could write things down that we talked about.

Who knew what we were going to establish today? A few minutes passed, Ms. Dayton played around with her things, and she was ready to begin our session. She started the timer she uses so we don't go over the scheduled time. It was one of those timers you used to bake with. She let out a big sigh before looking up at me.

"How are you today, Emma? Tell me about your week." Ms. Dayton's voice shrieked through the walls, startling me.

"Well, I had a shower. I visited my friend. My mom took me to the grocery store." I listed off things that happened to me that were somewhat eventful that occurred to me the last few days. Of course, nothing I did was ever eventful, but we always talked about it at the beginning of therapy. She may not think it was eventful, but I thought it was. I then decided to add something else.

"I'm— I'm going back to school next week."

"Okay, that's a good start. Tell me about your feelings about going back to school." Ms. Dayton said, writing things down as she went. I gulped.

"Well... I'm nervous. I don't want to be around all the crowds." I said, picking at the skin under my nails again.
"Why is that?" Ms. Dayton asked. I didn't know how to answer her question. All I did was shrug. That was the only answer I could give. "What makes you nervous?"
"I guess, being away from my bed," I answered. That was all I could give. Ms. Dayton picked up her pen, annoyingly clicking it to begin writing down everything.
"Signs of depression." She mumbled. I wasn't sure if she knew I could hear what she said, but I ignored it. I shook my head, scoffing at her comment. My leg began to bounce up and down.
I didn't have depression. Did I?
"Now, you mentioned seeing a friend a few days ago."
I nodded in response to Ms. Dayton.
"Tell me about that." I gulped again.
"Well," I started. "We used to be best friends, but we found different people to associate with. So, this was the first time she and I hung out in a long time." I explained. I was starting well. Somewhat.
"Were you happy to see her?" Ms. Dayton asked. I scrunched my brows. What kind of question was that?
"Um, yeah," I replied. I would make my fingers bleed if I didn't stop picking. I didn't know how to answer that question. Yes, I was happy to see Leah. It had been ages since we did something together, but that didn't mean it was special.
"Who is the friend?"
"Leah," I replied.
I saw the disappointment in my therapist's eyes. For what, though? That was my friend. Ms. Dayton knew that Leah was Cheyanne's younger sister. I had mentioned many things about her in my previous sessions.
"Being at your deceased friend's house doesn't help much with grieving." Ms. Dayton said. I squinted.

As right as she was, I didn't care about that. I needed a friend, and Leah was that friend that I needed. I shrugged in response. Ms. Dayton was acting like I was not allowed to have specific friends. It made me a bit angry. Was I not supposed to have friends and find happiness? I guess not.

"'Can I not have friends?" I asked with a harsh demeanor.

"Pardon?" Ms. Dayton asked, putting her black pen down, wanting me to respond. My anger began to grow. *Why do I get frustrated when I talk to this woman? She stirs the pot.*

It must be her job to get under her patient's skin.

"Well, you tell me to make friends, connect with others, and grow from the past. I do that, but you look at me with disappointment as if I haven't done that." I started to ramble on like I usually do at my sessions. At some point, my sessions turned into me just freaking out. I kept going.

"Leah was my friend first before I met Cheyanne. So why can't I be around the only person who makes me remember who Cheyanne was and makes me feel close to her? I went to Leah's house a couple of days ago, entered Cheyanne's room, and felt close to her. But I felt sad because I missed her so much, which still shows me that I am not okay." I rambled, realizing how much I had just said. I had to stop myself.

I sighed again, looking up at my therapist, who listened intently to what I was saying. She had that same disappointed look in her eyes again. Ms. Dayton picked up her pen and started writing in her notebook.

Oh no. What was she writing down? It's probably how crazy I was. If I was being honest, I was surprised she hadn't locked me up yet.

"Okay, I will give you an idea to help with coping. One of my older patients did this, and it helped her cope with her mom's passing. It may help you." Ms. Dayton sounded like she was tired of my shit. I nodded, open to any ideas at this point. Ms. Dayton stood up, taking the paper to the front desk.

"This girl wrote letters to her mom after she died. It helped her get past the hard times she faced. I suggest you try this out. Buy a journal and write to Cheyanne. See how it goes. Give it a try." Ms. Dayton handed me the paper. It looked like instructions. She was acting like this was a school project. But it was an idea I was willing to try.

Before I knew it, our session was over.

9

Another week of therapy.

I felt a hint of relief, but it didn't last long. I knew I'd have to go back again next week. I dreaded it.

Sitting in my car, I thought about getting myself back into school. Who would have my back? Leah? Yes, she would, but she had her friends to worry about. Being in public again scared me. My heart beat a mile a minute when I thought about it. But everybody is right. I couldn't sit around and make myself feel worse. I had to go back to school.

I pulled the paper out of the hoodie pocket that Ms. Dayton had given me. It had instructions on what to do about this whole *"letter"* thing. Writing letters to a dead person sounded crazier than what I already was. I wasn't so sure about it. I began reading.

"Until you begin feeling like yourself again, write in a journal about how you feel. Writing your emotions out helps with built-up anger.

"Contact your instructor/therapist about how the project is going and making you feel."

I sighed at that piece of paper. A project? It sounded nonsensical to me. Was therapy supposed to be another class for me? I said I'd try anything, at least for my family.

I set the paper down on the passenger's side seat when I heard my phone buzzing in the cup holder. I looked down to see Vada's name on my screen with a picture of the two of us.

I raised my brow. I haven't spoken to Vada in days. It was strange she was calling me out of the blue.

Do I answer? Of course.

I picked the phone up and clicked the green button to answer.

"Hey." It was all that came out of my mouth.

"Hey, Emma! How are you?" Vada sounded cheerful, jumping at her voice. She always had an upbeat tone when she spoke. It made things stranger. I gulped a bit, starting my car up.

"I'm— I'm good." I stuttered.

"You had therapy today, so I wondered how it went! You know I always ask."

This was true. Vada always called me on therapy days, asking how things went. That was another reason to add to my list of what made her a good friend. I smiled softly at her kindness.

"Yeah, no, it was good. I talked about my week... and... going back to school next week." I added, smiling through the phone, even though she couldn't see me. I felt accomplished from doing something that scared me.

I wouldn't say I liked school, even before.

"Emma, that's amazing. It would help if you were going back to school to be around others. I'm so proud of you." Vada said, and I could practically see the smile on her face from how chipper she was acting. "You are doing so good." She added.

"Thanks," I spoke, confidence shooting through my veins. "I am doing my best."

"You are, and I couldn't be prouder. Maybe next week we can get together after you're out of school and have a late lunch. That's sound, okay?" She asked.

I heard some noise in the background wherever she was. It sounded like someone banging around and slamming pots and pans. I was confused, but I ignored it.

"Yeah, of course. It's a date." I said as I started driving out of the parking lot.

"Okay, great. Well... I must run. I love you, and have a great weekend! I'll see you soon!" Vada hung up after that.

I didn't even get a chance to say I love you back.

I went to our messages, wrote, "I love you too," and sent it so she knows.

After sending my message, I let out a sigh. I caught a glimpse of myself in my rearview mirror. I had bags under my eyes, and I looked restless. My skin looked oily. I cringed at myself.

I looked abominable.

However, I'd been looking like that most days.

I made my way to the store. I needed a journal if I wanted to do this letter-writing thing. As stupid as it sounded, it might help. It would not hurt to give it a try.

I parked my car at a spot in the Target parking lot. I could run inside to get what I needed. I just wanted to go home and relax. Not to mention, I needed to get some stuff for school next week. It had been almost a month and a half since I'd been to school. I have been doing my courses online since Cheyanne died.

As I hopped out of my car, I walked inside Target, seeing nothing but rich people checking out, with their totals being almost $400. I rolled my eyes.

My mom never shopped at Target.

I went because they always had cute journals and school supplies. If I was going to do this, I needed to get at least what I wanted.

I grabbed myself a small basket to carry around in the store. I did a run of the things I needed. I started pulling out things I would need for school as I got to the home office section—a planner, some folders, binders, pens, pencils, and more. I loved the home office section. It always had a simple yet casual smell of paper and markers.

I could hear squealing girls in the next aisle over from me. I knew that squeal anywhere, though. I groaned in annoyance.

Stacey Milton.

She was one of the most popular girls in my grade. She and I didn't get along. She was friends with Leah. I bet Leah was probably with her. Do you remember when I said Leah befriended a group I didn't get along with? This is that group.

I ignored it and just kept looking at my journals.

I saw a couple I liked. They had prominent journals, but some were too girly for me. I scrunched my nose up at all of them. I saw one that had sunflowers all over it. When I examined the rest, it was the last journal with those flowers. I smiled softly, picking it up—Cheyanne's favorite flower.

Perfect, I couldn't resist.

It saddened me, but it told me that this was Cheyanne's journal.

"Well, well—" I heard from my left to see Stacey Milton standing beside me. Her blonde hair was in bouncy curls, and a silver necklace bedazzled her neck with her name. Her outfit looked trashy; she wore a loose pink blouse and a gold skirt. Her face was caked in make-up while snacking her teeth on the piece of gun she probably worked on for 2 hours. She looked gross, in my opinion, but everybody found her fabulous.

"Isn't it, Ms. Debbie Downer?"

I grimaced at her insult. It was trashy.

Stacey and I never had any issues with each other. She just wasn't nice to anybody. She made fun of people in a way that could hurt them mentally or physically. After Cheyanne died, her insults grew worse. It made her feel good. I tried not to let it get to me.

"Sad not seeing you in school." She spoke. "We just miss your... Well, we just don't miss you at all." I looked over to see Leah standing behind one of the other girls. She couldn't even look at me. This was one of the reasons why Leah and I stopped talking. She can't admit that we are friends with her group.

I nodded, acknowledging the situation, pressing my lips into a thin line.

"I don't care, Stacey," I said, setting the journal down in my basket. "I don't even think about your existence."

"I know you've thought about me at least for a minute," Stacey said. I shook my head, showing the annoyance in my eyes. She did not get the memo I was going for. I was silent, hoping she would get the picture.

"Well, I'm so sorry about your friend. Not that I cared to know—"

"I don't have time to talk to trash right now. If you would excuse me, I'm busy, and you are wasting my time and space. And keep Cheyanne's existence out of your pitiful mouth. You don't know her." I'd had enough of her idiocy.

She made me angry. I cut her off and pushed through her. I couldn't help but make eye contact with Leah, who looked like she had nothing to say.

"And you. To let someone as trashy as her talk badly about Cheyanne. Screw you, and you can forget about what we talked about a couple of days ago." I pushed through her and made my way to the checkout. I didn't even let Leah make a sound.

I didn't need Leah to figure out who killed Cheyanne. I could do it by myself without help. Hell, I didn't even need help from Vada.

After checking my things out, I left the store and drove home.

10

I sat at my desk. I needed to figure out where to start or what to write. My mind was blank, like the paper in front of me.

I sighed.

I started to feel defeated, and my heart began pounding. How do you start writing to someone who will never read whatever you put on that paper? Do I start from the very beginning? From the beginning of when the accident happened?

Suddenly, it hit me.

The night of the accident.

***

When I say how fast I was driving. I could have gone to jail.

My anxiety was going through the roof. Everything seemed like it was going 100 miles an hour. I don't know if it

was adrenaline or if it was. The words Leah spoke kept playing through my head.
"You better come quick—" was echoing through my mind. Dammit.
I pulled into the hospital, found a parking space, and almost forgot to shut the car off.
Slow down, Emma. I could not control myself. This was all too much.
I got out of the car and busted through the hospital doors. Everybody thought I was hurt.
"Cheyanne Wrangler!" I called. "I'm looking for Cheyanne Wrangler." I couldn't stop yelling. So many nurses and doctors came up to me to calm me down. It wasn't working, but they were still trying their hardest.
They told me to lower my voice or said they would check that name. I didn't care. I wanted answers. I was frantic.
"Emma!" I heard my name.
I turned around to see Vada walking right to me. She looked dressed up a bit, not in pajamas like I was. I couldn't help but look her up and down.
"Vada-"She hugged and pulled me away from all the doctors who were frantically trying to get me to calm down.
"Thank you. I got her." She started walking me down the hall. I couldn't even ask what was going on. Vada already started.
"She is in surgery right now. Doctors said she looked critical, but that's all I know. I got here not too long ago. It's a waiting game, so we must sit tight." I shook my head, beginning to pull at my hair as a coping mechanism for my anxiety
Why was she not freaking out?
"How can you be so calm?!" I asked, pulling myself off her. "And why do you look like it doesn't bother you that our best friend is on the table!" My voice was loud as we entered the waiting room. I saw Leah stand up, looking over at us. She

looked torn, tears soaking her flushed cheeks and her chest pulsing from crying.
That is when I realized my chaos was not helping anyone.
Vada sighed but did not answer me when I asked her a question. I could see Cheyanne's parents sitting by Leah. Her mom was crying, wiping her eyes every second she got.
"Emma, we aren't going to get any answers if you come in here screaming at people, so if you want answers, you will have to lower your voice." Vada snapped slightly. I was angry with how calm Vada was acting. But it wasn't good to lash out in front of Cheyanne's family at this time.
Vada was right.
I took a couple of deep breaths, forcing myself to calm down.

* * *

I was back to reality, taking the same deep breaths in as I was when Vada snapped at me. I sat at my desk with tears forming in the corner of my eyes. I could not help but remember when I arrived at the hospital with no sort of answer from her.

I heard my phone buzz, breaking my concentration. It was Leah. I skimmed her message, and "Can we talk?"

I ignored it.

That was the fifth message tonight that she has sent to me. I'm still mad at her for Stacey's situation today. Stacey ran her mouth about Cheyanne, and Leah didn't even stick up for her.

I grabbed my pen, clicking it open to begin. I was ready.

Aimee Lynn

***

Dear Cheyanne,

I know you would say how stupid this sounds, but this is my first letter to you, so be kind.

Things here in Hillsboro have been all out of sorts. My life is spiraling out of control. I miss you, and I wish you were still here. The night I heard you were in an accident, I felt like a rope wrapped around my throat, and I was suffocating.

Mom has been making me go to therapy. I hate it so much; I wish you understood. Of course, you don't. Sometimes, forcing people to talk about things isn't the best route. Since your funeral, I have not been to school. I'm going back on Monday. I'm nervous, but Mom says: "I need to stop being so antisocial during this time of need."

Whatever.

I yelled at Leah today. Screw her for letting Stacey Milton make assumptions about you and your death. It made me mad. But why would Leah be friends with someone like that? I don't know. It's not important right now.

I want to discuss the elephant in the room, though, while I'm writing.

Why am I seeing your spirit? You are dead. As much as you don't want me to, I need your answer. It's real soon. Before I lose my mind, my mother locks me up in a crazy house.

Anyway, I guess that's all for me. It's not much of a first letter, but it's a start.

I will talk to you soon

Love, Emma.

* * *

A splash of tears dropped onto that sheet of paper. Writing my first letter to my deceased friend had me emotional. My heart was beating so fast through my chest after finishing this letter. I would have to do this right here; it was about to be something new. It is not going to be easy, but maybe it will help me grieve a bit. I wiped my eyes, sniffling softly, trying to pull myself together. I gulped down the lump stuck in the back of my throat.

I then felt a gush of wind from behind me, taking my breath away. I turned to see Cheyanne sitting on my bed again. I froze for a moment. I didn't react like I did the first time. She had a slight smile with the same dirty blonde hair. She was wearing a plain white sweater with black sweats—comfy clothes for being dead, but also better than what I saw her the first time.

"You need to stop coming up on me like that," I mumbled, turning and closing the journal I just wrote in. I placed the pen right next to it.

"I loved your letter," Cheyanne spoke. "Thank you for sticking up to me with Leah's friends." She added, giving me the sweet smile I deeply miss. I closed my eyes, wanting to tear up from that smile. I felt angry that she was here. It was not helping the fact that I was grieving.

"Cheyanne, I can't keep seeing you. It's not helping me mentally. Please, go away." I said, sitting down on my bed with my back facing her. It was silent for a couple of minutes. I turned around, and she was not sitting there anymore. She was walking around my room, looking at everything, running her fingers over my things.

I asked her to go away.

"Cheyanne—"

"You do not want me gone, and if you want to find out who hit me with their car, you need me here more than ever."

My heart felt like it had stopped for a minute.

That same honest tone she always gave you came flying out with her words. I could not be mad at her for it. It hurt slightly, but I was right about why she was here. She was here to help me figure out who hurt her.

But why?

"I do want to know." We're the only words that came out. Now, I felt obligated to watch her every move. I felt like I needed more information every chance I got with her. Cheyanne nodded.

"Okay, then call my sister." She said, as my face tightened. I did not want Leah's help anymore.

"I'm good, thanks."

"Emma Jean, Leah still wants to find out too, and she's sorry for what happened today." Cheyanne pointed at my phone, which had been buzzing. I rolled my eyes, shaking my head.

"Why not Vada?"

Cheyanne stopped walking around the room when I said Vada's name. Her whole tone had changed, and the room's mood did, too. Cheyanne seemed angry with Vada. I watched her reaction. It seemed like the two of them had unfinished business before she died. It's sad. You'd think they both would have restated their tensions when things went south for them.

"No, she does not need to know." Cheyanne snapped, looking towards me.

I blinked at her words, and then Cheyanne was gone. My heart started hurting. Did I upset her to the point where she wanted to be away from me? I also felt anxiety boiling slowly. It made tears start to form.

I tried to keep it together, but this time was challenging. I felt myself begin to grieve again.

I missed my friend.

After speaking to Cheyanne for that little time, I couldn't help but lay down, crying myself to sleep.

11

The sun blinded me as I woke up from a 7-hour slumber. It didn't feel like enough. My body was sore, and I wondered why. My hands felt numb since they always looked so swollen in the mornings. It is strange why my hands are always swollen when I wake up.

I rolled over to shut off the alarm blasting through my phone. It screamed 6:30 AM on my lock screen. I was not too fond of the thought of getting up and going back to school. I don't have any friends now. Even though she's tried apologizing, I'm still mad at Leah. I still don't want that toxic energy around me. I have had enough of it.

I rubbed my eyes harshly before exiting my bed to see my reflection in my mirror. I didn't look too bad. My hair was a mess, but that's normal. I glanced at my dresser to see the arranged clothes I picked out last night for school.

Yes, I was that girl.

I didn't want to leave my warm bed. I felt cozy and safe. The thought of getting up out of bed to leave the house dropped my mood. I don't want to go to school.

It's the least of my worries. It will make my mom smile if I attempt to go through a day of school.

I slugged out from my bed, dragging my feet towards my dresser. I wasn't feeling a shower; I'd fall back asleep in there. I changed into the outfit on my dresser while applying some deodorant and perfume.

I had on a light pink sweatshirt with a pair of light blue jeggings. Of course, I added a pair of back converses and some jewelry to finish the outfit—a necklace with an E and two rings. One is on my right index finger, and one is on my left middle finger. My earrings were already in my ears.

I slugged into the bathroom to brush my teeth and wash my face. I needed to make myself look more presentable to be around a crowd. I pulled my hair up in a half-up, half-down look, the bottom part falling to my lower back.

I quickly finished getting ready and returned to the room to pack my bag for school. I started throwing everything into the pack as soon as I could. Everything was still inside its packaging. I didn't care.

I glanced over at my desk to see Cheyanne's journal. Maybe the start of a letter wouldn't hurt me. I shrugged. I walked over to sit down and opened it up. I glanced at the letter I wrote last night, smiling softly. I turned the page to see a blank one.

***

Dear Cheyanne,

How's heaven? I bet it's better than here. Today, I'm doing something I genuinely don't want to do. But it will get me out of this sad shell I'm living in.

I'm going back to school.

Do I like the idea? No. I guess it will show my mom that I'm somewhat okay. Even though I'm not. I'm tired. My body is so sore. I'm unsure why, but I wouldn't say I liked it.

I don't understand why I am so against school now. Everything seems to be moving slowly for me recently. Maybe that is why I wasn't too fond of it.

I know I am going to have to see Leah today. She's going to want to talk to me. I don't want to. She's fake, like everybody else on this planet. Maybe I am saying that because I'm mad at her for not sticking up for you. I know Leah is not fake; never has been, but my anger gets the best of me when people talk about your death.

Ugh. This sucks.

It does suck not having you here. I miss-

***

My writing paused when my mom called me, emphasizing that I would be late.

I glanced at the time on my phone to see it was only 6:45. I groaned.

Why am I so nervous to go to school? There's nothing special.

I closed my journal, slid my pen onto the page I was writing on, and placed it inside my bag. I grabbed it and made my way downstairs.

I could hear my mom in the kitchen being loud. She is always this loud in the mornings. It sounded like she was making breakfast. I scoffed when I turned the corner to see a plate of eggs, bacon, and toast on the island counter. She also had a black and pink lunch box beside my food. My old lunch box from middle school.

I rolled my eyes at her kindness. I should be thankful for it, but it was too much for me.

"Mom, you know I don't eat breakfast," I mumbled, walking over to sit down. I glanced at the big glass of orange juice sitting there, too. My mom has always been extra. But I knew my body needed Vitamin C from the lack of sun.

"Well, it is for your first day back. I thought it would be nice to give you a big breakfast." My mom replied.

I had to be nice about it.

I scrunched my nose at the big plate of food beside me. I picked a piece of toast and took the most petite bite ever.

"Thanks, Mom." I acknowledged, slowly eating my food. There was a slight hint of silence. I could only hear the news playing in the living room on the other side of the house.

I was examining my mom a bit. She was still in her bathrobe like she had just woken up. My mom was pouring herself a big cup of coffee, which broke the silence.

"So, you ready for today?" She asked, standing across from me by the sink. I could feel her eyes sinking into me with a stare. I scrunched my nose again at her movement. I shrugged in response, my bottom lip slightly popping out.

"I guess. It's school." I replied, taking another bite of my toast before grabbing the glass of orange juice.

"Yeah? You nervous?" My mom asked.

I wondered if she was trying to converse with me to break the heavy silence that crawled through the kitchen. But it was awkward. My mom and I used to be close, but after she started working long days and nights, we stopped being so close.

I shook my head at her question. I was nervous.

"I'm fine."

It has been a month and a half, almost two months, since I entered the school. I hated my school. It was filled with nothing but jocks, popular kids, and outcasts. Which one am I? It shouldn't be too hard to take a wild guess.

I was staring at the clock on the microwave, waiting for it to say 7:00 so I could leave and head to school. I had to be there by 7:15 to get in and go to the office to get what I needed. It was only 6:55. Maybe leaving five minutes early won't kill me.

"Well, I got to go." I took one last bite of the toast before hopping off the chair and grabbing my bag.

"Wait, Emma, you didn't finish your breakfast." My mom said, practically chasing after me. I rolled my eyes.

"I'm fine, Mom. I have to go so I can get my papers for class." I said sincerely, trying to walk away from her to leave the house. But she kept following me. I could hear the swishing of her scrubs rubbing as she walked.

"But Emma-"

"Mom, seriously, I'm fine. Thank you for breakfast. I'll see you later." I said before walking right out of the door.

I left her standing there clueless and worried. She shouldn't push me to eat if I didn't want to. She was a pusher. She had always been.

I got inside my car and drove ten minutes down the road before making it to school.

***

I made it to school. I drove to the parking lot.

I could see a bunch of familiar faces already walking inside. They like to meet up with their friends in the cafeteria and gossip about the parties that happened throughout the weekend—typical high school gossip.

I've been thinking a lot of things are annoying today. It must be my mood today. I knew I had to get there so I wasn't late. I had gone to the front office to get some paperwork done and get my schedule for the year. I hated how lovely the office ladies always were to you. I used to enjoy it, but not anymore recently. I dislike people who bring positive energy into my bubble.

I couldn't help but watch all the familiar faces that passed my car. They were staring at me, knowing exactly who I was. Of course, they couldn't forget about me.

I threw a meltdown at school the day Cheyanne passed. Yeah, I just remembered that I need to add that part. I got in trouble for that meltdown. All those faces were most likely wondering when the subsequent collapse was. It was sad.

Finally, it was time to get out of the car.

12

As I shut the driver's side door of my car, I could hear the murmurs of every person around me. It made me angry. It took everything in my power to contain that anger. Walking to that door into the cafeteria would feel like a long sidewalk to hell. I scoffed, just hearing everyone's whispers.

I saw a few familiar faces that were gossiping.

Dylan Summers – baseball and football jock.

We were friends before he became one of the other popular kids. Our friendship existed when we were little. Of course, we grow up and become different people. He grew into an ass. He was the kid who would look at you and tell you through his eyes that you weren't worthy of a friendship. Becoming a popular kid went to your head.

Piper Shay – Cheer Captain. That was all this girl did; she is still at Stacey Milton's top.

They are enemies.

Long story short, Stacey slept with Dylan, who was, in fact, Piper's boyfriend today. Piper dumped Dylan but still managed to stay with him for what he did to her. Piper was truthfully friendly in a way, but she still had that widespread attitude. She had short, straight, thin blonde hair and was tall. She was the one who was always at the top of the cheer pyramids because of her long, pale legs.

I saw Lucy Lovegood, Tracy Austyn, and Carrie Swindler, known as intelligent outcasts. They are the kind of girls who would participate in the STEM Festivals, Robotics Clubs, and Scholastic Decathlons.

A few other unfamiliar faces were looking in my direction, too. They looked like they belonged to the outcasts. I ignored every single one of them.

I was stopped by Dylan, who was chuckling to himself. His friends surrounded us with big smiles on their faces. It made me roll my eyes. I questioned why suddenly; he wanted to harass me like this when we used to be friends.

"Look who it is... Emma O'Connor. How was the insane asylum?" All his friends laughed at me.

It made me angry but also disappointed in him for his actions. Never once did Dylan ever act like this with me. What's sad is he thought it was okay to make fun of me. I was trying so hard to ignore it, but since that day when I went crazy finding out Cheyanne died. I've become the crazy girl of my school. But let's talk about how appalling his insults are. They were awful

"Bite me," I mumbled, pushing through him. All his friends did their *"oohs"* and *"ahhs."* I hated teenage boys with a passion. They find themselves hysterical and clever. I was stopped again by him. I kept walking, but he was trying so hard to stop me.

"What's the matter? Can't handle a joke?" He asked with his friends walking behind me. I scoffed at him. I could hear Piper yelling for him to stop it, but he didn't listen.

What boy would ever listen to a girl?

"I can handle a joke from you, thank you." I hissed. "I just don't want to talk to someone as rude as you." I finished before pushing through him again, causing him to stumble a bit before entering the cafeteria. I could hear Piper behind me telling Dylan he should've left me alone.

Typical Piper was trying to be the good girl in this and sticking up for me.

As I entered the cafeteria, all eyes were on me. It made me sick to my stomach. Luckily, I wasn't staying here. I made my way out of the cafeteria and to the front office. As I walked in, I saw an unfamiliar female sitting in the office. She looked happy, almost too happy for my liking.

Her dark brown hair was set back into two loose fishtail braids. She looked new to me. As I walked up to the desk, Mrs. Jones, the front desk lady, looked up at me with a smile.

"And what can I do for you?" She asked, with a bright and cheerful voice. It made me cringe slightly. I tried to be polite myself.

"I'm picking up my schedule and papers. Emma-Jean O'Connor." I said to the lady. I saw her typing my name on the keyboard before clicking the enter button.

"Okay, if you just have a seat, I'll print it all out for you and get you out into class," She said. I thanked her before walking over to sit next to the happy girl. We were silent for a moment before she turned towards me.

"You new?" She asked. Her voice was slightly low, but it was still cheerful.

I slowly turned my head towards her and shook my head. She stared at me like she was waiting for an answer besides shaking my head. I cleared my throat.

"No, I was on leave," I mumbled, looking down to start playing with my phone. Truthfully, I didn't want to talk to her. She was too bubbly for me right now. At 7 AM, it wasn't my time to be very friendly. It never has been.

"Well, wonderful to meet you." She said, holding her hand out. "I'm Tia. Tia Coleman." I looked over at this girl. "I just moved here from North Carolina. My mom was transferred here from her job." She was trying to be friendly. It was clear that she was new here and she was trying to make a friend. Of course, I was the one that got put into the situation to become her friend. She was friendly, I guess. I slowly put my hand out, touching hers gently.

"Emma." It was all that came out of my mouth. Our hands collided as she shook it gently.

"Wonderful to meet you, Emma!" Tia squeaked slightly as she looked around the room, letting out a small giggle. "This place seems friendly." She said as I couldn't help but look at her with a disgusted look glued to my face.

"Don't get used to it," I murmured, looking back at my phone.

"What grade are you in?" Tia spoke more. I could hear her bracelets clinking as she fumbled in her seat.

"Senior. You?" I asked, knowing now I was engulfed in conversation with this girl.

"Me too! Maybe we will have a few classes together." She spoke with excitement; I was thinking the opposite. Then again, maybe her positive energy is good for me.

"Yeah, me too. I could use a friend." I attempted to spill out kindly with a small smile. That was when Mrs. Jones called Tia's name.

"Got to run! I hope to see you around." She said before grabbing her papers and scampering off. Thank God that was over. As lovely as she was, it wasn't the same mood I felt right now. Maybe later, I'll be a little more friendly.

I chuckled to myself. Who am I kidding? No, I won't.

"Emma O'Connor." Mrs. Jones called out, holding up a stack of papers for me as well. I stood up and dragged her over to her desk.

"Okay, the top paper is your schedule, locker number, and combination. Looks like you are on the bottom floor with all the other seniors for your locker. Next, these are your syllabus for each class, even though you probably already have them. And you are all set. Have a wonderful day back." Mrs. Jones said before going back to doing her work. I thanked her with a head nod before turning to walk out. I started going to find my locker to get to my 1st period. I looked to see it was Algebra 3. I'm not too fond of math this early in the morning. It gave my body a headache.

I walked halfway from the office before finding the same locker I had two months ago. The number and combination were the same. Nothing about this school changed. I kept getting attention on myself as I was walking past. It made me mad. Of course, everybody looks at the crazy girl who threw her tantrum a few months ago.

Moving on.

As I looked around, trying to find my locker, I felt something impacting my shoulder. It caused me to lash back and fall onto the ground. The minute I fell, I was angry. Then I realized that I had run into someone. I was not paying attention to where I was going when looking around for my locker.

"Whoa. My apologies." I heard a deep voice from above me. I looked up to see a boy. He did not look familiar to me, but he seemed quite charming. His smile was wide and bright. I was drawn to him, but I needed to wake up. He had his hand out to help me up. I gratefully took his hand, both of us pulling me back up. I wiped myself off. I felt appalled falling in front of a cute boy. It wasn't very comfortable.

"Do I know you?" He asked me, breaking the silence between the both of us. It was awkward. I didn't think I could find someone as charming as him from this school. It was fascinating to see. My thoughts gathered, causing me to shake my head at the answer to his question.

"I don't believe so," I replied, fixing my hair to stay out of my face.

"Well, I'm sorry for running into you. I don't want to be late for my first class." The mysterious boy said. I nodded, refusing to make eye contact with him. "I'm Ben Coleman. It's nice to meet you. I'm new."

I looked up for a second, hearing his name. It sounded familiar. But while staring out into space for a minute, it clicked on me. This handsome boy was Tia Coleman's brother. It had to be. I scrunched my eyebrows.

"Do you know Tia?" I asked. He nodded.

"Yeah, that's my sister. We're twins." He spoke. It made sense. All I did was nod, smiling at the cute boy named Ben.

"I met her in the office. I'm sorry for cutting this short, but I must get to class, so it was nice to meet you." I said before sliding past the boy. I left him standing there. I felt stupid. He was trying to be nice to me, but I couldn't. I was not in the right mind to let a boy come into my life.

I went down the hall to find my locker, getting in with my day back at the place I hated the most.

13

The first week of school was not easy.
I made it through. I could not tell you how often I ran into awkward moments with students giving me dirty looks or running from me. I didn't feel bullied; I only misunderstood.

Tia Coleman wouldn't leave me alone all week. I mean, I appreciated her company, but it wasn't necessary. She kept saying that Ben wouldn't stop asking about me. I wasn't interested; I didn't know how often I had to tell him. I didn't have time for a relationship.

It was Friday. My late-night therapy session was canceled.

I had planned to have a late lunch with Vada. It has been a week since I've seen her. She has been hanging around with her new boyfriend all week. Finally, Vada reached out to me on Wednesday, wanting to do lunch like she promised. I missed having Vada around. I feel like ever since Cheyanne died, she had wanted nothing to do with anybody.

I have heard many things about her new boyfriend, Ezra. I've heard he's rude, a cheater, and a drug user. I've also heard he's abusive. Dylan was talking to his friend about him in class one day. He said how Ezra used to date Piper last year, which didn't end well for both. It became too toxic and abusive. Dylan even said Piper's parents got a restraining order on Ezra for his actions toward her. The topic was brought up by Ezra trying to reach out to Piper a few months ago. This must have been while Vada and he were starting together.

I was sitting outside at a small café waiting for Vada to arrive. She is always fashionably late when it comes to plans. I was sipping some green tea, enjoying the beautiful day. While waiting, I finished that letter to Cheyanne that I had been working on since Monday. I got a bit behind on it and never finished it. I pulled out the journal and pen, opening the page to the unfinished letter.

I left off saying, 'I miss you.'

***

It's been a couple of days, which is my fault—my first week of school wrecked me. I'm sitting at the café in town, waiting for Vada to arrive. You know how she is when it comes to time.

For most of the week, I was harassed and stared at. Especially by Dylan Summers, the ex-friend I've always told you about.

I got piled with so much homework that I still need to work on.

I did meet a couple of friends. I can call them that. They are twins, both new to the school, and of course, they befriend the crazy girl.

First, Tia.

She's nice. She is one of those girly girls with name-brand purses and outfits. You'd think I'd hate a girl like that, but she's not bad. Believe it or not, she and I have some things in common regarding choosing books, music, and movies. She's a pretty good friend.

Then, her brother, Ben. Oh god, he is something. He's got a smile that will make your heart stop. His eyes are blue that you can't stop staring at.

My problem is—I can't date. Mentally, I am not stable for it.

What if it leads to disaster, and I'm left with the wreck I already face? Being around him makes me feel happy and warm. I don't know what to do about it.

Anyway, that's been my week. I hope heaven is treating you like the queen you are. I wish you were here

Dear Cheyanne

to give me the guidance I truthfully need. Until the following letter...

Love,

Emma

* * *

I closed the journal, letting out a big sigh. The second letter is down. It still wasn't easy to write these. Sure, it makes me feel like I'm talking to her still, but it wasn't the same.

I felt a blast of air past me and saw a brunette sitting before me.

That would be Vada.

As I looked her up and down, my eyes couldn't help but stay glued to her. She looked rough. It's been almost two weeks since I saw her, and I could not believe it.

Her hair looked like she tried to do something with it but failed. Her skin looked pale and clammy, with bags on her under her eyes. She looked as if she was sick and hadn't slept. I also noticed a couple of bruises on her arms that looked like fingerprints. That drew my attention more. I could hear her talking, but I focused on how bad she looked. Ezra has got to be abusing her and or making her use drugs.

Vada has never used drugs in the past. So why now?

""Emma?" My thoughts were shaken away, looking up at her. I smiled at her, shaking off my focus.

"Sorry, it's been a long week, and I'm so tired. What were you saying?" I responded, putting my journal in my bag to talk to her. She opened the menu on the table, looking it over.

"I was apologizing for being late. I was stuck at a job interview." She said. I couldn't help but look her up and down, questioning if that was what she wore at a job interview. She looked homeless. I didn't acknowledge it.

"Oh, no problem. That's more important." I said, taking sips of my tea. Our waitress came over and started taking Vada's order. She got an iced coffee and an avocado chipotle chicken sandwich.

That sounded good.

I ordered the same sandwich. We thanked her as she walked away.

"So, how have you been?" She asked, sitting back a bit in her chair. She stared, playing with the ends of her hair, waiting for my response. I shrugged. I wasn't sure where to start my week. I just went on my week with Cheyanne's letter.

"Um... good. The school was okay. I met a couple of friends." I replied.

Honestly, I couldn't help but keep staring at Vada's marks on her pale skin. They were very noticeable. She looked different from Cheyanne's funeral, more sunken in. I could see her smile softly when I mentioned meeting new friends.

"We'll tell me about them!" She said in an excited tone. It made both of us laugh. The waitress brought Vada her iced coffee right when I was about to talk.

Servers constantly interrupt conversations to bring you something. It wasn't them being nosy; it was just how they worked.

"Well, they are twins. Ben and Tia Coleman." I started. I could see a smirk growing when I mentioned Ben. It caused me to feel hot on my cheek. Oh no, I was blushing. Focus

Emma. I threw my hand up while a giggle escaped through my lips. "Relax. We are only friends." I spoke.

Vada smirked again. "Yeah, okay. Sure. You have to tell me, at least, if he is cute." Vada spoke, taking another sip of her iced coffee. Not too long after our joking around, our food came out. My mouth was drooling for food. This last month, I only ate one meal a day, if that. I have been trying to do better. I have probably lost a lot of weight from not eating.

"How have you been?" I asked her. I could see her biting the inside of her cheek, a nervous tick she's had since I could remember.

"I'm good. I've been trying to find a job," Vada paused, continuously biting the inside of her cheek more. I swear, she's going to chew her skin raw. "Plus, Ezra is working through a lot of shit, so it's been a frustrating time for the two of us."

My skin began itching with the questions. I could not help but become nosy within seconds. I took a couple of bites of my food and sips of my tea.

"The two of us?" I asked curiously.

Vada nodded to my question. "Of course. We are partners. That means everything that happens between one of us involves the other. You would understand if you were in a relationship."

Vada's words sounded harsh when I believed they weren't meant to be.

I gapped my mouth open and closed before staring directly at her for a moment, food sitting in my mouth.

For the safety of the two of us, I decided to let that one slide.

"I've heard some things about him," I murmured, chewing the rest of my food and swallowing hard. I grabbed my tea, wrapping my lips around the cup to take a few small sips.

Vada's expressions seemed to be a pleasure that everyone knew about him.

"Yeah? Like what?" She asked, eating and sipping on her coffee. I cleared my throat, wiping my mouth with a napkin.

"Well," I started, worried about how this would finish, "He used to date one of my old classmates. Piper Shay—"

"Yeah, I heard she did him dirty." Vada interrupted. I froze, hearing the opposite from others. From what I gathered, he hurt her.

Then again, I don't know the whole story.

"I've also heard he gets around with his name and can be a bit harsh." I was finally out with it. Vada had no concern across her eyes. She shrugged, eating more.

"I don't know what you are talking about." She mumbled, now having trouble keeping her eyes on me. That's one way I knew she was lying. "He is good with me."

"Vada, can he be a bit harsh at times with you?" I blurted out.

Vada's body froze—like I was dumb enough not to notice things from her appearance and choice of words about him. Not to mention the things I have heard about Ezra around school. None of it was good.

She was acting dumbfounded by me, stumbling over her words.

""What? Emm-I don't— I mean— Where is this coming from?" She finally snapped out.

I've never seen a person be that much of an impulsive liar in a matter of seconds. She was trying to dodge this conversation fast. I couldn't help but chuckle. I needed to be honest with her.

"I mean, look at you." I motioned my hand toward her appearance. "You look like you don't sleep, haven't showered. You truthfully look like he's laid his hands on you, and you look... slim." Vada's face tensed up. "I mean, what are you trying to get at here?"

I already knew this conversation would fly south quickly with my last question. It already has. But she needed the truth.

"Are you doing drugs?" I blurted out. I watched as her head snapped at me, and her eyes popped. I watched as she became flustered within seconds.

"I think that it is none of your business." Vada snapped. She started shoveling her food. She was trying to dodge this conversation and fled our lunch date. I scoffed at her actions.

"Well, truthfully, it is my business, considering those bruises all over you are not from running into a wall." I folded my arms over my chest. How idiotic can she be?

"You don't know what you are talking about." Vada hissed, taking big sips of her coffee. "Did you bring me here to interrogate me?"

"Don't be ridiculous, Vada. I didn't know you looked this bad until I saw you." I spoke. I noticed I was aggravating Vada. "Plus, I do know what I'm talking about."

"Emma, you don't. You have no right to invade my privacy, and you certainly do not have any right to be asking about my life, considering you've barely spoken to me since Cheyanne died. Instead, you crawl into your hole and push everybody away from you. Maybe if you knew what was happening with me, you would come around more and be my friend."

I was at a loss for words.

Vada snapped at me in anger; I had never seen this side of her. She grabbed the money and threw it on the table like it was a stripper. She began gathering up her belongings from behind her chair aggressively. She was upset. I have figured her out. She can be mad all she wants, but it is true. She started to walk away, and I could not help but try to find a way to stop her.

"What happened to you and Cheyanne before she died?"

Vada stopped in her tracks. My heart was racing from the intensity in the air from the both of us. I already felt she would not tell me anything, let alone tell me the truth about her and Cheyanne's fight. She'd always lied about things—never had she told me the truth.

"We got into a fight. It didn't end well, and that's all you need to know. If you can't accept that, and if you can't accept my privacy, then maybe you are not my friend." Vada mumbled, walking away from me.

14

Here I am at the one place that brings out my sad side.

Cheyanne's grave.

I needed to talk to her. Even though I was seeing her ghost, she was not there. After lunch with Vada today, I needed to detox. I had her journal in one hand and some flowers in the other.

While walking up to her grave, anxiety started boiling. It looks like her parents had added things to the plot. I could already feel myself becoming emotional. Her grave looked beautiful.

Her gravestone was there, finally.

It had her name, birthdate, and the date she died. The stone was a beautiful grey color that shimmered in the sunlight. Just thinking about that day crushed my soul. There was also a picture of her on there. It looked very nice. Flowers of many different colors lined up in front of the gravestone. Red roses, purple lilies, yellow daisies. I added some sunflowers to the mix since they were her favorite. Nobody knew her favorite flower as well as I did.

"I brought you some sunflowers. I know they are your favorite." I spoke softly, laying them down by her grave.

I sat down in front of her stone, wanting nothing more than to have a good cry. I was fighting it too. I asked if Tia and Ben could meet me there. I had to be honest with them about my mental health, my dear friend, and my feelings. I was not okay; they both needed to know if they wanted to be my friends. Their company was reassuring, but I didn't want to drag them down with my sadness. I knew it was too much for some people.

Sitting in front of Cheyanne's grave, I was unsure what to say. I was going to read her my letters, but she'd already heard the first one, but not the second. I let out a small sigh before opening my journal to page two. I could hear crows cawing close to me. My ears rang from the obnoxious noise. Clearing my throat, I began reading letter two. I stumbled over some words while my nerves were starting to kick in.

Halfway through the letter, I saw Cheyanne's figure behind the stone. She was on her knees, elbows against the stone, smiling at me as I was reading. Something inside made me feel warm seeing her smile. I continued reading as the tears built up. I knew they were going to explode out of me like dynamite. I was doing everything to keep it together.

Finally, I finished. I looked up, making direct eye contact with Cheyanne and her beautiful golden-brown eyes.

"Beautiful." She spoke. "I hope these letters help you." She added, not taking her eyes off me. I sighed, gently shutting the journal and setting it down on my knees.

"I thought you would like it," I murmured. It was hard to think about if this was real or in my head.

"Of course. The sunflowers are a nice touch to it all. You know I love them."

I laughed softly, slowly glancing back up at her. She stared at my flowers, brushing her fingers over the yellow pedals. My head began to spin. After a couple of minutes of silence, I broke it.

"How are you here?" I asked, glancing up at her glistening face.

"What do you mean?" She replied.

"I mean, how is it that I can see you? I don't understand." I had to be honest. It was not that I didn't want to see her, but my mental state was still not strong enough for this. Cheyanne laughed softly, looking back up at me with soft eyes.

"Because you need me. I want to help you get better." She responded calmly. My chest hurt. She was right, but I still knew this was not normal.

"I am broken, damaged, and disoriented without you. Seeing you makes me miss you more. It makes me think you are still real. You will vanish one day, and I will return to square one."

"Emma, you will be okay one day. You need to accept that this is life." Cheyanne explained, her honesty building up in her more as she spoke. "Life sucks. We all must accept it."

"I don't want to accept it." My voice cracked partially as my tears began to brew in my tear ducts.

"You have no choice," Cheyanne said firmly. "You will find happiness again, and I will watch you become happy."

I sighed in frustration at her words. The truth poured out of her ghost self. It was terrifying. I would one day need to accept this.

"I see you getting better," Cheyanne said. I looked up at her, a small scoff escaping from my mouth.

"How?"

"You have made friends. You are going to your therapy sessions, taking your poison." I laughed softly. Cheyanne always thought that medication was poison to our bodies. She was not wrong about that.

"Yeah, two friends. When I am with Vada, all we do is fight now." I said, shaking my head at the idea of the amount of bickering we'd been doing. It had been happening since Cheyanne died. I heard Cheyanne scoff.

Emma won't be around her anymore. She has become someone that I don't think you should associate yourself with. She has made choices regarding choosing the people she wants to be around." Cheyanne's words made me question everything. She and Vada did have some issues before she died. "I'm surprised she came to my funeral." I scrunched my eyebrows.

"Cheyanne, she was there when you got to the hospital," I reassured, while a smirk came from Cheyanne's throat.

"Well, that is a shocker." Cheyanne snickered, my brow raising in confusion.

"Vada was there at the hospital when you woke up. Don't you remember?" I asked, but Cheyanne's focus wasn't on me. It was what was behind me.

I turned to see Ben and Tia parking their car. I was surprised they found me so quickly. Come to think, this was a small cemetery. I waved to them as they were getting out of the car. I turned back to see Cheyanne was gone. It broke my heart slightly to see she was gone. I sighed in sadness, wiping my face to get my emotions under control. Ben and Tia started walking toward me; Tia was running more than walking.

"Emma!" Tia shouted, causing me to cringe at her loudness. As they approached me, Ben glared at Tia, shaking his head.

Sis, you got to shout? You are going to disturb the dead." Ben barked at her in an annoyed tone. Tia shrugged, scrunching her face up at her mistake.

"I'm sorry; I just got excited when I saw her," Tia replied, gesturing toward me. Ben looked down at me, showing his white teeth with a smile. It was as if he was excited to see me.

"Hey, Emma." He said, sitting down next to me. Tia sat on the other side. "Is there a reason why you brought us to a creepy cemetery?" Ben asked in a confused tone. I laughed softly, nodding slowly to his question.

"Yes," I stated. "To understand me, there are some things I need to share with you both." The twins' facial expressions turned from happiness to confusion. I was not surprised. Bringing a person to a cemetery and wanting to talk about something doesn't sit well with anybody's stomach.

"Sure, Emma. What is it?" Tia asked in her higher-pitched voice, giving me a small smile and placing her hand on my shoulder. I let out a small sigh before turning my head toward Ben.

"Do you remember when everyone at school called me psychotic? How was I put in an insane asylum?" I asked them both. I could see them both give me a nod in response.

"I didn't like that, but go on," Ben answered. It made my heart flutter for his defense of me. It shook me for a second. I couldn't remember the last time I felt that softness in my chest.

"Well, there is a story behind it," I murmured. "I was not in an insane asylum —ever. Those are just rumors." I stated, looking at the twins, wanting to see how they would react.

"I could never imagine you being admitted to an insane asylum," Tia said.

"Good. You see that gravestone in front of us?" I pointed to Cheyanne's gravestone. Tia and Ben looked over where I was pointing, examining the headstone.

"Cheyanne Wrangler." I heard Tia's voice murmur to herself. It gave me chills to listen to her name from someone else.

"What about it?" Ben asked, looking at me.

"Well, this was my best friend. Nobody could ever replace her spot. She—" I started getting emotional again. A lump began to curl up in my throat, causing me to clear my throat softly.

"She died a few months ago. She was in a bad car accident coming home from work one night. They say it was a drunk driver, but I believe there is more to the story. She was in bad shape. At first, I had hope for her. She was awake, holding my hand, squeezing it tightly, and showing me she could have a chance. She had a seizure from a massive brain bleed, and she ended up being put into a coma for two weeks."

"That's awful," Tia said gently, grabbing my hand and holding it tightly. Ben used his fingertips to brush away the single tear sliding down my cheek.

"I was at school when I heard the news of her parents pulling the plug. I went crazy in math class. I flipped my desk and ran hysterically, crying out of the classroom. Everyone was scared but also laughed at my hysteria. The principal and vice principal had to chase me down in the courtyard and drag me back into the office. I was out of control. They called my mom to tell her about my meltdown. They thought I had bipolar disorder at the time, and well, those rumors began circling, too. I got suspended for two weeks for causing disruption in the class, assaulting a student because a desk hit a girl in the head, and running out onto school property without supervision."

Tia squeezed my hand tightly, running her fingers through my tied-up hair. It felt nice, but my emotions became the best of me, and tears began to pour. I always hated telling this story to anyone.

"I didn't care about the punishment." My shaky voice sighed. "It gave me space. The school recommended my mom take me to therapy and give me something for the outbursts. Which is what I'm living with right now. I am not crazy, suicidal, or bipolar. I was just devastated to hear the loss of my best friend, and I did not even get to say a proper goodbye."

This was the first time I had genuinely opened up to anyone like this. It made me feel warm and safe inside. I never realized how easy and refreshing it was to get it all out simultaneously. Therapy may be more accessible now I know this.

"Emma, we don't think you are crazy or any of that nonsense," Ben replied to my long story. Tia responded with a nod as she continued to run her fingers through my hair. "Losing a loved one is not something to be taken lightly, and sometimes, people are lucky enough just to have not experienced that kind of loss." This made me cry more.

"We lost our grandma two years ago. It was the first loss Ben and I ever went through. It was not easy at all. We both were devastated, but can I tell you something?" Tia asked. I slowly looked up at her, nodding softly to her question while Ben wiped my face dry.

"It gets better," Tia spoke. "Once you learn to cope correctly, things become simple again, easy, and pure. You will be sad for a while, but being around good people and happiness will make you realize that things are not so bad." Tia's words touched me, making me feel lively. Who knew having amazing people around you could make you feel something?

"I haven't had the support I need through all of this. I was being pushed to go to therapy, take medication, and live in a shell. You guys have helped me understand the benefits of friends again. Thank you."

The twins both reached out and bear-hugged me tightly. It was a bit too tight, but I didn't care or complain. A small laugh escaped my throat. I looked up to see Cheyanne smiling at me again. She did mean it when she said, "It gets better." As our talk ended, my phone started buzzing in my pocket. I reached to grab it to see Leah's name pop up. *Weirdly, she is calling me out of nowhere.*

"Sorry guys, let me take this quick. Hello?"

"Emma! Where are you?" Leah's voice shrieked through the speaker, causing me to wince.

"Erm, I'm at Cheyanne's grave. Why?" I was confused and dazed.

"You need to come over now! Cheyanne's case was reopened for investigation."

15

I was astonished. My head spun a mile a minute while driving to Leah's house. I was having trouble concentrating on the road. I scrambled to find my phone to dial my mom's number. It rang three times before she answered.

"Hey, Mom, I will miss out on dinner tonight. Leah needs me to come over." I heard my mom sigh over the phone.

Since when was she upset that I was going out with friends?

"Emma, your father, and your brother will be home for dinner tonight," I grumbled. She always wanted me home when my dad was not working. I got that. Family time mattered to her, but I was disrupted in thought when she mentioned something about my brother.

"Wait, David is home?" I asked in shock.

"Yes, he is home for a few days visiting. I would like us all to eat together." She replied to me. I groaned in frustration but was too impatient to wait for this news.

"Well, can we wait for like two more hours? Leah called and told me Cheyanne's case reopened, and she wants to tell me everything." I asked politely, thinking she would give in to my pleading. I heard her sigh over the phone.

"Mom, please. I need to know." I practically begged for her acceptance. She was silent for a moment before responding.

"Fine, you have two hours. But you better be home by seven o'clock, please." I smiled at her acceptance.

"Yes, I promise I will be home. Thank you. Thank you, Mom. I love you." I quickly hung up before glancing at the time. It was 4:00.

I had plenty of time to talk to Leah.

Pulling into the Wrangler's house, I saw a cop car sitting in the driveway with her parents' cars off in the grassy patch. I almost forgot to shut the car off yet again. I got out and quickly walked up to the door. Leah was already standing there waiting for me.

"Is it true? Are they reopening her case? Why? What made them change their minds?" I was bombarding Leah with questions as she let me inside, and adrenaline kicked in. I could hear her parents' chatter in the background as a cop stood in their living room.

"Detective Shepard found some information that may lead to the person responsible and if the person was drunk." The cop continued. I looked over at Leah, who was listening intently next to me.

"Is this happening?" I whispered in Leah's ear. She didn't respond. She just kept listening while I chose to do the same thing.

"Detective Shepard, what kind of information are you talking about?" Leah's mom asked, holding her husband's hand as they conversed. The detective sat in the rocking chair he was close to and opened his briefcase with many file folders and a computer.

"My team and I found some surveillance cameras from the streetlights in town and some traces of different fingerprints along the car that weren't hers. Of course, every fingerprint we found was examined for the first time, and we want to ask you about the names of these people. Shall we start from there?" The detective gave so much information that I couldn't understand with my spinning head.

"Yes." Leah's father responded. The detective opened up a file folder with Cheyanne's name and began.

"Thomas Avery. Leah Wrangler. Vada Graham. Kimberly Swanson. Kevin and Cathy Wrangler. Emma O'Connor. Ezra Hall. Justin Evans. Sophie Blake and Damion Troby." My thoughts came back when I heard my name. I gulped.

'Well, Leah and Emma are standing right over there. They are family. Thomas is an ex-boyfriend. We are Kevin and Cathy. Vada is one of her other good friends, Justin, Damion, and Sophie. The last three are her work friends, and Kimberly is an old high school friend." Cathy responded. It made me feel welcome that Cathy called me family.

"And none of those names are people we don't know or don't think would cause anything to happen to our little girl. We don't know about Ezra Hall." Kevin Wrangler added.

"Ezra is Vada's boyfriend." I chimed in. Everyone focused their attention on me. This made me uncomfortable, fast. I gulped, bowing my head to the ground. I could feel everyone's eyes on me, even Leah's.

"Ms. O'Connor. How well do you know Mr. Hall?" I heard the deep voice of the detective ask me. I looked back up, silent momentarily, before shrugging my shoulders lightly.

"Um, I-I've never met him. I've only heard Vada talk about him. I've heard he is... troubled." I responded, folding my hands into a ball in front of me.

The detective nodded and slowly closed his folder, removing his glasses from the tip of his nose. I could feel Leah's eyes scanning me.

"We will look more into this Ezra Hall, but until then, we need to do one thing at a time, starting with Ezra's background and the cameras. We do not quite have the footage yet, but once we develop it, we will get back to you, Mr. and Mrs. Wrangler. Ms. O'Connor, thank you for the help. I will continue with this case until we find something out." The detective said gently, knowing that was the tone needed in this room. As the detective started packing up his briefcase again, I stepped forward.

"Excuse me, sir?" The detective looked up at me. "If you find anything on Ezra, can he not know I said anything?" I was too concerned about having drama with Vada and dealing with Ezra. If this man did assault Vada, I didn't want the confrontation. The detective nodded, giving me a reassuring smile.

"I promise nobody will know this. Whatever was talked about in this room stays." He announced, looking at everyone toward the end. Everyone agreed as the detective and cop left shortly after.

* * *

I was sitting outside with Leah after they left. It was only 5:30, and I still had time to talk to her. The last time we spoke was before the outburst with Stacey Milton in the store. We were silent for a moment before she started the conversation.

"This is crazy, isn't it?" She asked, looking at me with a slight smile on her face. I looked back, giving her a nod as I sat with my arms around my knees.

"Yes, but it's good, right?" I asked her.

"Of course. I want to find out who did this to my sister." Leah responded. I gave her a small 'humph' at her comment before we grew silent again.

All I could hear was the slight breeze flowing in the air. Things with Leah had been incredibly awkward since our fight. I felt terrible and wanted to talk about it, but I did not want to cause more drama between her and me over a little thing that Stacey had caused. Leah sighed, breaking the silence.

"Look, Emma, I want to apologize for what happened between us. I should not have let someone talk badly about my sister. The guilt has been awful inside of me since that happened. I should have stepped up like you, and well, I am sorry." she said resolutely, looking at me with sincere eyes. I was silent, biting my bottom lip as she spoke. I was not mad at Leah anymore. It was the past, and I seemed to be building a warmer heart.

"It's okay, Leah. I forgive you. I am sorry I have been such a sorehead with everything. It was hard for me to lose Cheyanne. She was all I had that made me happy, and I know you feel the same way as me." I replied, giving her a small smile. Leah laughed, looking down toward the ground, her smile dissipating.

"She is my sister. I will never get over that this happened to her." Leah replied. The silence came back before I stood up, looking down at her.

"Well, I hate to run out. My mom is expecting me. David and my dad are home tonight, and she wants a family dinner. I will see you around."

"David's home?" Leah asked just like I did, causing me to giggle.

"I know how shocking is that."

After Leah and I said goodbye, the car ride home felt long but dreamy. It was exciting that someone would be doing something for Cheyanne's case.

Dinner with the family was average. Mom made chicken, mashed potatoes, and broccoli. It was always my brother's favorite. She always knew how to impress him when he came home from school. We talked about how school was between him and me. Dad talked about work and the type of surgeries he did. Mom asked me how I was but did not ask what happened at Leah's. I could not tell them anything anyway; I promised Detective Shepard that I wouldn't mention anything discussed. It was hard to bite my tongue.

After dinner, I decided to go to my room and write a letter to Cheyanne.

***

Dear Cheyanne,

Today was surprisingly enjoyable. We talked at your grave. Your case was reopened, and I helped the detectives figure out who Ezra was.

Things are lighter with life. You were right about things getting better. I am starting to feel warm, but not 100% yet. I am sure you know that. Ben and Tia are becoming my close friends, but nothing compares to what you and I had.

I see my therapist in two days. I can't wait to tell her everything. That's something I would not have said one month ago.

David came home today. He will be here for the next few days. I remember when he had the biggest crush on you. He thinks I've forgotten about that. He said classes are going well. For someone who's becoming an accountant, I can't even imagine the hard work he has put into his school. For the first time in forever, we had a nice family dinner. David and I conversed a few times; it wasn't much, and that's okay. That's more than what I've ever gotten.

Anyway, I will cut this letter short and go to bed. I am tired from the long day I have had.

Until next time,

Emma

16

My bed was so warm and comfy. My sleepwear comprised an oversized grey hoodie and red and black plaid pajama pants. My hair was in a low ponytail over my shoulder. My dreams were, in fact, peaceful.

Who knew sleep could be so exquisite?

I needed this sleep, considering I had school tomorrow. The weekend went by so fast after all the news from Friday.

I started feeling my bed vibrate. I slowly opened my eyes but did not acknowledge the buzzing from my phone that was going off. It was probably a scam call. I was too tired and comfy even to answer. After my phone stopped buzzing, I quickly fell back asleep.

I started feeling my bed vibrate. I slowly opened my eyes but did not acknowledge the buzzing from my phone going off. It was probably a scam call. I was too tired and comfy to answer. After my phone stopped buzzing, I quickly fell back asleep.

That was until it started ringing again. I groaned, reaching over to see who was sending me messages and calling me.

That's when I saw it.
Emma, are you awake?

Emma, please respond.

Call 911.

I need help.

EMMA, PLEASE!!!!!

    My eyes focused more as I shot up in my bed. My instant reaction was to call her back. The last time I had a text or call like this was when Cheyanne got into her accident.
    It brought back a lot of trauma33.
    I quickly dialed Vada's number with shaky hands. I put the phone to my ear, but it only rang once.
    I could hear someone's shaky breath through the other line.
    "Emma?" Vada's voice shot through the phone a bit harshly.
    "Yes, Vada? What is it?" I sounded rude, but it was 1 in the morning, and she was blowing up my phone and making me panic. I couldn't even wrap my head into consciousness before she started yelling.
    "Emma, I need you to call my parents. Ezra and I got into a fight that turned violent and physical. There was so much blood, and I-I am at the hospital, and I just... I NEED YOU HERE, EMMA. PLEASE COME!"
    I quickly jumped up without changing clothes and entered my mom's room. This time, I decided to tell her to take me. I hung up right away as I got into her room. I woke her and told her everything. As we ran into the car, Mom got in contact with her parents, who, on the other line, sounded foolish. My mom drove fast. She saw Vada as

another daughter, as she did with Cheyanne. I was baffled at the situation but also enraged with the issue.

I knew Ezra wasn't a good man. I was nervous to see what I was walking into at the hospital.

"Her parents are already there." Mom's voice chimed into the mix of my thoughts. I looked over at her and nodded, sighing in frustration.

"I told her to get out of it," I grumbled loud enough for my mom to hear.

"What is it?" She asked me.

"She's been seeing this guy who hurts her, and I saw it when we went to lunch. I tried to tell her this was unhealthy, but 'I knew nothing, and I needed to stay out of it. '" I explained to my mom, who had disappointed eyes for Vada. I had the same look in mine.

"Why would she put herself in harm's way like that?" My mom asked. My response was a scoff, shaking my head in my hands.

When we arrived at the hospital, we found Vada quickly. Her parents were yelling at her about these issues.

"This is why you aren't allowed back home." I heard her mom yell as she stormed out of the room. I didn't even acknowledge her. My mom was the person to stop her parents from shouting.

"Mr. and Mrs. Graham, what is going on? Emma got a call from Vada saying she got into a fight with her boyfriend." My mom asked attentively; I stood next to her as she asked questions. Vada's dad scoffed with a moody expression.

"Yeah, a fight that turned violent with guns and knives. Not to mention, she tested positive for cocaine and marijuana in her system. This is why she isn't stepping back into our house."

The news I received dumbfounded me. I had no idea she was kicked out of her parents, but I also didn't know she was strung out on drugs. This had Ezra written all over it. I grumbled in frustration, leaving the conversation.

Vada was lying in the hospital bed, needles and wires attached to her. Her head looked stitched up, with a piece of dressing covering the wound. She had bruises all over her face and arms. Her legs were covered with blankets, but I bet they were covered in bruises, too. She had a larger dressing wrapped around her left arm, and a nurse was bandaging up a large and deep cut that sliced across her stomach. She had blood on her hair, fingernails, and face.

The sight made me want to throw up.

This was different from the Vada I used to know.

"What the hell happened?!" I hissed loudly. My mom came in after me. I shook my head and turned toward my mom. "I need a minute with her." I requested before my mom and the nurse left after finishing her job. I practically slammed the door shut, causing Vada to jump.

"Emma, please, I have a headache." She mumbled, grabbing her head.

"I do not care, Vada Graham. I told you— I told you he was no good, and you did not listen, and this is where you are!" I was mean to her, but if this was the way to get to her head, I guess this interrogation needed to happen. Vada groaned, closing her eyes.

"I know. My mom already laid into me." She replied, playing with the dressings that were attached to her. "I don't need to hear it again."

"Leave those alone!" I yelled, causing her to remove her hands quickly. I was in disbelief with the girl. Vada only listens to Vada and nobody else. I could feel my face burning up with anger.

"You need to hear it again because it is not getting into your thick skull!" Vada's eyes shot toward me like I was the devil. I could see the fire burn in her eyes from my comment. I crossed my arms over my chest, letting out a loud sigh before walking over to her to gently cover her up with blankets.

"I am sorry, Vada, but I hate seeing you like this as your friend, knowing a man did this to you." Vada clicked her tongue against her teeth, glancing down at her blankets.

"I love him, Emma. Others misunderstand him," Vada spoke softly. I couldn't even talk to her for a minute. "I just wish you could see that. I am happy."

"This is not happiness, Vada," I mumbled, getting up from her bed. "None of this is happiness." Vada's parents had come back into the room with sour looks glued to their faces. It looked like they wanted to have a serious talk with her.

"Would you like me to—?" I asked slowly, backing away toward the door.

"No, sweetheart, you can stay." Vada's mom said before her parents slugged over to her bedside.

"Vada, I think you need to come home with us. Sober yourself up and get yourself enrolled in college. You need to be home, not going around on drugs and having violent outbursts with this guy we don't even know."

"Mom, you can get to know him. I promise he isn't always like this." Vada said defensively.

Why did she not want to be at home in a better environment? Before she knew it, she would be homeless, and her parents would not care.

"We don't want to get to know him. We want him away from you. Which is why we are filing a restraining order against him." Her dad said. My eyes widened, as did Vada's. Her eyes were filled with anger, while mine were filled with joy. I could already tell this talk was going to fly south. I let them all talk as I made my way out of the room. I walked down the hall, hearing the yelling start.

As I passed each room, I could hear a loud cough come from one of them. It looked like an older woman getting picked up into her bed by a nurse. Another room had a sleeping man wrapped up in warm blankets and his TV blasting.

As I passed each room, I noticed one of the rooms had a very familiar name on the door. Ezra Hall. I did not think; I just slid the curtain open to see him. Finally, I saw him for the first time. He was very built with a stern facial expression on his face. His dark brown hair was slicked back from lying on the hospital pillow, and his dark brown eyes stared back at me. His eyes even looked dark. He had a few cuts and dressings on him, too, from Vada attacking him back.

"Can I help you?" His deep voice rang out like I was interrupting him. I cleared my throat harshly, crossing my arms over my chest. There was no way I was going to show this man fear.

"Ezra Hall?"

"That's what it says on my door." He spoke sarcastically, pointing out towards the hallway. I could see this man curl a clever smile across his lips, looking at me. "You must be Emma." He said as my heart stopped beating. The fact he knew my name made me sick to my stomach.

"Yes, I am," I hissed. "And you had no right to do what you did to Vada." Ezra chuckled, shaking his head. This man didn't even wince at the pain his body showed.

"Well, you do not know everything."

"I know that Vada was clean and well before she met you. Now, she looks dead. The fact you do these things to women is not okay. You are an abuser." I did not realize how harsh and how close I was getting to him. As much as I was not showing him fear, he did not look phased by my words.

"Boy, you sound like a lunatic." Ezra's demeanor was unbothered. "I can't wait to tell Vada you came after me." A smile crooked onto his lips, showing the evil this man had in him. My jaw dropped open, dumbfounded at how rude and obnoxious he was. What did Vada see in this boy?

"Says the man who put her in hospital."

"Have you forgotten that she stays after everything I put her through? She wants me, and there is nothing anybody can do about that. So, you will have to deal with it or get out of her life."

I could not stay any longer. I had to leave his room before he dropped any more on me. This man made me so sick to my stomach. I could not see what Vada saw in this man. I wanted to burst into tears for her. I wanted to scream at the top of my lungs, "HE IS NOT GOOD FOR YOU! HE IS A BAD MAN!" into Vada's face. She would not listen. She thought he was just misunderstood. I thought she was delusional.

After composing myself, I went to find my mom, and we drove home, mainly because I had school tomorrow.

When I got home, I brushed my teeth again. I brushed so hard that I made my gums bleed. The amount of anger I had in me was horrendous. Ezra blindsided Vada, and he was an abuser and proud of it. That was the part that made me sick.

As I went back to bed, the nightmares came back that night with Vada and Ezra brutally hurting each other.

17

After that call from Vada, it had been a crazy couple of days. To my surprise, my mom let me skip school that next day since I was awakened by a crazy night. Instead, I helped her around the house by deep cleaning and taking a long, refreshing walk. The walk did not last long. It was getting colder outside, and winter was coming fast here in Oregon.

Our winters consist of more rain than snow.

It had been a couple of days since that day, and today, I had therapy around 1:00. I was going to leave early for school, which I was not complaining about. I would rather see Ms. Dayton than stay in school. I left right after my sociology class, which I wished I could have missed. Sociology was so dull to me.

The drive seemed so quick. For some strange reason, I was excited about my appointment with my therapist today. I felt the abrupt urge to talk since I told the twins everything. I parked in the same parking lot in front of the dull building; nothing changed. I exited the car and checked myself in at the front desk. It was like these receptionists were starting to remember me more and more each session.

"Okay, Ms. O'Connor, you are good to go to Ms. Dayton's room."

I thanked the receptionist and started the long walk to her office.

* * *

"You seem eager." Ms. Dayton commented, sitting at her desk.

I was pinching the tips of my fingers in a nervous tick. I never knew what Ms. Dayton would think of me when I wanted to tell her about what was happening. It could go two ways; she could be proud or disappointed in me. I sighed, giving her a slight nod.

"I'm ready," I said, sitting straight on the loveseat. Ms. Dayton gave me a cheery smile, setting her pen down and leaning back. It seemed like she was enthusiastic to hear what I had to say.

This was new.

"Well, we got some good news about Cheyanne's case." I started, observing Ms. Dayton's expressions. After saying this about Cheyanne's case, she seemed intrigued to listen. "They opened it up again."

"You are kidding!" Ms. Dayton jumped in her voice with a smile. This caused me to smile at her happiness. "What made them decide to reopen it?" I shrugged, clicking my teeth at her question.

"I'm— I was there when her family talked to the detective. I guess they found more interesting information on her case that made reopening it beneficial. They weren't sure of surveillance cameras from traffic lights and fingerprints on her car. I was one of the fingerprints, but I was not surprised."

"Wow— "Ms. Dayton commented. "Looks like they are going to be finally cracking something open."

"Yes, but who knows what they will find," I said. I was not wrong. They were determined to find something the first time but ended up just closing the case. It was like they gave up on her. "I just want her to find peace."

"Do you think she is at peace?" Ms. Dayton asked in an honest tone. I scoffed, shaking my head at her question without answering for a moment.

"No, I don't."

"Why do you think that?"

"You will laugh at me, think I am crazy, and lock me up." This was it. I felt confident enough to tell someone that was not Leah. I thought I should but also thought I would be locked up.

"I'm all ears." Ms. Dayton replied. The room was silent for a minute as I sat to think about what I would say next. My head started to spin again from anxiety. I sighed, composing myself to make words with my mouth finally.

"Ms. Dayton, do you believe in ghosts?" I asked. She returned to her seat, thinking about what she would say next.

"Well, I've never experienced anything involving ghosts, but I've heard they exist. Why do you ask?"

"Well— I— okay, this sounds crazy, but I've been talking to Cheyanne."

Ms. Dayton looked up at me, her eyes unsure what to think. She began writing fast before placing her pen down next to the notebook. My heart started beating a mile a minute.

"I've heard worse, Emma." She replied, making me feel better about my statement. I sighed, my hand placed over my chest softly. "Tell me more."

"She does not seem to be at peace. She seemed angry and sad." I replied, feeling slightly more confident telling my therapist I was seeing spirits. Ms. Dayton sighed, removing her glasses from her face to her head. "You think I am crazy?" I asked gently, attempting not to show panic.

"No, I don't think so." Ms. Dayton replied. "As I said, I've heard worse. So, tell me— has she said anything concerning you?"

"Yes, but no," I replied, not giving a solid answer. "She just tells me to stay away from our old pal Vada Graham and her boyfriend," I spoke honestly.

"Vada. I remember her. Do you have any theories of why she says this?" Ms. Dayton asked. I shook my head.

"No. Her boyfriend seems crazy. Not to mention, both are in the hospital after an argument turned violent."

It felt wrong to be explaining Vada's personal life to my therapist. Some things should be left unsaid. I shook my head quickly, stopping myself from saying anything more personal about someone that was not me. My therapist continued to write as I sat momentarily, collecting my thoughts again.

"My apologies," I said. "This is supposed to be about me, not someone else."

"I understand. You just got carried away. This is a new Emma to me. I have never seen her before. And I like it." Ms. Dayton commented. "So, how is school going? Any new friends?"

"Not really. The only two I have are Tia and Ben Coleman. I told them everything about Cheyanne." I replied, changing the subject like a dirty sheet.

"I remember them. How did they feel about it?" Ms. Dayton asked.

"Well—supportive, I guess," I replied, twisting my lips. "They understood the grief of losing someone you love. They are there for me more than anyone else has been. They hugged me and gave me their condolences, but not in a way that said, 'I'm sorry for your loss.' Which—I liked."

I finished ranting while Ms. Dayton wrote down everything. She nodded softly after I stopped talking. I kept looking up at the time, counting down to when I could be done. Just because I was talkative today did not mean that I was enjoying myself. Truthfully, I was tired and wanted to go home to take a nice long nap.

Before I knew it, our time was up, and the rest of our session was based on Cheyanne's case reopening. The drive home seemed long but wasn't. My mom was already home with my brother. Sometimes, I forget he was home for a few days—who knows when he was returning home. Dad was in major surgery tonight and was not going to be home till past midnight. At dinner, Mom mentioned him staying overnight in an on-call room or hotel and driving back tomorrow morning when he had the energy.

After dinner, I did my bedtime routine and wrote another letter. I needed to catch up on the letters. My body had been too tired to try to write. I missed talking to Cheyanne. The last time I saw her was a few days ago at her grave when I met Vada for lunch. Ben and Tia decided to meet up with me. I pulled the chair out at my desk, opened my journal, and began—

* * *

Dear Cheyanne,

Can we discuss Vada for the past couple of days? Boy, do I have a story for you?

She and Ezra got into this crazy fight a couple of nights ago.

She called me at 1 AM, having a meltdown from him physically assaulting her. She assaulted him, too. I wish that Vada would open her eyes. This boy is so toxic, and it makes my stomach turn. Of course, I went to the hospital and freaked out on her.

I was angry.

I also met Ezra.

He was different from other guys and seemed to have a darker energy. I went crazy on him, too.

I saw my therapist today and had a good session. I was more talkative than usual. It concerned her with how much I talked. This woman has never seen my lips move a mile a minute like they were.

I felt myself connecting with her when we discussed things. I am unsure if that is what therapy truly is about, but I only cared about making progress.

I could stop going after a while.

I doubt that.

The school year is about halfway done. Winter is coming, and you know how winter is in Oregon. Rain. Rain. Rain. It's mixed with some snow, but no promises there. This state makes me hate the rain each year I am still here.

Dear Cheyanne

I have been thinking about colleges and my career. If I want to do something with cosmetology or a medical assistant, I'm stuck. I've been thinking about going to school in Texas or California. I haven't entirely decided yet, if you can't tell. I'm trying to get a jump on with my life. Truthfully, I want to get out of Oregon. This place makes me sad, and I feel more miserable every year I stay.

Getting out of here and starting fresh is an excellent way to go.

Mom will probably be mad about it, considering my brother is never home, but I have a life I need to work on.

I need to get myself into gear for the real world alone.

Anyway, I am done with this letter. It is longer than the others, but that is because it has been a little while.

As always, I miss you a lot.

Love,

Emma

* * *

I shut my journal and crawled into my warm bed, drifting off into a deep slumber until the following day.

18

It was Monday morning, the start of a new week, and hopefully a better one. Last week was horrible with Vada's situation, thoughts of Cheyanne's case, and even my encounter with Ezra. It was like one thing happening after another. It was also like living an adult life.

It was 1st period, and I was sitting in Math class listening to my Algebra 3 teacher talk about Parabolas. I was unsure why we were even learning about those; I thought they were in geometry.

Then again, I am not the smartest at math like a teacher would be. Today was tiring and draining like any other Monday. For some reason, I was having some trouble sleeping last night. I kept having dreams about Vada getting hurt by Ezra. I mean, he pulled her to the point where he almost killed her. That was my worst nightmare, to not only have my best friend gone but to hear my other best friend let a man dictate her life so severely he beat her to death. The thought sent chills throughout my body.

Ben was sitting next to me, listening intently to our teacher. He seemed to be enjoying learning about Parabolas. He could teach me since I was not paying the slightest bit of attention. It wasn't because I didn't understand; I was daydreaming about Ben. I could not help but daydream every day in Math. I could use so many kind words to describe Ben; we would be here for days. He had been a fantastic friend but understood my background and why I am the way I am. Ben was a huge part of my life, letting me see the good again.

I genuinely think I am starting to fall for a boy—I am not ready to date.

Not to mention, I didn't even know how he felt about me. We kept glancing at each other, giving the biggest smiles throughout math class. His smile gave me butterflies in my stomach.

Before I knew it, class was over. I was gathering my books while Ben waited for me. It was constant; we waited for each other and walked to our next class. I met Tia at my locker for my next class, and we walked together. It was nice to have friends like them; it almost made me feel better about the past. I stood up from my chair with my books, and Ben was beside me.

"So, what did you think of the math lesson today?" Ben engaged in conversation. It was not something I was dying to talk about, but I went with it. Any discussion with Ben is better than none.

"Erm—confusing. I hate parabolas." I replied, organizing my books in my arms.

"Well, maybe I could help you understand it better." My stomach churned at his words. It was like he was trying to make a move.

"You may have to. God, I hate math." I said pretty harshly but in a joking manner.

"It is not so bad once you truly understand it." Ben and I squeezed through the tiny classroom door together, our shoulders nudging from the small space we had just encountered.

"Well, maybe you'll just have to teach me," I joked, but I wasn't kidding. I was asking for help with math. I was sucking today with comebacks.

"It's a date," Ben said, causing me to stop.

"What?" I blurted out.

"Nothing. Sorry, that was a bit overblown. I meant to say, "Are you doing anything on Friday?" Ben's words caught me off guard this time, but I could not tell if it was in a good or bad way. I didn't answer for a moment, and we just stood in the hallway looking at each other. Ben's face became worrisome when I didn't answer him directly.

Get it together, Emma; he is asking you a question.

"Um, I'm sorry, I blacked out for a moment. I'm not doing anything. I have a clear schedule." I said, giving him a reassuring smile. It was a buildup of him trying to ask me out on a date Friday night. He smiled back, feeling much better about his question.

"Okay, cool. Would you like to go out together maybe on Friday? I know this is a nice place in Portland. Italian food?" Ben asked confidently. I couldn't help but chuckle softly. He was asking me out, and my cheeks were burning. I bet they were rose red right now. I could not believe I was being asked out on a date.

"That sounds amazing, Ben. I'd love to go out with you." My demeanor became calm when I knew he was trying to ask me out without making it obvious. "Maybe we can eat, then do something after?" I suggested.

"Yeah, sure. That sounds like a lot of fun." Ben said with enthusiasm. It was almost too cute not to smile at his excitement.

"Okay then, it is a date," I spoke softly. We started walking side by side again to my locker so I could meet up with Tia. Ben's cheeks were pink. I couldn't help but stare at them.

Dear Cheyanne

"So, what kind of movies do you like?" I asked gently, not to scare him. He was like a small dog that could scare at any time. That was what made him Ben. I only tried to keep our conversation going until we reached my locker.

"Well, I am more of a comedy guy," Ben replied, giving me a small smile. "No scary movies."

"Me too. I don't care for scary movies. I know they are fake, but I still don't see a purpose in them." I replied. He nodded in agreement.

"Exactly. The same thing happens every time. It's all about people dying, having sex, and obnoxious scare scenes." I laughed out loud at his representation of a scary movie. He was not wrong. Every frightening film is almost the same. Some are not like that, but I bet you that 80% of scary movies always end in everyone dying.

"You know, I couldn't agree more. That is why I don't like them. Too much of the same thing is happening. It's boring." I started, watching Ben nod from the corner of my eyes. I enjoyed how much we were on the same page over scary movies.

"Now I know for next time." Next time? We stopped close to my locker to finish our discussion. I saw Tia waiting patiently for me, knowing exactly what her brother was doing. "I can see my sister staring at us," Ben added.

"I bet she will ask me what we talked about." I thought out loud. Ben smirked, looking at the ground momentarily before backing up at me.

"So Friday, I'll pick you up around seven," Ben stated. I nodded in agreement.

"It's a date," I said before walking away toward Tia, who was leaning against my locker. I could feel Ben's eyes glued to me after I had walked away from him. My cheeks were on fire at this point. When I got to my locker, Tia moved away so I could open it. She had a big smile on her face as well. She helped him go through with this.

"So, what did you and Ben talk about?" She asked, her arms wrapped around her books tightly. I laughed softly, turning the dial on my combination in my locker. 24, 39, 15. Open.

"Nothing important. He wants to hang out on Friday." I replied, exchanging my books for my next class. French. I always hated French, but in my first year, I failed Spanish, and I didn't want to continue with it and ruin my GPA. I understood French more, and I found it fascinating.

"You know he has been dying to ask you out for some time now?" Tia said, leaning against the locker next to mine. I shook my head, placing my old books into my locker and grabbing the new ones.

"Oh, I am sure," I replied. "I said yes." Tia's teeth showed beautifully in her smile when I mentioned saying yes to Ben's proposal. It even made me smile. "Okay, okay, don't make a scene," I spoke.

"I'm excited for you two. You must let me come over and doll you up." Tia's definition of dolling me up made my throat tighten. She was one of those girly girls, and I was not. That was where Tia and I grew apart in similarities. Her smile brightened more, but I guess one night was fine, being glammed up for a boy. It was something I had never done before. Maybe one night wouldn't be so bad.

"Fine, but just this once, Tia. You know how I feel about make-up. Just don't make me look cakey." I commanded, shutting my locker behind me. We started walking opposite from where I had come from before. The language classrooms were upstairs in one area. My school enjoyed setting up classrooms by subject.

"You have my word," Tia promised. "So, what happened with Vada?" I had forgotten I told Tia about the incident with Vada and Ezra. I sighed, rolling my eyes in a motion as we turned the corner to head up the stairs.

"Oh, Tia. It was a drama fest." I started. "I guess the two of them got into a fight. It got violent, involving knives.

Vada called the cops, and when they got there, both had gashes from their assault. She called me, and when I got to the hospital, she looked awful. Bruises, dry blood, scratches, and her wounds from him. I will say she got him good, too."

"Wait, you met him?" Tia asked, shocked by my story. I nodded in response.

"Yes, he is intimidating. I don't like him. Vada was trying to find an excuse to stick up for him. They are just so—"

"—Toxic." Tia interrupted. I could not agree with her more. She read my mind well.

"Exactly. I can't help her anymore if she can't see how bad he is for her. It is sad, but again, I can't keep putting myself into drama when I am trying to fix myself and my mental health." I explained. Tia's eyes grew wide with agreement, and she nodded as we turned down the hallway to our classroom. It was three doors down on the right, but we stopped to finish our discussion.

"Maybe distancing yourself from her is the best option," Tia suggested. I had thought about getting away from Vada for a while, possibly excluding myself from our friendship and focusing on better things.

"You might be right." We got to the classroom quickly and walked in to see the classroom piling up fast. "We can talk later."

Tia and I separated to our assigned seats and waited for the final bell to ring for class to begin.

* * *

The day went by quickly. I was sitting in the study hall for the last period of the day. I finished my homework for the day, which gave me time to relax. Before I knew it, the final bell rang, and school was over. I was exhausted and ready to go home. I walked to my locker to pack up my bookbag. There was not much I needed to bring home. Most of my nights are spent studying.

As I was packing my things, I felt someone standing behind me. They were hovering. I turned my head to see Leah's blonde hair frizzed out. I smiled at her before shutting my locker and zipping my book bag up.

"Walk with me." She said softly.

"What's going on?" I asked, slinging my bookbag over my shoulder.

"So last night, I overheard my parents talking to the detectives over the phone about a possible lead." She said softly. She was probably watching what she was saying in case someone around us knew something. It wasn't very confident, but it could happen.

"Okay, give me details." I harped.

"So apparently, they caught Cheyanne's car on a surveillance camera on Main St. When she was at a red light, a black Honda Accord sped through one of the side streets when the light turned green on her. They almost T-boned her, which is another situation to figure out later. They ran the car's plates, but the name that popped up was unfamiliar." Leah explained. We opened the doors to the front of the school and began making our way out to the student parking lot.

"Who was the name? Maybe I know." I asked, but Leah shook her head in a dubious reply.

"You don't know them because I don't, but the name was Regina Hall," Leah exclaimed. I stopped in the middle of the walkway to stare at her. I did not know the name at all.

"I don't know," I stated.

"Well, here is where it is dicey. Regina Hall was an older woman who died last year. They are still looking through how she died. They never officially said of what." My eyes widened, already knowing what this meant for the case. More digging had to happen.

"So, the car was stolen?" I questioned hesitantly, but Leah nodded to my unknown question.

"That would be correct," Leah mumbled as we walked to my car again.

"So now what?" I asked softly, seeing my car from a distance. Leah shrugged.

"I don't know, but they have more work to do in figuring out if anyone in the area related to a Regina Hall could have that car," Leah explained again before heading over to her car sitting in front of us.

After Leah and I split off, I walked back to my car and crawled inside. I let out a small sigh before starting it up to go home.

19

It had been two days since I had heard from Leah about the case. I could not help but sit and think about the name "Regina Hall." I'd never heard of anybody with that name, but the fact that she died a year ago proves that the car was stolen, and this piece of information just made the case difficult.

I decided to skip school today and see Vada. Mom had been riding me on going to see her.

Why? I don't know.

She was still in the hospital since they claimed she was a domestic violence victim and was not allowed to leave for ten days. Who knew if that was the real thing? I wanted to go and have a calm discussion with her about Ezra. He was not good for her.

Now that it had been a few days, her withdrawal stage for her drug abuse should be cleared out. She would have a sober mind, and I could speak to her without hearing objections.

I already knew I would be dead when my mom found out I ditched school. I just needed the day off.

I started out getting ready for the day after slugging out of bed. I brushed my teeth, washed my face, and threw on my deodorant. I decided not to shower since I took one last night. I brushed my hair in a high ponytail, still hanging to my mid-back.

My outfit choice was a blue pullover hoodie and light blue jeans. I was becoming decent in my outfit choices again. This made me feel complete. I put some body spray on to finish the look before heading downstairs to the hospital. My mom had already left for work. My brother was asleep on the couch while my dad was sitting on the kitchen island, having coffee and reading the newspaper.

"Emma, aren't you supposed to be at school?" My dad asked me. I stopped while my head circled inside, thinking of something to tell him.

"Yeah, I have a doctor's appointment. I am going in late." I replied.

My dad believed my lie and sent me on my way. I quickly went to my car to start it up. It was chilly this morning, and my windows were fogged from the rain we got last night. I used my wipers to get some of it away, but I had to wait until the car was warm. While I waited, I got a text from Leah asking where I was today. I sighed, lying once again.

"My mom let me miss today. Be there tomorrow."

I placed my phone in the cup holder and began backing out of the driveway. I made my way toward the hospital. I wondered how Vada was doing, especially with being sober. Everything was dragging along today, and it was only nine in the morning: the people, the cars, even me.

I decided to stop at the store to get some flowers for Vada. It seemed like the right thing to do, considering the last few times that I saw her, we got into it. As we had many outbursts with each other and in our friendship, I couldn't help but feel bad. Many people have told me I needed to cut her from my life, but it could be problematic, considering she was my last connection to Cheyanne.

I stopped at the nearest store, quickly approaching the flower section that was out front. I thought hard about what kind of flowers seemed right for her. I looked at every single one: Dandelions, lilies, roses, sunflowers, and more. I found some multi-colored flowers that looked right for the occasion. I picked them up, making my way to the checkout line. I got to the cashier, who rang the flowers up, inspecting them.

"Pretty choice." The cashier spoke, giving me a small smile.

"Thanks," I said while pulling my wallet from my jacket pocket.

"That will be $6.50."

I gave the cashier $7, encouraging her to keep the .50 cents. I took my flowers and waited for a receipt from her. She flashed me a smile while handing me the thin white paper.

"Thank you for stopping in! Hopefully, whoever those flowers are for loves them." I turned to give the cashier a fake smile before walking out of the store. I jogged to the car, waiting impatiently for it to warm up. I could not believe how cold it was starting to become outside. It was bone-chilling.

I started making my way to the hospital—the one place I did not want to be. The hospital makes me think of Cheyanne, and I could not help but think about it.

***

The waiting room was disturbingly quiet. Cheyanne's family was sitting on the far side of me with Vada; I was alone. My mom went to get me something to eat from the cafeteria. She knew I wouldn't eat it, but it was the thought that counted for her. The day felt dark. Cheyanne had been out of surgery for a few hours, and it was just a waiting game to see if she woke up.

From my understanding, she had a shattered leg that was fixed, and her shoulder was also fractured. She had some broken ribs and cuts all over her from the glass. She had hit her head when she crashed, and they couldn't see any swelling. This did not mean it was not there.

The doctors acted like she was going to be okay, but she was a "ticking time bomb," as they mentioned until they knew there was no swelling in the brain.

Her mom walked over to me with dry tears sticking to her cheek, clearing her throat for my attention.

"Cheyanne's awake. Would you like to come to see her with us?" Her mom asked. I nodded quickly before standing up to follow everyone to the room. Vada came to my side, wrapping her arm around mine. She looked thrilled to see Cheyanne like I was. When we entered the room, she was lying there still. Her arm was in a sling, her leg wrapped in many layers of bandages and was propped up onto a pillow. Her head was bandaged up from where she connected with the steering wheel. She looked brainless for a moment. Her mom walked over first.

"Chey? Honey, we are all here with you." She looked around the room, not saying a word. She looked at me and motioned for only me to approach her. I let go of Vada, leaving her to stand behind everyone, and I was immediately at her side.

"I'm here, Chey," I whispered, grabbing her free hand. She smiled softly, squeezing my hand tightly while I noticed some tears started to flow down her cheeks. Her mom wiped them away. She would not look at Vada, who came to her other side.

"Do you need anything, honey?" Her mom asked.

"No." Cheyanne choked, keeping her eyes on me. *Vada tried to get her attention, but Cheyanne would not look at her.*

Little did I know that would be the last day I would hear her voice.

***

My thoughts came back as I entered the front doors of the hospital. It was nothing but white, and everything looked so calm. That shows that there was going to be something crazy coming in soon. It could never be that calm in there. I checked in and was told where to go. They moved Vada to a different room, a private room.

I got inside the elevator and pressed the button beside the number two. Patiently waiting, the doors opened, and I followed the signs until I reached her room. I knocked first before entering. Vada was sitting in bed watching a local channel on her TV. When I saw her, she looked different. It was not in her looks; it was her whole mood. She looked calm, happy, and sober. She smiled at me before turning her TV down. They must have given her medicine to calm her down, considering she couldn't see Ezra.

"Oh, hey, Emma. I was not expecting you." She said, her voice sounding smooth and nonchalant. I smiled in response, slowly walking over to her side.

"Hi. These are for you." I handed her the flowers when I got to her bedside. She smiled wide with her teeth, grabbing them gently from me and wafting in their scent.

"These are so pretty. Thank you." She spoke before setting them down in her lap. "I will see if the nurse can get me a vase for them." She reassured me to have a seat in the chair that was sitting next to her bed. I took a seat, looking around the room.

"Nice and private," I spoke. She giggled softly, looking around as well.

"Yeah, it's a nice room. It is peaceful, too, until the nurses come to check on me." She said, sounding annoyed when she mentioned the nurses.

"How much longer do you have here?"

"I can come home tomorrow. Sadly, I must go home to my parents, but hopefully, they will let me get out and see people I want to see." I scrunched my brows together, wondering who she was in such a hurry to see. I had a fair guess.

"You in a hurry to see someone?" I asked curiously. She nodded, looking down at her flowers.

"Yeah, erm... Ezra got out a week ago and has been dying to see me. Unfortunately, my parents have that restraining order, and he cannot come here." She explained as my thoughts were taken back. I couldn't put myself in the toxicity of their relationship. It was sickening to hear.

"I see." Was all that came from my mouth before I looked down at my lap. I wanted to see what I could get out of her from the information I had heard a while ago from the detectives. I cleared my throat, pushing my hair behind my ear.

"So, I have something I want to ask you," I murmured to her, trying not to be too loud that it spooked her.

"Sure, what's up?"

"So, have you, Cheyanne, and Ezra ever hung out together?" I asked, biting the inside of my cheek, dreading the answer. But she nodded, giving me a small smile.

"Yeah! I remember it being a fun time. Cheyanne and Ezra got along well." My eyes bulged from my sockets at the answer. I recalled Cheyanne and Ezra hating each other. But Vada kept going. "They clicked so well and had a lot in common. He was devastated, too, when she died. She was the one that went crazy that night."

I felt like I was going to hurl. Why was everything that was coming out of her mouth a lie?

"She went crazy?" I asked in a questionable tone.

"I don't know what happened. He came to me and told me that we had ordered some food when she was at work. Then she saw him and started yelling and threatening him. He said she was obscene with him. He even got taken aback by it."

I could not believe what I was hearing. It was so hard to keep my mouth shut with this one. I never recall her threatening him; it was the other way around. I couldn't possibly wrap my head around everything that was being said. It was hard to sit and listen to this.

"Oh, I see," I replied before changing the subject. "Anyways, are you feeling any better than you were?" I asked, perking myself up again.

"Yes, I am feeling much better. I cannot wait to go home." She replied. The nurse then came into the room to take Vada's vitals. "One second." She mumbled to me.

"Good morning. How are you today?" The nurse asked Vada.

"Good, thanks. Just doing what I must do." Vada replied, sitting still to let the nurse do what she had to do. It was marvelous to watch Vada be as still as she was. She looked like a statue while the nurse checked her out. It only took five minutes to do. After finishing up, the nurse took her stethoscope out of her ears, wrapping it around the back of her neck.

"Okay, you sound good. I will be back in three hours to check on you."

"Thanks." Vada thanked the nurse while she was leaving the room. She sighed, shaking her head at me. "These nurses are so annoying sometimes."

"They are just doing their jobs," I mumbled, writing notes on my phone to tell Leah.

My biggest question was why Vada was lying straight through her teeth. At this moment, I wanted to be the bigger person for what I was about to do.

"So—I wanted to come here to see how you were doing but also apologize for my outburst the night you arrived. I was being protective of you. I want to see you happy." I pushed the words out of my throat, placing a cheesy grin across my lips.

Vada loved the words I spat at her. She grinned back at me.

"It's okay, Emma—no reason to be sorry. I'm also sorry for snapping at you at lunch. I'm just glad you were able to meet Ezra when you did. That way, you could see the kind of person he is." My eyes shot up, looking at her with curiosity. How did she know I met him?

"Wait—" I said, taken back a bit. "You know I went into his room?" I asked. Vada nodded with a smile. It was like she was told the opposite of what happened between us.

"Oh yes. He snuck in here late last night to see me. He told me you were wonderful and I should bring you around more." Vada explained. "Maybe we can build our friendship and hang out with him like I did with Cheyanne." I wanted to hurl when those words came out of Vada's mouth. I didn't want to end up in the same situation as Cheyanne did with Ezra. Who knows what getting to know Ezra enough could do to me?

At this moment, I wanted to leave this place. I made up some excuse of my mom asking for me at home.

"Okay! I hope to see you soon. I will also put these flowers in a vase as soon as possible!" Vada chirped. It was as if she was happy with the idea she gave me. I didn't say much when I left, only running to the car.

This made me leave the hospital questioning everything.

20

It had been a couple of days since my talk with Vada. I hadn't told anyone about our conversation yet. I have been waiting to tell Leah everything. The situation with Vada was the least of my concerns. I had a date with Ben in two days that I was not even remotely prepared for. I needed more time, but there was so much to do to look presentable. Tia was supposed to be my assistant for that.

Vada was discharged from the hospital yesterday. I helped her home to her parents. She begged me to drive her to Ezra's, but I said no. I was not going to be the one to get screamed at for taking her to the one place she was not supposed to be. She got livid with me, but I didn't care. It was for her good.

I was standing at my locker, thinking about the homework I had to pack up. I slept during my study hall today. I didn't sleep well last night, considering my nightmares returned the past couple of days. That is another thing I needed to discuss with Ms. Dayton. I was packing everything up when I saw Leah come up behind me. We have been walking to our cars together every day. It has become a routine.

"Homework? I thought you finished everything in study hall." Leah pointed out. I sighed at her, shutting my locker gently after I zipped up my backpack.

"I couldn't sleep last night. I ended up taking a nap." I replied as we started walking toward the front entrance of the school.

"Nightmares again?" She asked. She already knew me so well. I nodded to her question.

"Yeah. I'm unsure what from, but I hope I sleep better tonight." My thoughts had been rolling at night since I saw Ezra at the hospital. I could barely process the fact he enjoyed being the kind of person he was. It makes me question what he is truly capable of.

"I'm stacked with homework myself. Sadly, I don't get my study hall toward the end of the day." Leah spoke, her finger sliding down her phone like she was trying to call someone. We walked through the front doors to leave. I felt free when I left school.

"Oh, it is the best thing ever. What do you have plans for tonight?" I asked, forgetting for a split second that she already mentioned homework. She began telling me her plans, but I focused on someone in front of the school. He looked familiar. He looked frantic—like he was trying to find someone. As he turned around, my eyes widened with surprise.

Thomas Avery. He was Cheyanne's ex-boyfriend. They broke up a couple of months before Cheyanne's accident. He attended her funeral and then disappeared shortly after. Vada told me that he took her death hard, even more complex than me. Leah was still talking, not paying attention to the fact that Tomas was in front of the school. I stopped her from speaking, pointing in his direction.

"Leah, isn't that Thomas?" I asked. She looked over and took a split second to realize who it was.

"Oh my god, what is he doing here?" Leah asked, walking toward him. He then saw Leah, giving her a small smile. I followed Leah closely as she ran toward him. When we approached him, Leah hugged him tightly around his waist. He was taller than us, which made him tower.

"Thomas! Where have you been?" Leah squealed as he wrapped his arms around her neck to hug her back. The two let go of each other before he hugged me as well. It had been a long time since Thomas had shown his face.

"I needed some time away after everything. I'm still working on it." He replied, sighing like he was trying to compose himself. "Considering the past couple of months."

"We both are," Leah replied, nudging toward me.

"So, what made you come back?" I asked.

"Well, I came to talk to the both of you. I got a call from a detective saying, "Cheyanne's case has been reopened?" He asked in a questionable tone. He crossed his arms over his chest, waiting for our response.

"Yeah, they found some more evidence," I replied. Thomas stood hunched over like he was trying to contain his thoughts. It seemed like this was too much information for him to handle.

"They said that they found my fingerprints in her car. They wanted to talk to me." Thomas spoke.

"You have nothing to worry about. Our fingerprints are on her car, too." Leah reassured. Thomas then leaned toward us more so he could whisper.

"Could we go somewhere that's not school and talk?" He asked. As Leah and I agreed to talk, we walked to our cars to meet at our destination.

* * *

We decided on the park in town, considering it was a decent day outside. What better way to soak up our last nice day for a while? We were sitting at a picnic table by the playground. Thomas was sitting on the table while Leah and I were sitting on the bench. He had so many questions about Cheyanne's case. Leah had more answers for him than I did, considering she had heard her parents talk more.

My thoughts were somewhere else, and it was a place where so many questions lingered, but I was interrupted by Leah's voice.

"I'm sorry, guys. I need to go. I will catch up with you all later." Leah grabbed her belongings and started walking to her car quickly. Her parents probably wanted her to come home. It was just Thomas and I sitting together. After Leah was out of sight, he sighed, looking down in my direction.

"I didn't want to talk to you with her here. I thought this would trigger her." Thomas mumbled, inching down to my level on the bench. I was confused about what he meant, but I went with it.

"What are you talking about?" I asked politely.

"Well, there is some information that you need to know about Cheyanne and Vada. I know it is crazy, but I am the only one who will tell the truth, considering Cheyanne is not here anymore." Thomas' voice broke each time he said Cheyanne's name. It broke my heart to pieces. He was still in anguish at her death. He loved her very much, and this was hard for him.

"Okay, go for it." I pleaded.

"So, I was at her work the night she got into that accident. I was waiting for her to get off her shift. We were going to discuss getting back together—"

"Wait, you guys got back together the night she died?" I asked, shocked. I was happy for the two, which could be why

Thomas took her death hard. He shook his head at my question.

"It never got discussed." His voice broke, and his eyes started to well up with tears. "We were interrupted," He grumbled. I looked in his direction in confusion.

"That night, Vada and her boyfriend came in to get food. Considering how rude and malicious he was to her, Cheyanne did not want to serve him. Vada's boyfriend harassed Cheyanne, and then she and Vada got into a heated argument that the manager had to come out to make them leave to harass her. When they were fighting, he was threatening her too."

"So, what are you trying to say?" I asked, confused and trying to put the pieces together of what Thomas was talking about. But then it clicked.

"Oh god, Ezra threatened her the night she crashed." It finally came out of me. How strange it is that all this fits together? It was too bad that Thomas and Cheyanne never fixed their differences that night because of them. Thomas pointed at me with confidence. It was like we put a couple of puzzle pieces together.

"Correct. Ezra did threaten Cheyanne. I remember it clearly. But the thing is, Cheyanne did not want to see Vada, and that is where it started. Why would Cheyanne not want to see Vada?" Thomas asked in confusion. He was beginning to wrap his head around all the information that was brought up. Even I was trying my hardest. Everything was slowly starting to be pieced together.

"She was mad at Vada because she chose a boy over their friendship. That started when Vada and Ezra began to date." I explained to Thomas slowly so he understood everything better.

"A few days before the accident, I stayed with Cheyanne that weekend because my mom went with my dad to Portland. We talked, and she mentioned something about Vada choosing him over their friendship. It was like she didn't care what Vada chose. She knew who the real ones were in her life. But I could also tell it upset her—they had been best friends for as long as I can remember. Don't forget I knew Leah first."

"Yeah, you're right. This whole thing is just drama." Thomas said. I nodded in agreement. "Hey, listen, I must get going. I have a job interview in an hour. If you need or hear anything, please don't hesitate to call me."

Thomas handed me a small piece of paper with his phone number written down. I examined it for a moment before placing it in my coat pocket.

"So, are you back?" I asked softly but quickly. He shrugged, his face unsure of the choices he had made.

"We will see." He whispered. I smiled at him before he started walking away. I was left alone again. It was not anything new for me. I sat for a moment, thinking everything over. Ezra was determined to end Vada and Cheyanne's friendship and did a pretty good job. I'm sure it hurt Vada to see her best friend dying after a fight. These thoughts were making me nauseous.

Just then, I heard a familiar laugh coming from the playground. I saw Piper Shay chasing a small boy on the playground with her boyfriend, Dylan. That must be one of their little brothers. It must be Dylan's; they could pass as twins. Not to mention, the boy looked like Dylan when he was younger. Piper looked happy, her smile beaming from over here. I thought for a minute before standing up and gliding my feet toward the two of them.

I needed to talk to Piper.

21

"Piper!" I called out.

She stopped in her tracks, turning toward me harshly. Her facial expressions changed from happy to stunned. Dylan looked my way, too, cautiously grabbing the boy's hand. I examined Piper for just a moment. She wasn't in her usual cheer uniform like I see at school. She wore black leggings and an oversized black sweatshirt that looked like it belonged to Dylan. Her shoulder-length hair was tied back into a low ponytail that swung over her shoulder. She looked laid back for once.

"What do you want, freak?" Dylan's tone was harsh, but Piper didn't even blink at his remark. She just stared intensely at me, waiting for me to speak. I glared at Dylan when I approached closer to them.

"As much as that doesn't hurt me like you think it does, I need to talk to Piper about something."

"She doesn't want to speak to—"

"Excuse me, is your name Piper? No, I didn't think so." My eyes glanced back at Piper. "Can I talk to you about something? It's important." She was silent momentarily before looking over toward Dylan and then at me. She gave me a slight nod.

"Yeah, we can talk. I'll be back." She spoke softly before walking toward the same park bench I was sitting at. She left Dylan and the boy alone at the playground. We went to sit down, and I hit her with it.

"I know this happened to you in the past, but I need your help understanding him more—Ezra Hall. My friend is with him, and I think she is in danger." When I said his name, Piper's eyes widened, and her body became stiff. At first, it seemed she didn't want to talk from her body language. It made me nervous, thinking there was more to Ezra than meets the eye.

"I-I need you to understand that this was a bad time for me, and no judgment needs to happen. This is a dark past of mine that I wish never happened, and speaking on this needs to be kept between us. Got it?" Piper snapped slightly, which made me nod quickly, letting out a small laugh.

"Piper, I have no room for judgment here. Remember what I have done?" I commented, making her smirk softly. She sat and began playing with the ends of her hair while thinking about what to say. This boy must make her nervous. A small sigh escaped her lips before she began.

"I was with Ezra for a year. We broke things off right around the time I met Dylan. He hates it when I speak about him, so I decided to come over here. At the time, I had no idea what real love was. I didn't know how I should be treated and when enough was enough. When I was with Ezra, I thought he loved me, but that was not the case. I thought everything was a dream with him, only to end in a nightmare. This boy is not the boy you think he is."

It was like I was in her shoes, seeing everything that had happened to her and Ezra as she spoke.

"Ezra was 20, and I was 16. Being with an older boy would make me stand in the crowd more at school and give me a reason to be popular with power. At first, everything was great. He bought me flowers every day. He would pick me up from school and take me to the mall to buy me whatever I wanted. I thought that was love, spoiling and pampering me with things I enjoyed.

"I was young. I didn't understand what abuse was, and I didn't know when to quit. It had been five months together, and we got into our first fight. It was over him talking to a girl he used to fool around with. You don't know her, but I was angry he was doing it. When I confronted him, he called me crazy and told me I needed to watch how I spoke to him, or it would get bad for me. That was only the first fight."

Piper sighed, looking down at the wooden table we were sitting at. It was like she needed a pause, but I understood. Everything she was saying to me took my breath away. She was 16 and treated like this. I can't imagine the trust issues she gained from him.

"It started to get better until I went to his house one evening, and he was hanging out with some friends. They were sitting in the living room doing drugs. This was around the time his mother died, and he began acting out. They all encouraged me to try, but I said no. They forced me to do them, and Ezra threatened me. He said I'd be sorry later if I didn't do what he said. I don't know what kind of drugs I did, but I grew addicted to them. I did drugs every day for three months. He would shoot the drugs into my veins for me at that point because I would get so high. I am lucky I didn't overdose because I had no idea what I was taking. He just told me to trust him.

"The last night I ever took any drugs was a Friday night. I had a football game I had to cheer on. I had just shot up before the game and was all over the place. It was so bad that my coach forced me to leave the game. I ended up living with him instead of my parents. He took me to his friend's house, and we also ended up drinking. I started to spiral out of control, and one thing led to another. I slept with him. Two months later, I found out I was pregnant with his child."

My eyes widened, but I tried not to show any sign of judgment. Her story shocked me to my core, but I sat and listened.

"I didn't even know you were ever pregnant," I mumbled calmly, not to spook her. She nodded, clearing her throat. I knew there was so much more to say in this story.

"Yes, I was, at least. I went to tell him I was pregnant. I was eight weeks by the time I told him, and he freaked out. He started yelling at me, cursing, and well—beating me senselessly. I was so scared. I knew at that point I had lost the baby, considering he kicked me so hard in my stomach, and the next morning, I had blood running down my legs. At that point, I could see the man he truly was—a monster that no longer cared for me. I was afraid of him."

"I went home to tell my parents everything. I told them I was pregnant, what he did to me, and the drugs. From that moment on, my parents put a restraining order on him, and he had multiple charges from me. Domestic violence and a sexual assault charge were against him. Even though I let him have me, I was a minor. My parents acted off that right away. They also sent me to a psych ward for two months so I could get my act together. I did lose the baby. I'd love to be a mom someday, but I don't think I could ever have a baby with someone like him.

"There was more to our relationship than what I am telling you, but those are the most important parts of the story. Ezra Hall needs to be stopped and put away. I'd probably be dead if I didn't tell my parents. Things got better when I returned to school and got closer to Dylan. I was happier. I didn't look like a shriveled-up pepper anymore. I just . . . I wish I never met him."

I took a minute to soak up everything Piper told me. I almost wanted to cry for her, but it was too much. I think my tears were dried out from crying over Cheyanne's death. I licked my lips slowly, preparing to speak after Piper told me her story.

"Piper, I am so sorry this happened to you. I remember you left for two months and didn't return for nine weeks. You looked so different after you came back—in a good way. I am just glad you got out of it when you did. I appreciate you talking to me." I explained. She gave me a small smile while she sat with me a little longer. She turned to see Dylan playing with his little brother.

"It's okay. I ended up finding someone who loves me for me. Dylan helped me become the person I am today." She spoke gently, smiling over at him. Dylan turned to her and smiled at her back. His smile was gentle and sweet, almost as if he did care for her. "I know you and him don't see eye to eye, but he is gentle."

"I know he is. He is just protective at times. After my outbursts, I have brought the nickname freak into my vocabulary." I glanced over Piper's shoulder to see Dylan getting ready to come here.

"Emma, whoever your friend is, she needs to get away from him. She will end up dead if she does not get out of that relationship. I don't think you understand how dangerous he can be. She needs to leave him." Piper stood her ground on her statement. I listened while Dylan came to her side. I could tell from his posture he knew we were discussing Ezra.

"I've tried. She won't listen to any of us, and I don't know how to keep her away from him without locking her up. I don't know what to do at this point. They have already had it out violently." I explained, the stress for Vada evident on my face. She did not care she was with someone so dangerous. Piper sighed, shaking her head and shutting her eyes. She looked like she was trying to think of something to help me.

"Maybe locking her up is the best option for you. Please don't give up on her, but don't bring yourself into her drama. You don't need to be getting wrapped up in him too."

"You ready, sweetheart?" Dylan asked before looking up at me, although not with the eyes he had for me before Piper and I spoke. Piper nodded, standing up from the bench. "Tyler over here is getting hungry, and we promised to take him out."

"Hey, Piper?" I called out again, standing up and looking in her direction. "Thanks for talking to me."

"You're welcome—anything to help someone in my shoes. Don't forget to stay away from him. He is dangerous, okay?" She said before picking Tyler up.

"Go ahead and take him to the car. I'll be right there." Dylan insisted, kissing Piper on the side of her head. As Piper said goodbye, she walked with Tyler to the car, leaving Dylan and me alone. I didn't know what to expect from this one.

"What was that about?" He asked in a harsh tone, but not as harsh as before. I wouldn't lie to him, considering Piper would probably tell him everything.

"I needed some answers on Ezra Hall," I admitted. His demeanor changed when I said his name.

"You don't associate with him, do you?" Dylan asked, his body stiffening and his fist clenching hard. I shook my head quickly, watching as his body relaxed more. "Well, stay away from him."

"That's the plan. I'm trying to get my friend away from him." I stated, swaying back and forth on my feet while I was talking. Dylan smirked, shaking his head and looking at the ground.

"There's no hope for her. You are better off without her."

"Thanks for your input," I grumbled. We exchanged evil glares before he started walking to his car. I started gathering some stuff and headed to my car, driving home and thinking about what was discussed that day.

"Hey," I looked up to see Dylan standing there again. I raised my brow at him, eager to know what he wanted to say. "Sorry about your first day back. That was uncalled for from my end, and I hope it's something that can be forgiven and forgotten." Dylan's apology took me back for a moment. I was surprised he was even talking to me about that. I sighed.

"It's okay, don't worry about it," I replied, giving him a small smile. He exchanged one back before raising his finger at me.

"I do mean it; stay away from him, and don't put yourself into a situation that involves him, okay?" Dylan warned.

"Okay, thank you ." I nodded before he finally turned and made his way to the car.

So much information for one day.

22

It was the following evening. I was sitting up in my room doing homework. I was slammed with it today, considering I slept again in the study hall. I'm over these sleepless nights. I hoped they would end soon. I went from always sleeping to tossing and turning now. My stomach was churning all night. Mom made tacos for dinner, and it was not a meal I should have eaten.

I was working on my French assignments, texting Tia about plans for tomorrow. My nerves were beginning to intensify, and that was the reason for my upset stomach. My date with Ben was tomorrow, and I was nervous. I had never been on a date before. Ben was my first. What do I expect? Will he kiss me? What will my night end like, but most importantly, will he like me for me?

My French homework only took me 20 minutes, which flew by quickly. Next was math. This was the last of my schoolwork that I had to accomplish. Luckily, it was a breeze. After finishing my homework, I decided to pull out my journal and write to Cheyanne. It has been a couple of days since I've entirely written.

***

Dear Cheyanne,

The past couple of days have been crazy.

I wish you were here so I could tell you everything. I found out about a lot of crazy things. I can't believe you didn't tell me about you and Thomas' attempt to get back together. I'm not mad at you for it, but I was dumbfounded when I heard it from Thomas. Is this true? I always knew you two had a strong connection!

Now, about this girl I went to school with, Piper Shay. I don't know if you have a clue about her from Leah, but I heard something from her about Ezra. Gosh, I wish Vada would run from him. He sounds like a monster. Piper was only 16 whenever she was with him, but to add that she was pregnant with his baby was downright traumatizing to hear. If you could have seen how broken this girl looks, telling me all of this. I cried for her. It made me feel for her.

If only Vada knew these things. She would even consider leaving him if she knew these things. She acts like she needs to stay with him. Oh well, there's nothing I can do. I've done what I can.

School is going well. I have a date tomorrow with Ben Coleman. My nerves are shot right now. I could throw up. I have never been on a date and am finally going on one. It makes me want to cancel. Luckily, his sister is making me go and have a fun time. I will keep you in the loop on how it goes tomorrow.

Anyway, I think that's it. I will keep you posted.

As always,

Emma

* * *

I was finished. I closed the journal, placing it back inside my bookbag to keep it away from my mom. Considering she liked to go through my stuff when I was not there.

Suddenly, I felt a blast of cold air behind me, causing my baby hairs to flow over my shoulders. I turned to see

Cheyanne sitting on my bed. I sighed, almost relieved that it was her I was seeing.

"You scared me," I mumbled, zipping up my bookbag to hide the journal.

"I'm sorry. I wasn't trying to scare you." Cheyanne replied. She had a regular outfit that she used to wear. It is better than what I have seen her in previously. The hospital gown was getting depressing. She wore a pair of light blue jeans and a black hoodie. Her hair was wavy and stayed the same as before. She looked perfect. It was like she never left. "Are you about to go to sleep?"

"No, I can't sleep again these days," I responded softly, rummaging through my desk and putting everything away. My books and binders from school were slipped back into my bookbag as Cheyanne sat, watching me fumble through my things.

"How come?"

"Erm—just thoughts in my head," I replied, cleaning up my laundry on my bedroom floor. "Any reason why you decided to pop in tonight?"

"I noticed you had a rough day," Cheyanne spoke, watching every move I made. I stopped momentarily, almost forgetting about my exciting day with Thomas and Piper. I sighed, turning toward her.

"Yeah, I spoke to Thomas and Piper Shay today," I said, sitting beside her. Cheyanne's eyes closed, letting out a small sigh after her eyes stayed shut.

"How is he?" She asked, hesitantly at first. I shrugged, looking toward the ground, wondering if I should be honest with her.

"He's. . . Thomas. He is doing his best. Besides, you left out telling me that you and he were working on your relationship." I stood up, going over to my desk again to rummage. Cheyanne sighed but let out a small laugh.

"Yeah, we kept it on the down-low until it was official," Cheyanne replied, rubbing her hands over her bright red face. She was embarrassed for trying to patch her relationship up with Thomas.

"You could have told me," I said, laughing softly as I returned to sit beside her.

"I didn't know if it was going to work out. I had to wait. Plus, it was hard to talk to you about my love life while dying in the process." Cheyanne spoke brutally but honestly. This was her usual demeanor. It stabbed me in the heart, hearing her talk about dying. I grew silent for a minute.

"Thomas told me something—about the night you died," I mumbled, changing the subject.

"Oh yeah? What did he tell you?" Cheyanne asked, her voice sounding surprised that I mentioned it.

"Well, he said that Ezra and Vada showed up at your work. Things escalated between you and Vada." I spoke, watching her reaction tense at me, mentioning the two people she couldn't stand. Cheyanne's response was a slight nod, puckering her lips like she wouldn't speak.

"No, he's right. That happened."

"Well—what happened?" I asked. Cheyanne seemed like she did not want to discuss that night. That night to her was a living hell, and discussing the night when her life ended was a huge thing to ask of her. Cheyanne sighed, silent for a minute before finally speaking.

"I was working. Thomas came in to see me, and I was supposed to be getting off within the hour. I told him to wait for me, and he saw everything. I was cleaning up my tables when they came in an hour before we closed. Vada asked for me as a server, but I did not want to serve her after the shit she'd pulled before. The hostess seated them in my section. I pleaded for someone else to take their order, but nobody else did. I had no choice.

"I went over to get their drinks, and Ezra started with his harassment. He was making comments about how he wanted a different server, but I politely told him he had no choice and I was the only server he had. The comments did not stop. If anything, they got worse, but the thing was, Vada thought the things he was saying were funny. That set me off."

"Wait, Vada encouraged his behavior?" I interrupted immediately. What Cheyanne was telling me was upsetting. Just hearing the things I had all day made me have questionable thoughts about whether Vada should even be in my life. I shook my head, getting a headache.

"Something like that—since she and I ended bad. I don't know if she feels bad about it, but she should. It was clear that night that she had chosen an obnoxious boy over a friendship. Anyways, after getting their drinks--"

I suddenly felt myself slipping into her story. I was sitting at a booth with Thomas, watching the whole conversation. Cheyanne must have brought me into her past somehow.

I never knew the dead could do that.

I turned around in the booth to see Ezra and Vada sitting across from each other. Cheyanne was standing at the table with a notepad in her hand. She wore an apron around her waist, a white tank top with the restaurant's name, and jean shorts. The bangs of her wavy hair were clipped back to keep out of her face. Since the restaurant she worked at was a bar, she had to dress the part of one.

Everything was silent, ringing slipping through my ears until it cleared up, and then I could hear the tiny sounds of glasses clinking, plates being placed on a table, and conversations from others in the restaurant.

"Okay, you guys ready to order?" I heard Cheyanne's soft voice from the table. She always had the best customer service voice.

"What, are you rushing me now?" Ezra's voice chimed up. I could see Cheyanne's jaw tense up from his rude input. I stood up and walked a little closer so I could hear better. I sat at the booth next to theirs. It was easier to hear things better from this point of view. Cheyanne scoffed, digging her pen into her notebook. You could tell she was already angry with the two.

"No, sir. I was asking if you were ready." Cheyanne hissed, trying to keep her professionalism to a bare minimum. I couldn't help but laugh to myself.

"Okay, well, I am not ready." Ezra groaned, smacking his hand down toward the menu. Cheyanne groaned, walking away from the table. I watched as Cheyanne walked away; her posture changed into a defensive stance. I overheard laughter coming from their table. Ezra's deep chuckles rang out like he wanted everyone to hear him.

"Damn, it's like I have to answer to a woman even when I'm not ready." Ezra whisper-yelled. He had his presence known as people were glaring at him. I turned to see Cheyanne talking to the hostess, glaring in his direction at his comment. She walked in a different direction to Thomas' table, leaning over to speak to him. He even looked angry.

My attention was brought back when I heard a small but girly laughter coming from the table. Vada. My stomach sank seeing her laugh at what he said. Nobody thought that was funny except for her. The two started conversing instead of looking over the menu.

"So, when we get done eating, we can head out to the car and hit a bump before going on a ride," Ezra mumbled, but it was enough for me to hear. I scrunched my eyebrows at his comment. What was a bump? After sitting and thinking for a moment, I realized a bump had something to do with drugs. My jaw dropped.

"You know I'm down," Vada smirked, looking back at her menu.

"Yeah, you better be," Ezra mumbled before silence fell over the two. I examined the room from where I was sitting. Cheyanne was still over talking with Thomas. Two couples sat at a different table, and two older men sat at the bar, discussing their married life and how much their wives got on their nerves. I was hearing everyone's conversation like I was a vampire. Suddenly, my body jumped at the loud voice of Ezra.

"Hey, waitress! I think we're ready over here! Quit talking to your boyfriend, and come take my order." My eyes widened with a jaw drop as I heard his comments. I turned to see Cheyanne tense, angry. At this point, there was no time for professionalism; this was accurate harassment. She walked over, standing in front of Ezra.

"For future reference, there's no need to treat me like a slave. I am not your girlfriend." Cheyanne snapped, getting her pen and notepad out. "Now, what can I get for you guys."

"I'd like a manager," Ezra grumbled. Cheyanne smirked, looking down at him.

"I don't think so. I feel harassed. There's no need to bring a manager into this."

"Well, I need a waitress who can do her job, not a bump on a log that's making rude comments against me because I'm catching you not doing your job." Ezra snapped back, looking up at her with a smirk. Vada sat quietly, watching the two have it out.

"Excuse me? Who do you think you are?" Cheyanne snapped more, putting her pen and notepad away.

"I'm a customer, and you must take my order."

"I don't take orders from you." Cheyanne snapped, snatching Vada's menu from her and attempting to grab Ezra's before he took it away from her.

"Cheyanne, stop. You are making a scene." Vada said, standing up so she was at eye level with Cheyanne. But Cheyanne turned to her, tears growing in her eyes. Seeing her friend defending a boy over her must have hurt her. It would kill me too.

"Don't Cheyanne me. Do you even remember me, Vada? Your best friend?! You are supposed to have my back more than anyone, and you sit here, letting this snake talk to me like I am a rag doll he can throw around. What is wrong with you?" Cheyanne was fuming. Her voice cracked with each word from the pain she felt. It made tears brim my eyes. I was at a loss for words.

"You are my best friend, and you are supposed to support everything I do, and I don't see that in you with this relationship. All you do is try to start arguments. I introduced you to him, thinking you would have a fair state of mind for him and make him feel welcome. But clearly, Emma should have been the one to meet him first." My heart stopped when I heard my name. What did I have to do with this? I wish I could have stopped this fight before it got out of hand. But this made Cheyanne angry, and I could see it.

"Don't you dare bring her into this? That's your escape for everything, to bring Emma into our fights for no reason. This is between you and me. She is not here to defend herself, so you must stop that." Everything was silent for a moment, and my anxiety was through the roof. I looked back to see a manager coming out from behind me. One of the workers must have gone back to get him. "I'm sorry, but I must ask you two to leave."

The manager came around and asked what was going on. Cheyanne explained the harassment situation before the manager looked over at the two.

"I'm sorry, but if you are harassing my employee, you need to leave. I don't tolerate abuse toward my workers. I don't care if you are friends or not. You need to leave."

Ezra slams his hand on the table, standing up and getting in Cheyanne's face. His expression looked evil and demented. Cheyanne's manager pulls her back by the arm, waiting for them to leave.

"You have lost a customer, then. I'll get you, Cheyanne." Ezra grabbed Vada's arm and pulled her out of the restaurant. Cheyanne was frozen momentarily while her manager dismissed her into the back for a quick break. Before I knew it, I was sucked back into reality. Cheyanne was still sitting in my bed with me, and everything was normal. I couldn't help but wipe the tears from my eyes. I was lost, not knowing what to say.

"Cheyanne, I—"

"—I know. It was rough. After I left that night, I wrecked my car. I don't remember anything after that. But when I crashed, it felt like someone meant to hit me. This was no accident. Someone meant to hit me."

23

It was Friday evening.

Tia was at my house while I prepared for my date with Ben. I was extremely nervous about tonight. I have never been on a date and don't know what to expect. I sat in my bed while Tia sat behind me, curling my hair. She had applied a small amount of make-up like I had asked for, to make me look less cold.

My nerves felt shot. I couldn't help but feel numb still about the events that happened the past few days. I was doing everything in my power to focus on this date.

Cheyanne's vision opened my eyes to the kind of person Ezra is. Not to mention how Vada encourages the behavior from him. It seems like she loves the bad boy side of him. I find that stuff very unattractive in a man. Treating a woman like they are nothing is not something someone should look for in their partner.

"You nervous?" Tia blurted into my head, shooting my thoughts back into reality.

"A little. I have never been on a date." I said, sighing from looking at the time on my alarm clock. I had 20 minutes before he got here.

"Oh, don't be nervous. It's only Ben. Think of it . . . as two best friends hanging out." Tia guided me gently as she finished curling my hair. I couldn't help but laugh at her pep talks. They helped slightly.

"Isn't that what a date is?" I asked.

"Oh, enough of the date talk. No matter what, you are going to have fun. Trust me on this." Tia spoke proudly, exiting the bed to unplug the curling iron. I nodded, letting out a small, shaky sigh with it.

I fumbled towards my closet to find something to wear. Tia picked out a spaghetti strap blue dress that hung to my knees and hugged my hips tightly. At first, I was against the wardrobe choice, but Tia insisted. I wondered why I had that dress, to begin with. She grabbed some matching blue heels to go with it and a white cardigan to keep me warm.

I was regretting this outfit choice. As I examined myself in the mirror, my heart was pounding. I've never seen myself this dressed up since before Cheyanne died. This was new, yet different to me.

Before I knew it, I was ready for my date, and Ben had just arrived at my house. My brain began to scatter.

"Okay, Emma, just remember, it's Ben. It's not some random stranger that you met on Tinder. You guys will have a lot of fun tonight, and you will leave this date the happiest you've ever been." Tia confirmed before I am emitted on my way with her brother. I took a couple of deep breaths before giving her a slight nod.

"I'm ready," I said to myself before heading downstairs. I heard the doorbell from the top of the stairs, making my heart thump. I skidded down the steps to the door, quickly opening the door to lay my gaze on Ben. He was speechless for a moment, trying to speak but couldn't. My cheeks were on fire from his reaction.

"Say something, brother. You are embarrassing yourself." Tia poked her head over my shoulder, smirking. Ben's cheeks also turned red, shaking his head.

"Wow, Emma. You look amazing." Ben finally said, rubbing the back of his neck while trying to speak. I smiled at him widely, considering I'd never been told things like that.

"Thank you. Shall we?" I asked, reaching for his hand. Ben nodded, grabbing onto my hand gently. We all stepped out of the house and walked toward his car. Tia went in the opposite direction to her car and left us for our date. Now, I was alone with him.

"So, what's the plan?" I asked as he helped me into the car. Ben shut the door before going to the driver's side, getting in gently, and starting the vehicle.

"We are going to drive to Portland," Ben spoke excitedly. My eyes widened. It had been so long since I took a trip to Portland. My last trip was with my mom to visit my dad seven months ago. It was to see my dad for dinner one evening. My expression showed how excited I was to get out for once.

"Portland? What are we going to do there?" I asked, buckling in as Ben started the car. He laughed softly before buckling himself in and putting the car in drive.

"You'll see," Ben whispered before speeding down my road. Before I knew it, we were on the highway heading to Portland. He was speeding, but it was a fun and safe kind of speeding. Was he trying to impress me? I couldn't help but smirk that I was on a date with a boy. This was something I had never thought about doing. Cheyanne would be proud of me. I used to believe that boys were gross.

"Okay, you must tell me what's going on. I'm itching to know." I groaned, leaning over the middle console and resting my head on Ben's shoulder. A smirk slipped onto his lips, looking over toward me. Our eyes connected as he drove before letting out a small sigh.

"Fine. First, I am taking you to a beautiful Italian restaurant, and next, ice cream for dessert." Ben explained his plan. My lips parted when he told me everything. This boy had to be a dream to me.

"My two favorite things. Italian and ice cream," I spoke, leaning away from him and relaxing against the leather seats. Ben chuckled, driving with his right hand propped up on the steering wheel. I couldn't help but study how attractive he looked when he drove. My heart began to skip a beat from my overthinking.

We were in Portland and arrived at one of the top-rated restaurants in the city—Mama Mia's. I have never been here, but my mom always told me it was the best place. My dad would bring her here when they had date nights. When Ben parked the car, he quickly got out before walking to my side to open the door.

What a gentleman.

I stepped out as he reached for my hand in assistance. His gesture made my cheeks burn with happiness. He kept a hold of my hand as we walked to the restaurant. His skin was soft. I wonder if my hands felt the same way.

"You have been here before?" He broke our silence. I shook my head at his question.

"No. But I've heard of this place. My dad used to take my mom here for date nights. She always said they had good fettuccine alfredo." I said, examining the city as we walked down the sidewalk to our destination. From a distance, it already looked busy. Considering it being a Friday night, I bet there would be a long wait. I stopped dead in my tracks, exhaling a small gasp.

"Oh no, looks like there is going to be a long wait," I mumbled, turning toward Ben. He had a broad smile painted across his face.

"Are you doubting me, Emma O'Connor?" He asked sarcastically before retaking my hand and pulling me inside, pushing past all the customers waiting around. As we approached the hostess counter, the woman in uniform kindly smiled at us. "Good evening. I had a reservation for Coleman." I scanned the room at all the angry faces looking toward us. It seemed like they had been waiting for a long time.

"Alright, you two. Your table is ready. Please follow me." The hostess grabbed two menus and walked us back toward an open booth. Everything was set up beautifully as we sat across from each other. There was even a small vase with a single red rose in the middle of the table and two plates in front of us. I sat comfortably in my seat, beginning to look over the menu. I had a good idea of what I wanted, but I still wanted to see what else they had.

"You have any idea of what you are getting?" I asked Ben, who was inspecting the menu like I was. He pursed his lips together as he flipped through.

"I'm thinking—Tour of Italy," Ben spoke, continuing to review the menu. Our waitress brought over some breadsticks, opening her small notepad.

"Good evening! My name is Grace, and I will care for you tonight. Would you like to start with something to drink?" She spoke clearly with every word.

"I'll take a water," I said shyly as Ben ordered a lemonade right after me.

"Perfect. I will get those for you, then return to take your order." As I looked up toward Ben, she walked away, laughing softly at ordering a lemonade.

"What are you laughing for?" Ben asked with a broad smile painted across his face. I shook my head, the heat rising to my cheeks, feeling how red they must be getting.

"Lemonade?" I asked, raising an eyebrow.

"Yeah. It sounded good. What is wrong with that?" He asked me in a soft tone. I couldn't help but look at him and see Ben's beauty. He has perfect eyes, lips, face—everything. He was the definition of perfection for me.

My heart began to flutter as he was smiling.

Before I could answer him, our waitress returned with our drinks, opening her notepad to place our order. She asked what we were thinking of ordering, looking at me first.

"I am going to have the fettuccine alfredo, please," I spoke shyly, closing my menu and looking over towards Ben so he could order.

"I am going to do the tour of Italy, please, and thank you," Ben said, closing his menu and handing it back to the waitress.

"Would you guys like salad?" The waitress asked, her smile standing out in her features. Her bright blonde hair also stood out in its tight ponytail. As a server, you must have the best customer service, considering most of your paychecks come with tips.

"Yes, please. And can we get a side of Alfredo for the breadsticks?" Ben asked, giving the waitress a warm smile. She nodded before walking off to put our order into the computers.

"Hm . . ." I hummed to myself, biting my bottom lip before speaking. "Great minds think alike. I was going to ask for the same sauce." I finished my sentence before picking up my straw to place inside my water and taking a small sip. Ben did the same thing with his lemonade. His face showed the drink's sourness, but he tried to keep it cool.

"So, tell me about you. Everything that I need to know." Ben rested back gently in his seat, shooting a wide smile my way. It gave me goosebumps when he smiled at me. This is what I was nervous about. What should I tell him? What is everything to him? I stayed silent momentarily, thinking of things to say to him.

"Well, there is not much to me that you already know. I mean . . . My dad is a cardiothoracic surgeon, my mom stays at home, and my brother is away in college. I use my free time to sleep, spend time with family, and read. I do like to read." I went on to talk about my family and my hobbies. I didn't have much of an idea of what to tell him about my hobbies. I was more of a loner.

"Although, when Cheyanne was still here, we used to go to the falls in town to swim, jump off the cliffs, and eat snacks. Now, that was fun. I do miss them days." I added, trying not to bring this dinner down in the dumps with my talk of Cheyanne, but it was true. Those were the days when I dared to be extreme. I knew what having fun was really like. I shook my head, reaching for my glass and taking a sip of water. I met Ben's gaze as he was listening intently to my thoughts.

"I have never been swimming at the cliffs in town," Ben said while sipping his lemonade.

"You've never been?" I asked in surprise. I kept forgetting that Ben and Tia were both new to town, and they had not been exploring as much as others.

"No, I have heard from kids at school how nice and relaxing it is there," Ben replied. He never took his eyes off me; no matter what I did, he always seemed to have his eyes on me. I could feel my cheeks getting hot.

To my surprise, the date was going perfectly.

*　*　*

Driving home was filled with nothing but conversation. I felt like I hadn't been quiet since we had ice cream—the night was filled with laughter and happiness. We rode with the windows down. My hair retracted from its curls now. I swear, I have not laughed this hard in so long. This boy is doing something to me but in a good way. The drive was quick, and we sat in front of my house. I didn't want to go home; I wanted to stay like this forever. I have never felt something so surreal for a boy in my life.

We got out, and Ben walked me up to my front porch. What a gentleman.

"I guess this is our final stop," Ben mumbled, his eyes meeting mine, showing sadness. I frowned slightly while reaching for his hand.

"This is the worst part," I replied, not taking my eyes off him as I spoke.

"I had a fun time with you," Ben spoke, giving me a warm smile that sent butterflies through my stomach. I nodded to his comment.

"Yes, I did too. Thank you." I wrapped my arms around him and hugged him. I could hear his heart racing as my head rested on his chest. "For everything. I had the best time. Can we do it again?"

"Absolutely," Ben said. He leaned down and gently kissed my cheek before walking to his car to head home. It hurt my heart to see him leave. This night was one I needed, and I was the happiest I had been in so long.

I loved this boy and everything about him.

24

The following day, my body awoke peacefully. There was no headache, pain, or reason for me to dread the coming day. I felt light and fresh. A smile was glued to my lips when I sat up, stretching. It felt so good to stretch.

I hadn't felt this happy in a long time. I inhaled the fresh scent of my room, then exhaled hard. This made me want to crawl out of bed and be productive. First things first, a nice hot shower. I found something to wear, throwing it down on the bed. I strolled out of my room and headed to the bathroom, immediately turning the water on so it got hot quickly. I took my hair down from its messy bun, letting it flow down my back. The loose curls from last night were still in tack. It almost looked too pretty to wash. I decided to throw my hair back up and leave it alone. I was feeling a braid today anyway.

I undressed quickly before stepping inside the shower. It was a quick one at that. After washing, I let the water run down my body. I could feel my muscles releasing from the tense pressure. My eyes rolled from how good the water felt. After standing there for a few minutes, I decided to get out. I turned the water off and wrapped my towel around my body tightly, drying off every inch of my skin. I scurried to my room, feeling a blast of cool air hit me when I opened the bathroom door.

I started dressing in the outfit I laid out on my bed: a pair of black leggings with a red T-shirt to go with it. I stood before my mirror, twisting my hair into two tight fishtail braids. Once I finished my hair, I felt the sudden urge to attempt putting some makeup on. It wasn't much, just some foundation, mascara, and lip gloss. For once, I looked like a girl. I looked like my old self. I'd missed this version of me. It gave me the energy to write to Cheyanne but write something positive.

After getting ready, I went downstairs, getting hit with the smell of coffee. Mom must be home. I decided to sit outside on this beautiful Saturday morning. I always loved sitting outside my house, watching all the cars go by. I parked myself on our swing on my porch, opened my journal to a blank page, and began writing--

* * *

Dear Cheyanne,

How do I explain the emotions I am feeling right now?

I feel good. For the first time in a long time, I feel amazing.

Dear Cheyanne

Last night was memorable; the entire night, I felt complete, like the missing piece of my puzzle was put back together. I've never felt this way about a boy. Ever. Ben made me feel like I was the only girl before him. We went to dinner in Portland and stopped for ice cream on the way home. We talked for so long, I swear I couldn't catch my breath when I got home.

The funny thing is that I woke up this morning feeling fresh. Like nothing terrible has happened, I can write you a letter for the first time and not feel angry and depressed. I feel new. This boy may be the key to new happiness. I hope things stay that way.

Therapy has gotten more accessible and easier to go to. Ms. Dayton and I are doing better. I remember wanting nothing to do with that woman and thought she was annoying. But now, things are good with her and me. For once, I feel alright going to my sessions. I don't cry during them anymore.

As for Vada, I don't know, Cheyanne. She is out of control. She only sees Ezra as her number one and the only person she can rely on. How can you rely on someone when they hurt you all the time? I don't get that. Does she love being treated that way? Is she just used to being brought down? No matter the situation, nobody deserves that. I wish she would listen to me, her parents, or anybody. The Vada we knew before is long gone, and I know it.

I wish I could've done more.

***

My writing was interrupted by my mother coming outside. She had two coffee cups in her hand. A small smile was on her face as I closed my journal.

"Hey, honey, what are you working on?" My mother asked, handing me a cup of coffee with cream inside. My mom knew me well. She sat beside me as I took a small sip of my coffee, trying not to burn my tongue. It tasted good. My mom made it perfectly.

"Oh, nothing. Just something for therapy." I replied, setting my journal down away from her. As confident as I was now with my journal, I was still not ready to show everyone what I was writing. I didn't think I could ever show someone this. My mom took small sips of her coffee, rocking the swing gently in rhythm.

"Your dad will be home tonight. Care to join us for dinner?" My mom asked. I nodded, always looking forward to my dad coming home from work. She then jumped straight into the obvious.

"So, how was your date?" She asked. I couldn't help but feel the burning sensation grow on my cheeks. From the look on her face, I was blushing. "It went well."

"It did. He took me to dinner and ice cream. It was the most fun I've had in a while. Since Cheyanne and everything." I spoke, sipping on my coffee harshly after saying Cheyanne's name. Hearing her name come from my mouth still hits me differently sometimes. I've learned how to control my emotions better throughout this experience.

"Wow. Seems like a nice guy. When will I meet him?" Mom asked, a smirk working its way across her face. I laughed softly, shaking my head.

"Soon, Mom, I promise. I need to see how this goes first." I spoke, eyeing her. She nodded, understanding where I was coming from. "I don't know, though."

"What do you mean?"

"Well, I've never had someone care for me as much as he does. It's scary. My problem is that I don't know if I am truly ready for a relationship." I explained, my heart hurting as the words flooded out of me. My mom watched me, showing interest in our conversation.

"Because of Cheyanne?" She asked. I couldn't answer her. All I did was nod, focusing on what was before me. Which was nothing, but I couldn't look at my mom right now. "Oh, honey. It's okay to feel confused right now. You've been through a lot these past few months. Your body is still tired and repairing the damage you've felt. That's nothing to be ashamed of. But I will tell you one thing—I met your father at a hard time in life, but I decided to keep going. Now look at us. We've been married for almost 20 years, and I am still as happy as I was the first time I met him. Don't give up on anything you love, even if your heart is broken from before. It just takes time to feel like you matter."

"I don't want him to see my depressed side. He already has, and even though he was so supportive, I want it to be happy from here on out." I explained, looking down at the coffee swirling around in my mug.

"Then you make sure that you keep things positive. This boy could be your forever flower," my mom said. I scrunched my eyebrows at her words. Forever flower? I had never heard anything like that. I couldn't help but ask.

"Forever flower?"

"Yeah, it's like a plastic flower. Those flowers never die out on you." My mom said. I thought long and hard about the words she said. A smile slowly appeared, sipping my coffee more until I finished it quickly. "I will say, you look good, Emma. Today, you look fresh—new—the best I've seen you since Cheyanne died. You look great, dear." After thinking about it, I sighed, getting up from the chair.

"Then I am going to see my forever flower," I replied, getting to my feet. I leaned down and hugged my mom for the first time in a long time. "Thank you for talking to me." She hugged me back, a sigh escaping her lips.

"Of course, dear. I am always here." We then broke off before I ran inside to grab my keys. I decided to head over to Ben's house to see him. I needed to tell him how I felt.

* * *

As I pulled up to his house, I parked on the street. I sat for a moment, containing myself before finally having the courage to get out. As I walked toward the house, their front door opened, and I saw Ben come out. My heart fluttered when I saw him. My smile grew wide, but he didn't see me. I started jogging up to him when.

No. This couldn't be what I was seeing. I stopped dead in my tracks, watching everything. She was a beautiful blonde that I didn't recognize. She was taller than Ben and looked older than him. My heart stopped. I could hear him talking.

"I'm glad you were able to make it out here. I just wanted to make sure we were still good." Ben said gently, looking up at the tall girl. I saw the girl nod, smiling wide at him.

"Of course. It's not every day I can come out to see you. You are looking good." The girl replied. Then, the two hugged tightly. My heart dropped, and so did my jaw. Tears began to burn in the corners of my eyes. I felt like my heart had shattered at the sight. I couldn't see this anymore; I had to leave. I turned quickly and started to walk back to my car. Then I heard it.

"Emma, wait!" Ben's voice echoed through my ears, but I shook my head. I got back in the car, starting it up quickly before speeding off. I left Ben in the streets, watching me drive away. My mind began to spin. This feeling—I recognized this feeling once again. What was this feeling?

This was the same feeling I had when Cheyanne died.

The wave of depression and anxiety rolled through me, leaving me feeling out of control.

Oh no.

25

My room was dark. Dusk was spread across the sky and flashing into my room. I felt nothing. The horrible feelings I once knew were rolling across my body again. I sat in my bed, staring at the emptiness I felt. I never thought Ben could make me feel like this. I had no idea who that girl was, but I didn't want to know. My phone sat on the other side of my room, vibrating every five minutes. It sounded like a good idea not getting on my phone. I didn't want to hear the excuses. Like Ben, Tia has not stopped trying to reach me. You would think by now they would leave me alone. I wonder if she knows what her brother did.

There was no way that I wanted to see him again. Once a cheater is always a cheater. Granite, I didn't need him to explain himself, but I know what I saw. One thing is sure: I needed to leave this house before I went crazy again. I needed to go somewhere.

Who do I call?

Leah?

I know she's always busy on Saturday nights. Thinking about the people I have, I could only think of one person that I know who would want to do something.

I sighed, pulling myself out of my bed and towards my phone. I scoffed at my phone, seeing six texts from Ben, eight from Tia, and seven missed calls between both. They are going to break my phone if they don't stop. I scrolled down to the bottom of my contacts, finding her name, clicking it, and the line began ringing. It didn't take long for her voice to come through the phone.

"Hello?" Vada's voice seemed calm and raspy. It sounded like she had just woken up. However, I wouldn't be surprised if she did.

"Hey. It's me. I know it's been a while, but do you have any plans tonight?" I politely asked before making it seem like she had to go out with me. The other end of the line was silent before her voice returned.

"No, I am free. Why did you want to do something?" Vada asked, a yawn escaping through her throat. I nodded like she was right in front of me.

"Yeah, I—I want to go out. Anyway, we can get into a club?" I asked, making it sound too apparent that I wanted a night to let loose.

"You want to drink?" Vada came out with the question. I didn't know what to say, but I couldn't be in denial any more.

"Yes, I do," I replied. I heard Vada laugh through the phone.

"Okay, I got just the thing for us. Come over around six and look decent. I will send you my new address. I'm not at home anymore." Vada spoke. I couldn't help but smile. It would be nice to spend some time with Vada. It is needed, and I think I could use a girl's night. I agreed before we both hung up the phone. But the million-dollar question was how would I get out of dinner tonight with my parents?

***

As I approached the address Vada had sent me, I couldn't help but scrunch my eyebrows at the sight of the house. It looked run down like someone hadn't lived in it for years.

Was Vada living here?

She is probably back here with Ezra. I cringed at the thought of his name. As I parked on the side of the street, I slowly got out and went to the front door. I knocked a couple of times before the door opened to the sight of Vada. When I saw her, my lips parted.

She looked completely different from when she was in the hospital. Her cheekbones were sunk in, and she had bags under her eyes. However, she managed to cover up those dark bags with makeup. She looked like she was using it again. I blinked a couple of times, snapping back into reality before she noticed my intentional staring. I was engulfed in Vada's arms before I could even speak. She had a strong smell of weed in her hair.

"Hey! It's so good to see you. How are you?" I could not speak momentarily when the pungent smell glided through my nostrils. It made me nauseous. I gulped loudly, clearing my throat and managing a smile.

"I'm okay. I just wanted to have a girl's night." I spoke. I was not ready to discuss Ben. Not to mention that Ezra was probably here, and I did not want him to know about my business. After our run-in at the hospital, I had bad feelings about him. Vada grabbed my arm and pulled me inside the house. It was small. You walked into the living room right when you walked in. The couch is lined as a sectional around the wall. Their TV was mounted to the wall, and their entertainment stand had small baggies, pipes, and cigarette buds sitting still.

"I'm down for--. "The both of us were startled by clattering coming from the kitchen. Ezra strolls into the living room, a cigarette hanging from his lips. He was eyeing both of us before smirking and sitting on the couch.

"We're about to head out, babe. This is Emma; I am sure you guys have met before." Vada spoke for a long time, grabbing her purse off the couch. Ezra grumbled, not paying attention to anything Vada said except he was staring at me. "Did you put them in my purse?"

"Yes, Vada," Ezra grumbled more, getting up and turning his game on. It looked like he was thrilled to have some time alone without Vada. The pit in my stomach made me feel extra nervous about him. Just being in their house made me uncomfortable.

"I'm going outside," I mumbled, turning towards the door, but Vada followed me.

"Don't be out too late. I am not coming to get you." Ezra demanded of Vada. I rolled my eyes, walking outside after hearing his commands. I heard Vada say something before she followed me.

"We are walking. There's a bar right down the road from here. I don't think it's a good idea for us to drive if we are going to drink." Vada spoke. I smirked to myself. That was the smartest thing I have ever heard come out of Vada's mouth.

"I agree. But how am I going to "

"Don't you worry about that?" Vada spoke, smirking at me. What did she have in mind?

***

"Are you kidding me? Fake IDs? How did you-?"

"Ezra made this for you. I already had one. This is how I have been getting into clubs. Don't worry; I have the best idea in getting you in." Vada was out of her mind. I am not trying to get so drunk I can't function. I grumbled to myself as we entered the bar. There were a lot of younger adults in here. People played pool, sat at the bar, danced, and mingled. My stomach was stirring more and more like I was going to throw up. As we approached the bartender, he smiled in our direction.

"Well, hello, Vada. How are you doing tonight? I see you brought a friend." The bartender spoke, looking in my direction. I scrunched my eyebrows. Vada must come here all the time.

"Yes, this is my friend Emma. It is her 21st birthday. Let's treat her well tonight!" *21st birthday?* This was her brilliant idea. One thing for sure is I am never coming back here again. I always hated lying, especially if it was illegal. I gulped, giving the bartender. I have never been drunk before. The bartender poured vodka into two shot glasses and then started making what looked like a fruity drink. He finished it quickly before splitting the drink into two tall glasses.

"Here you go! On the house. Happy birthday, Emma." Vada grabbed our drinks and shot glasses, handing me mine. The smell of alcohol reeked. I already regret this decision.

"What is this?" I asked Vada, but she already took her shot, giving it back to the bartender.

"Who cares! Just drink it." I sighed, taking the shot whole. The burning sensation travels through my gums and down my throat. My lips curled up, showing that it was my first time drinking. Vada giggled, taking my shot glass and giving mine back as well.

"Let's go sit and talk!"

I started sipping on my drink as we went to the dance floor. To my surprise, Vada was making this fun and letting me loose. We found a booth and sat next to each other.

"So, you want to tell me what's going on?" Vada asked as we continued having our drinks. I knew this question was coming. I kept drinking, and before I knew it, my drink was half gone, and I could already start feeling the alcohol get to me.

"I went on a date last night with Ben. It went well. I decided to see him today, and when I got to his house, I saw him hugging another girl. I didn't know what to do. I just left. I could have let him explain who she was, but my body just kept telling me to go home. So, I did, and here I am." I explained thoroughly, finishing my drink quicker than I thought. My head began to spin as Vada finished hers as well.

"Looks like we need another round." She said before getting up to order another round. She quickly returned with two more of the same drinks we had, letting out a small sigh.

"Boys are dumb. They never know what they want. Maybe it was a misunderstanding, and that girl meant nothing to him. But you will never figure it out until you talk to him. Maybe you should." Vada explained, looking directly at me as she spoke. "But don't run away from him. From what you have told me, he seems like a good guy."

We sat and discussed different things, catching up on our lives, considering it had been long since I'd seen her. We both had already hit our third drink at the time, and I was very drunk. The rest of the night was filled with laughter, dancing, and a wonderful time with Vada. But before I knew it, I was so drunk I don't remember leaving the bar.

***

Screaming. Thumping. Glass Shattering. Arguing.

I jumped inside a dark room, lying in a bed I did not recognize. But I did remember the scream escaping from the other side of the closed door. Vada. I was still drunk; I did not know what time it was. The room was spinning, and the loud noises made concentrating hard.

"Vada?" I mumbled, getting up from the bed and falling over as I did. All I could hear was Vada and Ezra yelling. I got to the door, cracking it open. Every light was on in the house, causing my eyesight to see white and purple specks.

"Will you shut your mouth? You are going to wake her up! I took a bump with you. Was that not good enough for you?" I heard Vada yelling in the distance. I could see the living room from where I was, and it sounded like she was on the other side of the house. I must be in a guest room. I got down on the floor, lying on my stomach to see what was happening. Heavy footsteps echoed through the house, sounding like they were approaching me. The rest of the conversation was hard to make out, considering I was heavily intoxicated.

The two came into my peripheral vision. Vada looked like she had taken a beat down while I was sleeping. Her hair was a mess, tangled up in a big knot. It looked like he grabbed her by the hair. Her dress was off, and all she had on was her bra and panties. It seemed like something was happening; Vada didn't want to, and Ezra was mad at her. Gross.

I breathed slowly so the two couldn't hear me. The next thing I knew, Ezra raised his hand and smacked Vada across the face while she was yelling at him. I gasped so loud, watching her head spin to the side from how hard the hit was. It looked as if he could have snapped her neck at the speed at which her head spun. I covered my mouth so the two of them couldn't hear me. At this point, I was drunk and scared. I wish I dared to climb out of a window, but I was afraid to move.

"You will NOT speak to me that way!" Ezra's voice chimed through the house and my ears. I covered them as the pounding headache grew worse from his voice. Vada slowly turned her head back, pausing momentarily before pushing Ezra, causing him to stumble back into a wall.

"I do what I want; you drug attic narcissist." Vada's voice was deep. I didn't even recognize her. Vada pawns him off as a good person when she talks terribly about him, too.

Something is going on here. Ezra laughed before getting back to his feet and shoving her back into what sounded like something breakable. I heard Vada yell. Ezra walked closer to her, seeing him grab her arm and bring her back into my vision, pinning her to the ground.

Tears started boiling in my eyes as I watched every hit Vada took. She looked weak and lifeless. She blacked out, and Ezra was swinging on her. I was right. He was beating her. One punch after another. Her limp body flailing around with every hit. I could even hear his fist connecting with her face. Ezra stopped after a couple more hits, leaning down and whispering something to her. He then got up and pushed her limp body to the side with his feet before sitting back down on the couch, playing a video game.

I wanted to throw up, scream for help, and cry so loud that they both could hear me. I stayed quiet on the floor for the rest of the night. The images I just saw replaying in my head repeatedly.

26

The following day, there was no way of sugarcoating the situation. I was still a bit drunk, but it was beginning to turn into a hangover.

The house was silent. I had been sitting against the door all night, not even trying to move. I could use my anxiety medication right now.

I needed to leave.

I could not even find my phone to look at the time. I bet my mom is worried sick. I told her I was only going out for an hour and coming home for dinner.

I never came home.

Oh, I am grounded for life.

The house was silent, and I heard nothing but creaking from the wind against the walls. My mind kept replaying the events that occurred last night. I could not get out of my head watching Ezra's fist wailing on Vada's face and her yells echoing through the walls.

I sat, blocking the doorway with my body and my knees pressed to my chest. I picked every piece of my skin around my fingernails, they were raw. My ears were ringing from the yelling and trauma. It was like hearing the news of Cheyanne all over again. I sighed to myself, squeezing my eyes shut.

"I told you. It's bad." My eyes shot open to see Cheyanne sitting in front of me.

Her facial expressions looked disappointed. I couldn't respond to her without wanting to cry. My sobs choked in the back of my throat before wiping my nose from the snot that was dripping.

"I didn't want to believe you. She—she is out there with that monster." I choked softly so neither Vada nor Ezra could hear I was awake, not that it mattered. From what I saw a few minutes ago, they were both out cold.

"You need to leave," Cheyanne whispers back to me.

I met her eyes; they looked pleading, like she was begging me to leave. I rubbed my wrists along the temples on my head, the headache growing relentless now. I sighed, standing up with a stumble. I forgot I felt drunk still. When I rose to my feet, the nausea escalated. I turned to open the door slowly, but when I turned back to Cheyanne, she was gone. I grew sad. I did not want to do this alone.

My footsteps were soft and quiet. The house creaked several times as I tip-toed toward the front door. When I got into the living room, I stopped, gasping at the sight I was seeing. My shaky hands reached into my jacket pocket for my phone, and I began taking pictures of the sight I was seeing. The drugs lined along the table, beer and liquor bottles scattered along the room, Ezra was passed out on the couch, and Vada was lying on her back against the floor.

Her face was bloody; I could not recognize her. I glanced at her hands, seeing her knuckles scrapped with blood. It looked like she was trying to defend herself the way that Ezra looked. He had a few cuts and bumps on his face.

I took pictures of the two. After finishing, I could not leave her there. I tip-toed to the kitchen, grabbing a dry washcloth. I put water on it to dampen it. I trailed back into the living room, beginning to wipe Vada's face and knuckles off. I was careful not to wake either of them up.

A light sob escaping from my mouth at the sight of her. I was scared for her. I was going to lose her like I did Cheyanne.

"I'm sorry," I whispered, dropping the washcloth beside her. I stood up quickly and ran out of the house. I ran to my car, quickly getting in and backing out of the driveway as fast as possible. Before the two could realize that I was gone. I promptly plugged my phone into the charger in my car so It could turn back on.

The entire ride home, I cried out loud.

I feared that Vada was going to get herself killed staying with this boy, and there was nothing I could do to convince her. Did she want to die at this point? I felt the nausea coming back. I probably shouldn't have been driving while still somewhat intoxicated. I had to pull over; I felt like I was going to be sick. When I pulled over and opened the door, I immediately felt the acid rising in my throat. It escaped through my lips, making the connection with the pavement beside me. After a minute, I felt better. A mixture of alcohol and the sight of Vada got too much for me. It made me feel so sick.

I slammed my door shut after my outburst, hearing my phone buzzing like crazy. My phone was back on again. I saw 12 missed calls from my mom, plenty of text messages between my dad, mom, and Ben, and 20 between Ben and Tia. I sighed. I felt horrible about Ben. I read one of the messages from Tia, and my heart stopped, and guilt rose in me.

"I don't know what you saw with Ben and that girl, but an old friend of his came to visit. They were best friends, and he had

never had feelings for her. He wanted to introduce the two of you to each other. He loves you, and he wants to talk to you. Please call him back."

After reading that message, I sighed, rubbing my eyes harshly. I screwed up something so wonderful with someone because I didn't let him explain who she was. Let alone introduce me to her like he wanted to. I sent a message to Ben before I made my way home, considering I knew my phone would be taken from my parents.

"Meet me tomorrow at the park after school."

I went to my mom's messages and could already tell I was in trouble. I hope she has not done anything too crazy by filing a missing person's report on me. I quickly drove home, and when I did, I could see my mom and dad both home.

Oh god.

I got out of the car and made my way inside the house. When I shut the door, I could hear footsteps racing from upstairs.

"Emma-Jean O'Connor, that better me you!" I heard my mom's voice through the house. I groaned, grabbing my head as it was pulsing with every loud noise. I was in so much trouble. When my parents came flying down the stairs, their expressions were scared yet angry.

"I'm sorry I—"

"Would you like to explain yourself, young lady?" My dad's voice roared as my mom pitched in with his.

"We were worried sick about you! Your phone is going straight to voicemail, and not coming home for dinner—like I asked you to do! Not to mention, I got a call from the school on Friday saying you did not show up for school last week. Would you care to explain that?"

My mom was furious. I could tell in her body language and facial expressions. I knew there was no hiding about ditching school last week and the events that occurred last night. Who knew my school calls parents about students not showing up?

"How—How did you know about school?" I stammered, my eyes burning. All I wanted to do was lie down, not be screamed at. This hangover was a buzzkill.

"Don't you worry about that young lady? Now, care to explain about last night?"

"Mom, please. I have a headache, which makes my eyes burn from the yelling." I groaned, covering my eyes with my hands. From my mom's expression, she knew exactly what was wrong with me. This ultimately made things worse on my end.

"Are you—Are you drunk, Emma?" My mom yelled more. I groaned again. "I can't—you—you are done. I have had it with your behavior. Your phone. Now. You are grounded."

I sighed, handing my phone off to my mom. I knew it was coming, and I would not argue about it.

"You will go to school and come home. No friends. No extracurricular activities. No boyfriend. Nothing. School and home. You understand?" My dad roared more. I nodded with my eyes shut.

"Yes. Now, can I go shower and go to sleep?" I asked softly. I could see how disappointed my parents were in me. I can't say I blame them. I hope they don't go through my phone and see those pictures I took. Then I'd be in more trouble than I already am. Oh no, the pictures.

"Go." My mom mumbled to me. I started climbing up the steps before turning towards them.

"Um—how long am I grounded for?" I asked curiously. I needed those pictures. I had to find a way to send them to Leah.

"When we say so! And don't even think about getting onto any electronics. They are out of your room." My dad snapped more. I sighed, turning back to head up the stairs.

"Noted," I mumbled, walking towards my room. It was empty, like usual. My laptop was gone, as well as my TV. What was I going to do now?

After showering, I crawled into bed to sleep off this hangover until dinner.

* * *

My mom's voice called from downstairs for my name. It was dinner time. I had been up in my room all day. Thankfully, I slept my hangover off, but my hunger escalated. I slugged out of bed and made my way downstairs. My dad must have left for work, leaving my mom alone with me. She was sitting on the island alone, eating dinner and drinking wine. I haven't seen my mom drink in such a long time. I must have driven her over the edge.

"Make a plate." She mumbled as she drank more. She watched my every move. I covered my plate in grilled chicken, mashed potatoes, and a vegetable combo he made. I grabbed some ranch for my chicken and went next to my mother. She didn't speak to me for a moment. I had decided to break the silence.

"I'm sorry, Mom. I was with Vada, and we got carried away with hanging out." I spoke, but my mom kept eating. I could tell she was listening to what I was saying, so I continued. "I wanted to drink, and she told me she would with me, so I went over to her house."

"You were not at her house. I called her parents, who told me she chose to live with her boyfriend. So, I will ask you now—all you did was drink? No weed? Heavy drugs? Cough syrup? Any of that?" My mom asked harshly. I could tell in her voice she was trying to stay calm. I shook my head honestly at her question.

"No drugs. I don't do that. I just drank, that's all." I confessed to her. She sighed, taking another sip of her wine. "I thought things were getting better, Emma." She mumbled, taking a bite of her mashed potatoes. I did the same, shrugging at her comment.

"It's complicated," I replied in a whispery voice. I could see my mom look over at me like she wanted answers. I knew she did. "It's nothing. I misunderstood something with Ben, and I probably screwed everything up, so—I need to go back to square one." I continued.

"Emma-Jean, don't give up on yourself so quickly. Maybe he will be considerate, but you should have let him explain himself if you misunderstood something."

"I know, Mom. I'm sorry for scaring you and dad. I promise that will not happen again, and I understand the consequences." I spoke. My mom smiled softly, giving me a nod as we both sat to finish dinner.

The night ended quietly, and I fell asleep for school tomorrow.

27

The last period came quicker than I'd imagined. Ben and I have not spoken. He didn't sit next to me in math class today, and we didn't share a peep. I felt bad for everything I had put him through already. Should I even try to fix this mess?

"Okay, class, don't forget to do your homework tonight. It is worth 40 points just for completing it. Please get it done." I quickly shuffled out of the room, my teacher's voice shouting through my ears. I had to meet Ben at the park. I'd rather discuss things there than in school, where everyone can hear. While packing my bag, I felt someone come up behind me. Oh man, I hope it is not Ben. As I turned around, I saw Tia standing there.

"Are you okay?" She asked softly. I nodded, retracting my arm from her grip.

"I'm fine. I need to talk to Ben and fix things." I replied to her before making my way towards the school exit. I quickly made my way out to the student parking lot, arranging to head to the park. I hope I get there before Ben does so; I have time to think.

Luckily, he had already arrived and was waiting for me. I sighed at the anxiety that was coming through me. I was never good with confrontation. All I need to do is let him explain what happened and who this girl was. While acting like Tia didn't already tell me. I walked up to where Ben was sitting, giving him a small smile. Ben smiled back, to my surprise. He looked almost happy to see me.

"Hey," I mumbled, sitting down next to him. He gave me a nod as a response. We sat in silence for a moment. I was chewing hard on my cheek, anxious for his response.

I did not know what to say to him or how to start this process of apologizing. I was in the wrong, and I knew it. I needed to make things right. I didn't know how to. We both stared into the grassy patch before us, eager to speak to each other.

"So—I want to explain what you saw that day. It was not what you think." Ben began to explain. I sat in silence, my eyes locked to the ground.

"Who was she?" I asked softly.

"Her name is Marissa. She was my best friend for a long time before I moved here. We never had a love connection; it was just a friendship. She wanted to visit me the weekend we had our date, but I could not blow both of you off. So, she flew in the morning after so we could have Saturday together and Sunday together before she came home. You saw her returning to her hotel for the night." I let Ben talk and explain to the girl.

"So—you two never—?" I stammered to speak to him. I didn't want to say anything that could upset or make him feel like I couldn't trust him. He responded by shaking his head, a chuckle escaping from him.

"No, never. She's like another sister to me, but not as annoying as Tia," Ben replied with a small smile. I sighed, rubbing my fingers along my face in exhaustion. Ben then started laughing out loud, rubbing his face. "I am just going to come out with it; Marissa has a thing for—women," Ben added, my eyes widened,

"Oh—" I grumbled. "So, she--?" I stammered with my words, wanting to be more respectful to his friend, considering I had already messed up.

"Yes. She always has been since we were in sixth grade." Ben replied, confident in his answer. I groaned at my embarrassing judgment. I felt stupid now.

"I'm sorry I misunderstood. I really should have let you explain." I apologize sincerely. "I am not good when it comes to being let down," I explained more, turning my head, hoping to see the sweet Ben I knew. Luckily, Ben's heart was kind enough to forgive my actions.

"It's okay. I would've freaked out, too. I do have a question for you." Ben spoke, becoming severe, for just a moment. I felt obligated to answer the question truthfully, considering he told me everything. "Where were you when we tried to reach you Saturday night?"

I froze at his question, the scenes I witnessed still new in my head. My lips parted as I wanted to explain it all to him, but PTSD got the best of me for a split second.

"Erm—" I started to say before shaking my head towards the ground.

"You can tell me. No matter what it is." Ben nurtured me, resting his hand on my shoulder. A small sigh escaped from my lips.

"I didn't cheat, if that is what you are asking," I replied, hoping he knew. "I was with Vada."

"Oh. I guess that's not bad at all." Ben spoke, smiling towards me. His smile kills me, making my heart pound against my chest. Unfortunately, he didn't know the whole story of Saturday night.

"Well, it's a complicated thing," I murmured, sighing yet again; I decided to come out with it. "I went drinking with her. I got drunk. Somehow, she brought me back to her place with her boyfriend, Ezra, and when I woke up, the two were arguing, and it got physical fast, and—it wasn't pretty." I stammered plenty of times, telling Ben all of this. His smile disappeared quickly as he reached down, grabbing my hand. "I took some pictures of everything when I left the next morning. They are brutal."

"Show me."

"I—I can't. I don't have my phone on me. I'm grounded." I stated. "Which I had coming."

I needed to get a hold of those pictures, mainly because they aren't something my mom needs to see if she's gone through my phone. I would be grounded for life if she saw those. "I need to figure out how to get to those pictures."

"Is your mom home?" Ben asked. As I thought about what day it was, I shook my head.

"No. She goes to a spin class today around this time. She won't be home till 5." I replied. Ben quickly stood up from the bench and pulled my hand with him.

"Come on. I have an idea." He spoke softly, pulling me towards our cars. "Let's get your phone, and you can send me the photos." He suggests. As we got to the car, his phone started ringing. He pulls it out from his pocket, wrinkling his eyebrows. When I looked down from his puzzled look, I saw Leah was calling him.

The two must have exchanged phone numbers at some point.

"Answer it." I barked, but he shook his head and handed the phone to me to answer. I sighed, hitting the green button and placing the phone against my ear.

"Hello?"

"Oh, Emma, good. I was hoping you were with Ben. I can't reach your phone." Leah spoke through the phone, her voice sounding raspier than usual.

"Yeah, um—I'm grounded, so that's why. But what's up?" I asked.

"Is there any way you could come to my house? I found something in this case, and I think you need to see it. They have a suspect in mind." Leah spoke. My eyes widened as I turned towards Ben, nodding quickly.

"Well, be there. I need to go get my phone first." I spoke.

"Okay, well, see you soon." I hung up the phone, giving it back to Ben, who had a confused look on his face.

"We need to drop my car off at my house, get my phone and go to Leah's. They have a name." I said to Ben.

He nodded as we got into our cars.

* * *

"Holy shit Emma these pictures are gruesome." Ben and I were sitting in front of my house after I got my phone. My parents sucked at hiding my belongings. They've hidden it all in the same spot for over ten years. It was nothing hard to find.

As Ben flipped through the pictures, he got to the one with Vada's beaten face. I gasped at the picture, turning my head away. It was still too hard to see, especially being the one who had to clean her face off.

"I cleaned her face off after taking those pictures. I couldn't leave her like that. I'm sure she knew." I murmured while watching Ben shake his head at the sight of the pictures he was seeing.

"This is absurd," Ben said.

"I know. Ezra did that to Vada. I wonder what he is truly capable of." I replied, flipping through the pictures with Ben. His eyes widened when we got to the picture of the drugs sitting on the table.

"Oh my god. You didn't—do any of this stuff, did you?" Ben asked, turning his whole body towards me like he wanted an answer. I scoffed, raising my eyebrow at him.

"Please. Saturday was the first time I've drank in a very long time. I'd never ruin my life with things like this." I spoke. Ben laughed, shaking his head and then sighing in relief.

"Good. I would have been distraught with you." Ben grumbled.

"I wouldn't blame you. Let's get to Leah's before my mom gets home and realizes I was gone. I have 1 hour until she gets back."

28

As Ben and I pulled up in front of Leah's house. I saw an unfamiliar car sitting in her driveway. I hope that's not a detective or something. The last time I was here, I was bombarded with questions like I was the one committing a crime.

"Okay I have one hour before I have to get home so let's make this quick." I relayed to Ben.

He nodded before getting out and making his way over to my side. He opened the door for me, smiling down at me. He is such a gentleman. How did I get so lucky? I couldn't help but smile back at his gesture. As we both made our way towards the front door. I knocked, waiting for Leah to answer but instead, I just heard her yell to come inside. As the two of us made our way through the front door, I walked directly into the living room to see Leah sitting on her couch and Thomas sitting on the floor in front of her. I gasped softly at the sight of Thomas. I'm surprised he is here.

"Thomas. Hi." I greeted surprised. He smiled softly, waving his hand up towards me. Ben comes up behind me, seeing Thomas and nodding his head at him. "So—what's going on?" I asked, sitting down next to Leah. Leah sighed, looking down at the papers scattered across her coffee table.

"Well, I was going through my parents' papers about the case wondering if they have found anything else after the last time the detectives came by and—they have a possible lead on someone." Leah explained. I gasped at the words 'possible lead'. Could they have finally found the person responsible for Cheyanne's death once and for all? My head was spinning. "And—I feel like this is something you need to know."

"Tell me." I pleaded.

Ben sat down next to me on the couch. Leah begins to rummage through the papers.

"So—do you remember that night when they came to my house asking questions of someone named Regina Hall? And how it was her car?" Leah asked, sitting there going back to that night. I nodded.

"Well turns out, this woman was 50 years old, and she died of a drug overdose. They thought she was an old lady, but she wasn't. Apparently, her death was called in by her oldest son Jeremy Hall, who lives in California. They called him in for questioning about the car and he said the car was with his younger brother." Leah paused after that, sighing. "I think you may know the younger brother."

I glared at Leah puzzled. I have no idea who the younger brother could potentially be.

"I—I don't know anybody." I replied to Leah. At this point, my brain was fried from all the digging and information that was given to me not too long ago. My head was not in the right space to even think about who Leah was talking about.

"Think Emma." As I sat thinking for a moment, I started thinking back of the day after Cheyanne died. I started asking myself if I had met anybody since then. I started naming them off in my head. Ben, Tia, Ezra, Piper. That's it. Ben and Tia Coleman; who could never hurt a fly. Piper Shay, which I barely spoke to. Then Ezra Hall.

Wait.

My eyes widened quickly, looking over at Leah. She could see that I knew exactly who she was talking about. She could see the wheels in my head begin to spin. Everything was starting to come into play.

"Don't tell me it's—"

Leah holds the paper out and it was clear that Regina Hall was Ezra's mother and she died from an overdose. My eyes were about to pop out of socket from what I'm seeing.

"Ezra apparently took his mother's death to heart, and he was acting out more than what he already has before. Ezra is the prime suspect that the police are looking towards right now." Leah explained more. I shook my head, setting the papers down.

"This is impossible. I didn't see a—" I picked up the papers looking to see the car that was allegedly the one that hit Cheyanne. "Black Honda Accord at their place when I was there on Saturday."

"Maybe it's hidden?" Thomas suggests. I thought for a moment, seeing where he was coming from with the idea. "Maybe he has the car hidden in the back of the house."

"Only way to find out is going to check it out." Leah spoke. Ben immediately steps in, volunteering for himself.

"I'll go."

"*No.*" I hissed. "I think I should. I can go check on Vada while I'm at it." I suggested. I could see the confusion on Leah's face when I talked about 'checking on Vada'. I sighed, not wanting to explain this situation again. Then again, explaining it would make more reasoning as to why I should be the one to go.

"On Saturday, I got drunk with Vada. While I was passed out, I woke up to her and Ezra screaming, and I watched him beat her. He doesn't know I saw it all but, I took these pictures of them the next morning." I gave my phone to Leah as she looked over the pictures with Thomas. The two of them look horrid seeing them.

"Why didn't you go to the police about this?" Leah asked, handing my phone back to me.

"I've been grounded. I couldn't. Plus, my mom doesn't know about this." I explained. The four of us sat in silence as I started looking through all these papers before blurting out. "My god, what if Vada knew about what Ezra did? What if she's known all this time?"

That was the last thing I wanted to think about.

"She was at the restaurant where Cheyanne works the night she was hit. Make sense. The three of them did have a heated moment together." Thomas explained. I looked up at him, almost forgetting that Cheyanne did show me what happened with the three of them. I pressed my lips together, wanting to tell Thomas that I knew. But it would make me sound crazy. I turned towards Leah.

"Cheyanne showed me that night. He isn't lying." I whispered softly so the boys didn't hear. Leah scrunched her eyebrows at me, scooting closer so we could talk better.

"Her ghost showed you?" She replied to me through a whispered tone. I nodded in her direction. I didn't forget that only Leah knew about seeing her ghost.

"What you two whispering about?" Thomas asked curiously. The two of us turned towards him, shaking our heads.

"Nothing. Girl talk." Leah answered him.

I couldn't help but smirk to myself before getting serious again. Ben raised his hand up, wanting to say something. We all turned towards him like he was the shy boy in class finally wanting to talk.

"For Emma going to Vada's, I don't think she should go alone." Ben suggested. I agreed with him, but I don't think he should be the one to go with me. This is potentially dangerous, considering Ezra is a prime suspect and I don't want Ben getting into any danger.

"I agree Ben, but you aren't coming with me." I stated. He turned towards me, dumbfounded at my comment. "I'm sorry but I think it should be Thomas. You have a big heart for me, and I can't have you there if this is a dangerous thing to do." I continued. Ben looked defeated that I didn't want him there.

I just wanted him safe.

I sighed, grabbing his hand, and squeezing it gently.

"It is not that I don't want you there. I just need someone to keep a look out for in case something goes wrong. You have love for me, and I don't think it should be you." I explained more, our eyes staring into each other as I spoke to him.

"I agree. I don't mind going. I'll make sure she's safe. You have my word." Thomas spoke towards Ben. Seeing how nurturing Thomas was about the situation clearly made Ben feel a little better about the idea of me going. Leah sat and listened to the conversation before adding onto it.

"Ben you can come here and help me out with looking through more information." Leah suggested her idea. Thinking a little bit, I smiled at Ben and then at Leah.

"Maybe Tia should come too. She's good with problem solving and figuring out clues. She's also good at hacking. Maybe she can help you guys' hack into cameras or any systems you need." I suggested.

This would also make Tia included, considering she is my friend too and I didn't want her to think I thought more of Ben than her.

"That's actually a good idea." Ben stated.

"Sadly, I can't do anything tonight. Maybe this weekend when school is over for the week. I need to get home before my mom does." I spoke. I started gathering things up, but my head was spinning.

"We will talk more throughout the week. You better get home before you get in more trouble." Leah suggested as Ben, and I made out way out to leave to his car. I couldn't believe that Ezra could have been the one to hit Cheyanne.

The big question I have is—how long has Vada known what he has done? Or if she even knows?

When Ben had dropped me off, I only had 10 minutes before my mom was going to be home. Before I got out of the car, Ben grabbed my arm, pulling me back in.

"Listen—why don't you send me those pictures on my email? I can have Tia print them out so you can turn them in when we get him. That will be more charges on him." I sat, listening to Ben's idea. It was a good one. I pulled my phone out, quickly sliding my finger across the glass to finally send it all over.

"That's a good idea. Thank you." I murmured to him. I leaned over and kissed his cheek before hoping out of the car. I needed to get my phone back in its hiding spot before my mom finds out I've been out. Ben drove off quickly as I made my way inside the house.

I ran upstairs, hearing a car pulling into our driveway. Mom. I quickly ran to her room, throwing my phone back into my mom's dresser. That was always her key spot to hide my belongings. It was like it was never touched. I scurried into my room, pulling out books like I had been studying this whole time. I heard the front door open, footsteps echoing through the house and up the stairs. I swallowed the lump in my throat, nervous that I would get busted for everything I did.

Then, my mom appeared in the doorway of my room. She had a smile on her face. She must be in a good mood.

"Hey honey. How was your day?" She asked, cheerfully more than normal. It scared me slightly. I shrugged, my body showing there was nothing too exciting that happened.

"It was fine." I replied.

"Dinner will be ready in about 45 minutes, okay?" My mom announced. I nodded, before going back to my blank pages I had in front of me. I let out a sigh of relief, happy I wasn't busted.

Though I couldn't help but think about the events that happened today. Who knew what was going to happen with Vada and Ezra. This had me more nervous than waiting for Cheyanne to get out of surgery.

29

It has been a week since my talk with Leah.

It was better to let things die down before I went over to bombard Vada. I could not stop thinking about Leah's hypothesis regarding Ezra and Vada. Could Vada have known what Ezra did this whole time? Or worse, was she part of the idea? All these questions are making me sick to my stomach. I was sitting at lunch with everybody, anxiety circling in me. Tia and Leah were carrying on their conversation while Ben was talking to one of his friends in his science class. As for me, I was staring off into space. My thoughts are scattered from the information received. I could hear the voices echoing in my head, mixed with my thoughts.

The biggest question I had in my head was—why? Why did Vada have to put herself in this situation? This was not like her to do. She enjoyed living the life she had, especially with us. I know Cheyanne's death took a toll on all of us, but she couldn't possibly be an acquaintance of Cheyanne's death.

I wanted to hurl at this thought.

What I didn't understand was the changes Vada perused. She used to be sweet and kind to everyone. We always had great times together when we all would get together. Nothing terrible would happen. We'd only watch movies in the pillow and blanket fort we made and eat popcorn. I miss those days.

Why did this have to turn south?

I felt as if there was more to what was going through Vada's mind than met the eyes, but she'd never tell.

"Emma—Emma—Emma-Jean! Are you even listening?" I snapped back into reality when I heard the screeching sound of Tia's voice next to me.

"What?" I spoke, obviously showing I was not listening. Leah rolled her eyes, looking across from Tia.

"I told you she wasn't listening." Leah sarcastically said, shoulder-bumping me with a laugh. A small smile came from my lips, but it didn't last long. I didn't realize Tia and Leah were now buddies.

"Sorry, I'm having a crazy day. What were you guys talking about?" I asked, getting back to reality once again.

"We were asking you if you did the French homework," Tia spoke, asking her question and holding up a packet that looked like the French homework. I nodded to her question, pulling mine out from my French folder. It looked like Leah didn't do her homework, considering she grabbed mine from my hand.

"You know, maybe you should try doing yours occasionally." I teased, crossing my arms over my chest. She looked over at me, rolling her eyes and copying it down.

"Don't judge me. I am not good at French." Leah grumbled. "I'm only doing it for an extra-curricular class." Tia and I laughed softly at her.

Whatever.

After lunch, the three of us made our way to French class. Leah stopped me before making our way in, telling Tia we would be right in. "So, is everything set for today?" She asked me. I nodded.

"Yes, I'm going to talk to Vada after school today," I replied, giving her a small smile. "Hopefully, our theories aren't true," I mumbled, frowning softly at her. I didn't want these theories about Ezra to be true. I only hoped that this was what you would call—a myth.

Maybe they aren't.

***

School flew by. Now, it was time for my confrontation with Vada. I was hoping that Ezra wasn't there so I could have a private conversation with her.

It's not like she would tell me the truth.

She defends that boy more than she does her steadfast friends. It's sad if you think about it. I was also worried for her safety. It makes me question if she enjoys being treated like that. It is toxic.

I was on my way to pick up Thomas at the library in town. He has been staying with a friend close by for now until he goes home. As I reached the library, I saw Thomas standing outside looking for me. He was wearing a loose white tank top with basketball shorts. His hat sat backward on his head, his hand holding it. He finally saw me and made his way to the car. When he got in, he sighed, giving me a small smile.

"Ready?" He asked. My hands squeezed the steering wheel tight, a breath escaping my lips. I shook my head honestly.

"No. But—I need to know." I murmured before driving off.

"Don't worry. As nerve-racking as it is, the person responsible must be put away. For Cheyanne." Thomas spoke, biting the inside of his bottom lip after speaking.

I nodded in agreement, anxiety still creeping up on me. I hope Ezra wasn't responsible.

"I agree. No matter who it is. I wish it weren't Ezra." I replied, stopping at a red light.

"How did you know about the confrontation with Cheyanne and Vada? Did Vada tell you?" Thomas asked the one question

I was trying to avoid it.

I looked over at him, slowly shaking my head in response.

"It's—a long story we don't have time for," I spoke. I started driving again when the light turned green. I turned off a side street. My heart began racing as we drew closer to Ezra's house.

'When we get there, I'll stay outside but hide so they can't see me." Thomas instructed. I nodded in agreement.

As I started approaching the area Ezra lived in, my stomach churned.

I have such horrific memories here of this place.

I was more nervous to see how Vada was doing and what she looked like. Though it has been a week, and she is probably cleaned up. I gulped when I pulled far back from the house so Thomas could stay hidden. I didn't see a car here; maybe Ezra isn't here. That makes me feel a bit better. It took me a minute to get out of the vehicle. When I did, I slowly approached the house, walking up the gravel driveway. I got to the door, hesitant to knock. I got over my fear and did so. It was a minute before the door opened to Vada.

I gasped at her appearance.

Her face was beaten in.

She had cuts along her lip, cheek, and eyebrow, as well as some bruising lining those cuts. Her lip was fat around the cut, making her look like she had had lip injections. Her eyes looked exhausted. She was crying out for help she didn't want or ask for. When she saw me, she smiled softly but was confused.

"What are you doing here?" She asked, shocked to be seeing me.

I needed clarification on her demeanor. It was like she didn't want me there. I just kept staring at the person in front of me. I didn't recognize her. It made me angry she was letting someone do this to her. I snapped out of my thoughts, clearing my throat before speaking.

"I was—coming to check on you. We can't act like I don't know what happened." I spoke the truth to her. She looked down at her feet, nodding.

She knew.

"Would you like to come in?" She asked. I hesitated, my eyes already asking the question she knew how to answer. "Don't worry, he is not here. He won't be back for a few hours."

"Oh, okay. Sure." I mumbled before stepping aside from her to get inside. The place looked cleaned up more than it was last time. The coffee table was cleaned off. I didn't see any sign of drugs lying out. It was like Vada got so bored she cleaned up. Though the place still smelled like weed. It upset my stomach and caused a headache to come. Vada shut the door gently behind me, causing me to jump.

"Listen, Emma, I want to apologize for what you saw last week. Ezra and I—we got into a fight after I brought you home, and things took a hard toll for the worse. I didn't want you to see whatever you saw. I was the one who started it, and—I'm just sorry you had to see that." Vada explained. I crossed my arms over the fact she was blaming herself for how Era was. Anger started to build in me hearing that.

"You can't blame yourself for his actions," I stated. She shook her head, clearing her head and showing that what I said was wrong. I rolled my eyes at her, disappointed in the idea of her blame.

"Well, I just wanted to apologize. I did have fun with you that night." Vada replied before she grabbed my arm.

"Thank you for cleaning me off. I know he didn't do that." She spoke sincerely with a smile.

I didn't say anything about it, only nodded at her, my headache brewing more. As I stood there, I started thinking of how I could get the two of us out back so I could look for this car. I chewed on my lips, looking around. As I did, I came up with a mischievous but truthful idea.

"Do you think we can go outside and talk? The smell of the weed is giving me a headache." I asked, hoping she would say yes. She nodded and motioned me to follow her out back. The plan was already going well.

"Sorry about the smell. Ezra smokes a lot." She muttered, gesturing me to the back porch. Sure, he does.

We made our way past the kitchen to the back porch. It was a spacious backyard. I was impressed with it; considering where the two lived in town, the backyard would be negligible. The only problem I have here is that it will be harder to see things because it's so spacious. I could hear Vada talking, but my focus was on one thing. A beaten-up black shed at the back looked big enough to fit a car. That had to be where Ezra stored the car.

"Emma?" I snapped back, seeing Vada staring at me, looking concerned for me. "Are you okay?"

"Yeah, I'm—I'm just impressed with how big this backyard is. I wouldn't expect it to be so big, considering you live right in the center of town." I spoke to her with a smile.

I needed to act like I was there to see her. I needed a more positive attitude than a sour one, especially if I was trying to find this car. Vada smiled, looking out that way at me.

"Oh yeah. I thought the same thing when I moved in here. I was surprised myself." She replied, motioning her hand out towards the yard. "I like it."

"Not to mention you have a shed over there too. It's good for more space. What do you guys put in it?" I asked.

My heart started racing when I asked that; I hoped she didn't grasp how nosy I was about the backyard.

Thankfully, she didn't notice.

She smiled and locked our elbows together to walk off the porch.

"Here, I'll show you." She said, pulling me along the tall grass towards the shed. I gulped, scared to see what was indeed behind the shed.

As we approached the entrance, sweat started beading on my forehead. My anxiety was starting to make me sweat profusely. As we turned the corner, I saw some outdoor machines, rakes, and shovels, and then a rugged tarp sat over something huge. It looked like a car. The sweat started coming out more and more. Vada let go of me, walking into the shed on her own. I stayed out at the entrance, staring at the tarp.

"It just looks like a normal shed," I mumbled, Vada hearing me as she nodded to my statement. "What's that?" I blurted out, pointing to the tarp. Vada looked at it and slowly started uncovering it.

There it was.

The car we were looking for and the car I was hoping for wasn't there. I gasped softly, freezing in so much emotion. What struck me was that the car was wrecked, clearing, and looking like a severe accident.

Oh my god.

I wanted to throw up. I tried so hard not to show my emotions.

"This was Ezra's mom's car. She died in a car accident, and Ezra wanted to keep it as memories. It's not good for him to do but to each their own." Vada lied to my face.

Nobody ever lets you keep a totaled car after an accident. I started puzzling at her, trying so hard not to snap. The words that came out of her mouth were lies she stupidly told me. I was angry, sad, defeated.

Everything we saw on those papers was true.

Ezra did this.

Vada is covering it up to save his ass. Why would she do that? Did she even know it was him? I felt so stuck and so disappointed. I watched Vada cover it back up like it was their prize possession. I could feel the nausea coming up.

"Are you okay? You don't look so good." Vada spoke, walking towards me and touching my sweaty face. "You are white as a ghost and dripping in sweat. Are you getting the flu?" She asked in a concerned manner. She had no reason to be concerned. I was just disgusted with her. I shrugged, licking my dry lips and blinking profusely.

"Maybe I am. Maybe I should go home and lay down." I suggested, wanting nothing more than to leave this place and never return. Vada nodded, linking my arms again and walking me out from the back to the car.

"Are you okay to drive?" She asked, concerned again. I grumbled at how nice she was trying to be.

She was a killer. I was angry with her.

She was Cheyanne's killer, and I wanted to scream. I nodded, pulling away from her and walking quickly to the car. "Call me when you get home!" She yelled from her driveway.

I didn't respond to her; I just got inside the car, turned it on, and drove off. Thomas was sitting waiting.

He could see how distraught I was.

"What? What happened?" He asked quickly.

Tears poured down my face. I was utterly heartbroken by what I saw. Not to mention, Vada lied straight to my face. I could *never* forgive her for this. It didn't matter if she knew; I feel like she did. But I also feel like she had something to do with it. We needed a plan to bust them.

"He did it." I stammered, having trouble concentrating on driving. Thomas quickly buckled himself in, considering my driving was not up to its standards. "The car was there."

What was frightening was that I would have to be the one to do it.

"We got to go back to Leah's," Thomas spoke, driving off.

I didn't listen to anything he said, let alone the car speeding off. My thoughts went to betrayal. How could this happen? Why would Vada let things get this bad? One things for sure, I needed to get in there to hear it from the both of them.

I already knew it would be a challenging site to bust.

30

My head was spinning while I was sitting in Leah's living room. I was in complete disgust with every event that had happened in the past 24 hours. I was sick to my stomach. We planned to confront her the next day after I visited with Vada.

I did not sleep the night before. I sat up all night crying and screaming into my pillow again. I felt like I did the day Cheyanne died. I knew I was going to have trust issues after this.

I wasn't doing this part alone.

Thomas was explaining everything to Ben and Leah, who were shocked. But not like I was. Truthfully, I am still in utter shock. I am nauseous. I sat on the floor, staring into space, hearing the voice muffled. Everyone's mouths were moving, but that muffledness turned to ringing in the ears.

I never believed the phrase, 'Everybody's got a dark side.'

What if the people I'm sitting with couldn't be trusted?

Oh, don't think like that, Emma.

These people are all you got. When I slowly raised my gaze to everyone, it looked like everyone was talking and using their hands. I could not concentrate. I tried so hard, but it was hard. All I could hear was the continued ringing in my ears.

My thoughts went to before Cheyanne died, and we were all close. We had a sleepover at Cheyanne's, played board games, and ate junk food. We laughed, threw popcorn at each other, and enjoyed our time together. We spent the entire night being ourselves and not questioning if we would ever become enemies. Now, one of us is dead, and the other is a killer. That curdled my stomach more. I miss those friends. I never imagined that friendship would turn into this.

"—being careful because we don't know what Ezra is capable of." I could hear Leah's voice chime in, pulling me back into reality.

"That is true, considering he did what he did," Thomas spoke. I watch everyone's lips move, not saying anything.

"Well, not to mention he does beat Vada. He's capable of a lot. He's an angry person." Ben chimed in. "So, what's the plan?" I was not focused on the conversations that were chiming through my ears.

I felt fuzzy.

"We got to get him to tell the truth without force. Maybe someone should try to get Vada to confess?" Leah spoke. From my eyes, it looked like everybody liked that idea. Then, all eyes were on me, which quickly made me uncomfortable. "Emma, any ideas?"

I shook my head, not knowing what to say. My head was pounding from the anxiety. I could hear my staggered breaths through my ears. Everyone's eyes were on me while I sat motionless. They looked concerned for me.

"She is in shock. Don't expect her to think about too much." Thomas mumbled. I looked over at him, realizing that she was right. I was in shock and needed to get myself together and do this for Cheyanne. This is why she has been coming to me. She wants me to lock him up for good, even Vada in my eyes. I nodded, finally back to reality.

I had an idea.

"Yes, we need to get them to confess it without being forceful. Both will know something Is up if we are forceful on it. Maybe I can try to talk to Vada first, see what I can get from her." I explained, taking a small breath. "I don't believe Vada would do something like this to Cheyanne. Then again, she did lie to me about it." Thomas smirked next to me.

"She lives." He spoke sarcastically. I scoffed at him.

"Leave her be. She's got a lot of her mind," Ben grumbled. I eyed Ben, telling him to be pleasant through my facial expression. "Someone needs to go with her in case things go south."

"I agree with Ben. It's risky going alone." I replied with Ben. I gave him a small smile as he gestured one back to me.

"Okay, so how about this—" Thomas started saying, clearing his throat. "I'll go with Emma. I'll stay outside while she talks to Vada. I think you should hide your phone and record the entire conversation. That way, It's her word against anything. You'll get more out of Vada than Ezra. Then, if things go south, I will be there to get you."

"I like that. Don't stop recording the entire time." Leah agreed. I nodded. I stood up, needing to move around. Suppose my parents could see me now. I'm risking my life to get answers. This could get dangerous fast.

"So, when should we do this?" I asked the one question I was scared to get an answer for. Everyone looked at each other, waiting for ideas to pour out. After a moment, Leah stepped up.

"We should do it tonight. Get it over with. It will be better than the anxiety building and waiting." Everyone nodded in agreement with Leah's suggestion. "The longer we sit on this, the longer it takes."

"The sooner, the better," I mumbled. "I want to get this over with." Everyone stood up as we gathered.

"If either of you need help. Do. Not. Hesitate to call, okay?" Leah spoke, looking towards both Thomas and me.

I nodded, and so did Thomas.

* * *

It has been two hours since our talk about our plan. We were getting ready to go, and I was jumpy. I did not know what to expect out of this. I pray it turns out okay and Vada gives us the information I want. I hope she doesn't throw herself under the bus instead of Ezra. Maybe I can convince her to run off and forget about Ezra. As I was getting ready to go, Ben grabbed my arm. He pulled me off to the side so we could talk alone.

"Why do you have to do this?" Ben whispered, looking around to make sure that nobody was listening. I sighed, understanding where he came from but needed to do this. I was the only one out of everyone that could get inside to talk with Vada. No one else would be able to step foot in the house. It had to be me.

"Ben, you don't understand—"

"No, I don't. I know you are doing this to find the truth. I want you safe." I smiled at Ben's protection. I reached down, grabbing his hand to hold gently. I wanted him to see that I would be okay and could do something good. The fact I have been depressed over wanting to know who did this, and I am here now, is impressive but scary. The only scary part was the unknown of what Ezra was capable of.

"I don't need you worrying about me. You need to stay here with Leah and wait. If you need a ride to get us, call

Tia." I comforted him gently, squeezing his hand tightly. He nodded, giving me a small smile.

"So—when are you going to let me kiss you?" He asked nonchalantly. I couldn't help but let a laugh escape. I was not one of those girls who wanted to give the boy I liked a kiss goodbye, especially to find out what happened to my best friend.

"When I come back," I whispered to him. I could see the inpatient look in Ben's eyes. It seemed like he was waiting for so long to kiss me. It was sweet, but I would not kiss him on the spur of the moment. I could see Thomas over Ben's shoulder, nodding that we needed to go.

"We got to get there before sundown," Thomas called out. I nodded, my eyes returning to Ben, telling him goodbye. I hugged him tightly before walking towards the car.

My anxiety was shot now.

At that moment, I knew I was not ready for this.

31

This time, I let Thomas drive from how jumpy my body was. We were going to be doing this. I was slowly starting to regret my decision to put myself through this. Granite, I would be talking to Vada, not Ezra, but thinking of the idea that Vada could have potentially known about this—there was a pit growing in my stomach.

It's more like nausea.

Everything that has led to this point in time was less worth it than I hoped. Maybe it is for Cheyanne, but for safety not. There was no question about it; I was uncomfortable with this. Why couldn't I have let the police do their job? Especially if they already had Ezra's name as a suspect. I groaned to myself with all these questions. It was giving me a migraine. I needed to know for myself. I needed to hear it come out of their mouths that they did this. I could see Thomas eyeing me.

"Hey—you have nothing to be nervous about." He mumbled, putting his hand on my shoulder to squeeze it tightly. I sighed. I had a lot to be nervous about.

"At least you don't have to go into the house," I replied softly. He slowly approached a red light. Once he stopped, he turned towards me.

"Look, I will be right there if something goes wrong. If it does, we will work together as a team to get the job done. Yes?" Thomas lectured.

His choice of words didn't soothe my nerves, but the enthusiasm of the pep talk was inspiring. I nodded, taking a breath in and out. We got this. "Okay, don't be nervous."

Thomas started driving again.

The more the car sped forward, the closer it got to my death. Oh, I should not say that. As I looked out the window, I saw it was growing cloudy. I forgot it was supposed to rain today. Great, there is another damper in the day. As we turned down the road Vada lived on, the lump in my throat closed. We stopped far back so they couldn't see where we parked. Thomas turned off the car, grabbed my hand, and slapped the keys into my hand.

"What is this?" I asked softly, looking down at the shiny objects in my hand.

"If things go south, I want you to run to the car and go straight to the police station. Don't look back, and don't stop." Thomas instructed. I shook my head, trying to return the keys to him, but he pushed them towards my stomach. "No. I don't want them. Just do it." He spoke more abruptly. I was in no mood to argue.

All I did was nod, stuffing them in my coat pocket.

"Okay, let's go," I mumbled before leaving the car.

The two of us shut outdoors gently so they could keep themselves quiet. Thomas went in front of me, stepping off into the side bushes so he could still be close. I took a big breath before making my way up that driveway again. It looked like Ezra's car was gone again. That was a good sign. I stopped in the driveway, grasping my phone from my back pocket to begin recording.

It was time.

I went to the door to knock, but the door blasted open, with Vada smiling wide. Her face still looked beaten, but bruises were beginning to form.

"Emma! Hey, are you feeling better?" Vada already started in conversation. I stared in confusion before remembering what happened yesterday. As I stood there, I got a strong scent of rain before the skies opened with water and thunder rumbling. This put a damper on everything.

"Yes. I'm feeling much better. Sorry, I hurried off so quickly. It hit me out of nowhere." I replied. Not only did my nose fill with rain, but it also smelled of weed from inside the house. I crinkled my nose at the smell.

"It's raining pretty good. Come in. Ezra will be back in a little bit." Vada offered.

I accepted her offer but stared out towards Thomas, who gave me a thumbs up as an okay to where he was. I felt terrible; he was about to stand in the rain, but his looks told me it was alright.

As I got inside, Vada invited me into her room. I watched her scurry to the coffee table in front of the couch. I noticed her fumbling around with something. When I got a clear look, a wrap was lit. That's where the smell of weed came from. She was putting it out in the ashtray that sat on the table.

"Shall we?" Vada requested, motioning towards the back bedroom. I accepted as we went down the hallway and sat together on the bed. "Sorry for the mess. I haven't cleaned yet."

"That's okay," I said, sitting on the bed and looking around the room. It was a plain room. White walls with red curtains and bed sheets. It had a strong smell to it like someone was burning wood. When I got a better look at what was on the dresser, it was an incent burning through the room.

"We won't be able to stay back here for long. Ezra hates it when people are back here. I don't know why; he is hostile about that." Vada went on while trying to clean up her mess on the floor. I looked around, keeping my hands before me and licking my lips nervously.

"That's okay, you don't have to clean up. I don't judge." I gestured towards Vada, bent over, shoving dirty clothes in a basket. I then went straight for it.

"So, hey—I came here because I had a question for you. About Cheyanne." I spoke gently, ensuring I wouldn't trigger her to react. I saw her face tense, but with a couple of breaths, she was calm again. She nodded in response to me. I took a deep breath. Here I go.

"Is it true you went to the bar she worked at the night she died?" I asked. It was like ripping the band-aid off a wound. She scrunched her eyebrows but didn't hesitate to answer me.

"Yeah, we did. We had a good time! That's why the night of her accident, I was dressed up at the hospital." Vada answered, but it wasn't as truthful as I knew. I didn't respond initially; I just nodded, pushing some hair behind my ear. I'm not sure what to believe now.

"I miss her. I wish she were still here." I sighed, looking down at the ground. She didn't say anything back to me.

"I miss her too," Vada whispered. "Even though she and I fought all the time, there is not a day where I don't miss her." I became eager with my questions. I felt as if she was lying more through her teeth now.

"What happened between you and Cheyanne? We've never really talked about it." I asked more. Only this time was I getting into it.

"Wow, you are asking many questions," Vada grumbled with a small laugh. I responded in laughter as well. It got awkward fast. I felt like I needed to act now.

"Yeah, sorry. I am just curious." I mumbled.

"Her and I just fell off, but that didn't mean I didn't care about her. Things like that happen, and I hope you can understand that." Vada answered. I decided to get straight into it. Enough questions of Cheyanne.

"That car you showed me—why was I seeing that was the car that hit her in the accident?" I blurted out. This took Vada off guard, and I could see the tenseness on her face.

"Excuse me? How do you even know the type of car that hit her?" Vada questioned, scooting away from me. Now, she was acting timid. I didn't answer her question; I ignored it.

"Why did I see the same car in Cheyanne's case, and why did I see that Ezra is a suspect? You know something, and I think you have known something for a long time." I started getting angry and mouthy with my words. I was ready now to get the answer out of her. Vada kept shaking her head, laughing to herself. She rose from her bed to where she stood before me.

"Do you think I am a killer Emma?" She asked, raising her voice slightly at me, pointing to herself. I didn't back down. I just laughed, standing up to her.

"No, but I think Ezra is. I think he did this, and you know it." I gritted my teeth, spitting out the words I had held in. Vada backed up from me, shaking her head. She tried to escape me by leaving the room, but I followed her. She did not think that one through.

"I'm sorry, but I am going to have to ask you to—"

"Leave? That's funny when I encounter you; you send me away when you hear things you don't want to hear. You do that to everybody." I could tell I was triggering anger in her. Her cheeks started turning bright red, and she shook her head and pointed to the door.

"Leave now." She spit at me. I've never seen Vada so angry. She was defending him. Why is she defending a killer? Is she still with him because she fears being lonely forever?

"Tell me the truth," I argued, refusing to leave.

"Emma, don't do this." Vada pleaded. My face stayed straight. I was not leaving until I heard what I wanted. I crossed my arms, waiting for a response. "Please don't make me do this." She whispered.

"Do what, Vada? Tell me the—"

Just as I was about to finish my sentence, the door was booted open. Ezra stormed in, holding Thomas by the back of his shirt. Both Vada and I let out a yelp when the door was kicked in. I stumbled back, my mouth covered from what I was seeing. Thomas looked defeated. It looked as if Ezra beat him to pieces.

"What do we have here? A lurker?" Ezra grumbled, shoving Thomas down onto the ground. I ran to his side, trying to help him off his back. "What were you doing looking into my house?" Ezra roared out, then his eyes panning to me. "And you—what are you doing here?"

I didn't respond.

I stayed by Thomas, making sure nothing happened to him. Thomas then spit at Ezra's feet, blood coating his spit. A smirk peered across Ezra's face as he shook his head. "We can do this the easy way—" He pulls a pistol out. My eyes widened, knowing this was going to go south quickly. Thomas sat up and shielded my body with his. "Or the hard way."

"What did you do to Cheyanne?" I blurted out.

Vada stood back, watching everything.

Vada's actions disenchanted me. She stood helpless, watching someone point a gun at the two of us. She didn't yell to stop or not to do it. She just stood there silently. Does this boy have that much control over her? Ezra gazed into my eyes, but all I could see from him was darkness. It frightened me. He chuckled, pivoting the gun around with his index finger.

"You were always so nosy about her." He grumbled. Ezra sighed loudly before glaring down at the two of us. "Okay, hard way it is. Graham, take her." My eyes widened as I watched Vada follow his commands. She is sired to him; no matter what this man did or said, she was at his side doing his tasks. Not to mention, he doesn't even call her by her first name.

"She has a name-"I grumbled to Ezra, who had no care in the world.

Thomas reached around, holding onto me tightly so I couldn't move.

"She is not going anywhere." Thomas hissed, pinning me against his back. Ezra chuckled more before walking towards us. As he passed Vada, he pushed her to the ground, causing a screech to escape from her mouth.

"Vada," I called out to her. "How dare you touch her!"

"I'll handle this since you are too chicken to do what I ask of you." Ezra roared more. He then leaned down, quickly pulling me out of Thomas' grip. I yelped, my arm feeling like it was pulled out from my sockets. Thomas whipped around, trying to grab my ankles. Ezra kept pulling me, and then I could see the barrel of his gun sitting against my shoulder, pointing at Thomas. My heart was racing.

"I suggest you let go before I shoot you right here. Right now." Ezra commanded. I struggled against his grip. He was stronger than I anticipated. I shook my head, eyeing Thomas, who still had a grip.

"Let. Go." I breathed out. Thomas did what I told him, and before I knew it, I was being pulled into the same back room that I was in the night Vada was beaten. My anxiety and PTSD began rising in me, causing my heart to beat faster.

"Wait." Ezra threw me into the room, slamming the door shut. I heard a click on the doorknob. I was locked in. I got up and started pulling on the door, trying to get it to open. I was pounding, yelling, and calling for Vada to help me.

Nobody came.

I heard yelling coming from behind the door. Thomas and Ezra's voice roared through the entire house. I tried so hard to scream out for help. My throat became scratchy. As the yelling escalated, I was taken aback by the sound of a gun exploding through the other side of the door. I yelped, covering my mouth as the tears began rolling down my cheek. I heard a thump on the floor underneath me while Vada gasped.

Silence filled from the other side. I already knew what this meant. I dropped to the floor, hysterically crying over the thoughts running through my head.

I was going to die.

One thing I didn't forget was I was still recording that whole time. I still plan on recording.

32

I lost track of time being locked inside this room.

I sat against the wall with my knees pressed to my chest. My face was damp from the tears soaking into my skin. There was no sugar coding in the situation. Thomas was dead. Ezra shot him.

It was silent from behind that door once again. I can't help but remember the feeling of that silence. All I wanted to do was call my friends, but I was too petrified to shift.

My arm was throbbing in pain from where Ezra was pulling me.

I gasped when I looked up to see Cheyanne sitting in the corner of the room. I needed to stay silent since I was still recording. I slowly began reaching back to grab my phone. As I did, footsteps rang in my ears, and they were coming closer. I slipped my phone back into my pocket, keeping the recording going.

I gulped when the door flung open.

Ezra came in first, then Vada stumbling in behind him. I gulped once more, the lump in my throat getting stuck. My eyes started to burn with tears again.

"Where is Thomas?" I stammered, my voice cracking through the choked sobs. Ezra smirked before sitting down on the end of the bed. He did not answer my question. He glared at Vada.

"Sit." He grumbled at her. She did follow everything he told her to do. It was sad.

"Answer the question." I spit through my teeth. "Now."

"Don't worry about him," Ezra replied. No emotion was plastering through his face. I kept thinking to myself how I was going to die in this house—a place where I didn't want to be.

I looked over in that same corner where Cheyanne was, and she was still there with fear in her eyes.

I was going to die a quick death like Thomas. Tears are streaming down my face more.

"No reason to cry. You are going to sit, listen, and not speak a word. If you do—" He pulls his gun out, holding it up. I looked towards Vada, who was sitting emotionless.

"Just do what he says, Emma," Vada demands. I nodded, not saying anything. All three of us sat in silence for a moment. The suspense was killing me.

"It was not intentional, but I was angry with her after our heated argument at Cheyanne's work. I knew she was not a good friend to Vada, considering she never supported our relationship." Ezra explained. Without thinking, I opened my mouth, scoffing.

"I don't blame her," I murmured, hoping he didn't hear that. I was wrong. He leaned forward, grabbing my cheeks and pulling me closer to him. I winced from his touch.

"I told you to be quiet." He breathed in my face. I groaned, tears forming once again. I never truly knew what this man was capable of. Now, I am seeing his true colors.

He threw me, my back connecting with the wall. He continued. I could see how sorry Vada looked in her eyes.

"I was so angry that I demanded Vada that we would stay and wait for her to get off work. I wanted to talk to her and tell her I didn't appreciate how she talked to me. She didn't stay around. She instantly started driving home. I had to follow her, and I think she was onto me. Of course, I wasn't thinking of the traffic cameras in town. I was using my mom's old car, which Vada told me you were curious about. That had to be why you wanted to come here last week to "see" Vada. To seek out the lost car?" I froze when he caught onto our sneaky visit. I gulped, looking over at Vada. I was angry that she told him about it. The entire time, she knew what I was planning. She still showed me how to look good by telling him.

"I hope that made you feel good, Vada," I grumbled to her. She said nothing at first until she crossed her arms, raising her eyebrow.

"Maybe you shouldn't use me against my boyfriend." She spoke back. My mouth dropped, wanting to scream at her.

How dare she.

"You are joking me, right?"

"Shut up! Both of you." Ezra roared, flaring his arms around to get our attention. I backed up from his outburst, worried he would lay his hand on me. "Will you let me talk?" I nodded.

"Anyways, I started following her home and how she was driving. I could tell she was getting suspicious of the car following her. She started a speed chase with me, going up and down roads trying to escape." Ezra explained. She didn't start anything; It was all him. How dare he blame her for being scared? Anger boiled in me. I noticed when looking over that Cheyanne had disappeared.

"I decided to keep my distance. I was angry at this point, and I wanted her to stop. So, I went a different route. I was coming up on the road that she would turn down to go home. Anger started getting the best of me, and I started speeding towards her head-on. Vada was screaming at me, telling me to stop and not hurt her. I couldn't help myself. She needed to be gone. I told Vada to jump out of the car. She was pissing me off yelling, so it made me speed faster and—BOOM!" I jumped, screaming at his car description and slamming into Cheyanne. I covered my mouth as the tears poured out of control. My body felt like it had dropped.

"I pulled over, and Vada screamed, running towards her car. I followed her over there. When I got there, her head was sitting on the steering wheel knocked out. She had some glass in her face, blood everywhere. Let's say she looked dead already. I grabbed Vada, pulled her into the car, and drove off. Someone must have found her and called 911. What a waste." I covered my ears, hearing my breaths growing heavy from anger. Something in me switched. I was not some sad, defeated teenager grieving over her friend. I was angry, ready to fight, wanting to scream at the top of my lungs. I slowly raised my head at both, Ezra smirking at me and Vada on the verge of breaking down.

"You. Are a coward!" I screamed, standing up and getting in his face. "YOU think that is funny to talk about? Do YOU think *killing* someone is a thrill? YOU are a piece of shit! And you know what? You are going to rot in jail because I am going to get out of here and tell them everything you just told me. I will NOT sit here and let you talk on my friend like that."

"—and *YOU*." I pointed towards Vada, who was now in tears. "You could have done something. You could have done everything to protect her. You could have stood your ground and called 911, but you ran. You've known about it the whole time and have done nothing. You are not a friend, Vada; you are a liar and a fake soul. You deserve everything that comes your way. I can't even look at you and call you a friend. You watched me grieve, fall into a depression, and fail at being a person because I was so sad over her loss. You sat and let it happen, not doing a damned thing about it. You are—" My arm was grabbed after yelling.

A force pushed me against the wall, causing me to fall. I weakened her and could see it in her face, but I did not care. Every word I said I meant.

"Alright, that's enough. YOU are not going to the cops because you are not going anywhere. If you even try anything, I will kill you." Ezra stood up, motioning for Vada to follow him.

A defeated Vada followed him out, slamming the door shut behind them. I could hear the door lock again. I fell to the ground, bringing my knees up to my chest. I was hyperventilating, screaming, and crying. I could not get Ezra's words about Cheyanne out of my head. The way he was describing everything was despicable.

I knew what I had to do.

I needed to get out of here, so I grabbed my phone. I stopped the recording and immediately dialed Leah's number. Only two rings, and I could hear her voice through the other line. I did nothing but cry on the phone. Both Ben and Leah were asking what was wrong.

"It's true. H-He did it. V-Vada was with h-him. He told me everything, and I got it on video. Leah—t-the way he talked about her. It was d-disgusting." I was stuttering with almost every word. "I'm locked in a bedroom."

"Call 911." Leah encourages. "Where's Thomas?"

Oh my god, Thomas.

"He's dead," I mumbled. I could hear Leah gasp through the phone. Her breath was shaking at the news.

"Emma, call 911 and get out of there now," Ben commanded.

"No," I grumbled, wiping my face from the tears. "No, I must go to the police station and show them this before Ezra knows. He doesn't know I have my phone. Meet me there.

Call Tia to give you guys a ride. I'll see you there." I stood up and started looking around the room. I stopped when my eyes connected with the window. I smirked. "I'm going to break out of here."

I hung up the phone and immediately went to my notes. I needed to write one thing.

Dear Cheyanne,

If I die, I hope your face is the first thing I see. I love you.

Emma

33

    I started looking around the room for something to cut the wire out from the window. I did this as quietly as I could so I could escape like I wanted to. Even though I could call 911 as Ben and Leah told me, I tried to deliver the evidence myself. They were going to meet me at the police station.
    As I rummaged through the room, I found a tiny needle that looked like it was used to inject drugs into their arms. I gagged, reaching for it. I should not be touching something like that, but I needed to get out. I tip-toed over to the window, opening it up slowly. It creaked slightly from being so old, but it wasn't loud enough to disturb anyone.
    I gritted my teeth as I opened it.
    When I finally opened it, a cold breeze blew at my face, filling my lungs. It smelled nicer than what I'd been inhaling. It was dark outside, with no sign of light except the streetlights and other houses.
    Suddenly, I jumped at the sound of loud yells and banging going on from behind the door. I stopped what I

was doing to see what was happening. I kept the window open so I could go right back to it. As I slowly creaked over to the door, I knelt to peek out the bottom of the door. I looked around, and my eyes stopped at the body lying in the middle of the ground face down.

It was Thomas.

I gasped softly, covering my mouth as my eyes stayed on his lifeless body.

Just then, Vada came into my view from where the yelling came from.

"I can't do this anymore." Vada sounded like she was begging between her soft sobs. "Just let her out." She must have been talking about me. I could not help but scoff at her sympathy.

"Vada, if I let her go, she is going to the police. Then you and I will be done. Do you want that? Do you want to go sit and rot in a jail cell?" Ezra was harsh with his words, but he was not yelling.

I heard Vada laugh like she had enough of this.

"Maybe we should!" Vada snaps, throwing her hands up in the air. "I'm tired of this. I've lost enough people in my life from this."

"I'm here." Ezra comforts in his way. I scoffed. He was trying to manipulate her, keeping her around. The only way he can do things is by smoothly telling her and then beating her to nothing.

"You killed someone, Ezra!"

"He deserved it! Nobody spies on my house!"

"Whatever." Vada scoffs before storming off to the other side of the house. Ezra followed. Perfect, this is the best time to make my escape. I looked around, taking the nightstand next to the door and pushing it in front so nobody could enter. That gave me time to get out. Once the nightstand was set, I stood silently, waiting to see if I had caught their attention. From the sounds of it, I didn't. I sighed in relief.

I continued planning my escape. I held the needle in my hand, still debating what it was doing here and what it was used for.

I shivered at the thought.

I pinched the needle into the screen part of the window and slowly looked at it open. I knew it would take a long time to do, but this was my only option. As I continued to see, I noticed I needed to get farther with this, and a needle would not work wonders for me. I threw the needle across the room, groaning in anger.

What was I going to do?

There was one other option. It was a horrible idea, but it was all I had to get out of here. I could always use the needle to unlock the door, run for a knife in the kitchen, come back, cut the screen, and climb out.

Or I could just run out of the house.

That sounded like a simple option. I reached up, slowly shutting the window again. I shivered at the breeze that hit me after I closed it. I then heard voices again coming from behind the door. I walked over to listen.

"Where are you going?" The sound of Vada's voice yelled across the house near the door.

"I'm going outside to smoke a cigarette. Are you coming?" Ezra replied in the same tone as I bent down to look out the bottom of the door. I saw both their feet shuffling to the front door. The screeching of the door echoed through the house as it became silent when the two went outside. Running outside was no longer an option; a knife in the window was.

I ran to the needle I threw, grabbing it with my sweaty yet shaking hands. I fumbled with the needle in the keyhole, attempting to unlock the door.

I've only done this once and never said I was a pro at it.

It took me only two minutes before I heard the door click. I got it unlocked. I was impressed with myself. I slowly pulled the door open. Luckily, it did not creak. I peeked my head out to hear Ezra and Vada's voices coming from outside the house. I sighed, thinking of a way to enter the kitchen without being seen. I just had to run for it. I did just that, making sure I shut the door behind me in case.

I scurried across the floor, getting to the kitchen quickly without being seen. I hid behind the wall, holding my breath so they couldn't hear me. I was also too scared to breathe, considering I could get caught easily. Nausea grew in me when I hit the wall. Thomas was still lying on the ground. They have not done anything with him yet. That's the first thing I will take care of when I get to the police station. I went to the counters quickly to find a block of knives sitting still. I sighed in relief, seeing how easy it could have been to grab one. I grabbed the biggest one, scurrying back to the same wall I rested on. I could hear the distant conversations between the two outside.

"How long do you expect her to stay in there?" Vada asked.

"As long as I say." I was about to run back to the door when I heard the screen from the front open. I immediately sucked in a breath, holding the knife to my side, waiting for them to pass. It was a good thing I shut that door. They would have been able to see right there that I was gone.

"Want to shower with me?" I heard Ezra's voice behind the wall.

"Sure. Then, after, we needed to let her out. Or give her some food." Vada replied. I rolled my eyes at the nice gestures she was trying to pull. There was no way I could forgive her after this. I could not try to regain friendship with her, whether she goes to jail or not.

"Fine," Ezra grumbled before I heard the two approach the back room. The shower faucet made the pipes throughout the house creak as the door shut. I then could only hear the muffled voices of the two. It was my time to run. I took another breath before running to the room. I opened the door quickly, then shut it quietly instead of slamming it.

I exhaled, slid down the door, and dropped the knife to my side. I wanted to burst into tears. The fact I was able to do something like this so swiftly was a significant anxiety kick. I felt like I was holding my breath for too long. I had to sit and contain myself before continuing my escape.

Never in my life have I thought I would be here. I was trapped in a bedroom with a killer on the other side of the door. What was I thinking? I could hear it now, especially from my friends and family. Plus, Cheyanne. Everything felt as if it was spinning. I needed to relax.

After a while, it had been a couple of minutes before they realized they would return here after their shower. I jumped up, heading back towards the window. I opened it up again, using the knife to cut through the screen, and it worked. I then started hearing footsteps walking around. How could they have been done already? I turned towards the door, breathing heavily and sweating down my face.

I started cutting faster before the screen was able to be lifted. I threw the knife down and pulled myself up to get out of the room. All my upper body strength went climbing out of this window. Half of my body was already out. I curled my head between my shoulders and rolled myself the rest of the way out. I fell onto the ground, covered in dirt. I could feel the pile of dirt flying up with dust. I groaned when my body hit the ground. If I didn't curl up, I probably would have broken my neck.

I stood back up, dusting myself off. I reached into my pocket, finding my phone and the keys Thomas gave me. It was a good thing he gave them back to me. I started running down the driveway, but a roaring man's voice stopped me. Ezra.

"Where did she go?" I heard the scream coming from the room I was in. I started breathing quickly, my heartbeat pulsing faster, before turning and running for my car. I wished I had parked closer. My feet shuffled underneath me as I ran.

Finally, I got to my car.

I unlocked it quickly, throwing myself inside as I slammed the door shut. Adrenaline was kicking in me fast. As I got the keys into the ignition, I suddenly jumped at the sound of bullets going off and hitting my car. I screamed, turning to see Ezra standing at the end of his driveway. The gun was pointing at me. My breaths quicken again, anger and frustration pulsing through me. I turned, trying to start my car with shaky hands.

"Come on. Come on!" My voice grew louder.

I got the car to start when suddenly, a burning sensation went through my arm, and warm liquid started pouring down it.

I was even afraid to look; I just stepped on the brake and drove away.

I needed to get to the police station.

34

The drive felt like it was taking forever. My arm was throbbing at this point. I could not bear to look down at it, for I already knew I had been shot at. I'm sure Ezra and Vada knew where I was going, and they probably were not far behind me.

Or at least Ezra.

As I drove, my hands would not stop shaking.

I reached into my pocket, pulled my phone off, and dialed Leah's number shakily. Like last time, it rang twice, and she answered.

"Emma, we are here waiting for you. Where are you?" Her voice sounded calm and collected. On the other hand, I was kicking with fear and adrenaline. My breath hicks in the back of my throat before I speak.

"I'm on my way. I got caught in something. I will have them behind me, so we must do this quickly. I don't know what Ezra will do." I explained. The sweat on my forehead became cold as the AC blasted on my face. I have not sweat this much since gym class. I hung up the phone before continuing to drive. It wasn't much longer until I was at the police station.

I just wanted this to all be over. I was done with this. I needed to move on, and I needed to attempt to be okay this time. I was done with sadness and danger. I've lived so young to see how violent and despicable this world can be. I was weak now. Mainly being shot in and in the arm, it wouldn't be long before I could feel it.

My mind went right to Thomas. I wonder what his last thoughts were before he was killed. I wanted to know what happened before he died. I didn't even get to say goodbye. I was crying again, tears slowly sliding down my cheek. Or maybe I was screaming from the pain I was feeling in my arm. I began to wince, looking down at my arm. The hole in it stayed while blood began to trickle out from the wound.

I gagged once more. Who knew my body could do that?

I had pulled into the police station. Leah, Ben, and Tia were standing outside waiting for me. Leah was taken aback by the speed at which I was going. She threw herself into the car as I parked. I swung my door open, climbing out and being greeted by the twins.

"God, Emma, you are bleeding." Tia pointed out. I could see the worry in Ben's eyes as Leah was at my side.

"No time. I need to do this." I murmured as I grabbed Leah's hand, pulling her inside the police station. Ben and Tia followed us in. As I was about to walk in, she stopped and turned to me so I was looking at her.

"Before we go in there, you must tell me everything." She commanded. I shook my head; my breaths finally became slow and steady.

"We do not have time. They will be right behind me." I mumbled.

"They?" I heard Ben from behind me. I did not have the energy to turn towards him, but I could see in Leah's eyes she knew who I meant.

"Ezra and Vada." She mumbled. She then grabbed my hand to pull me inside of the station. As we walked in, the lady at the front desk looked towards us.

"Can I help you children?" She asked sternly before looking towards my arm, seeing the blood. "Are you hurt, dear?" She asked, taking her glasses off and standing up from her chair. Now, she wanted to be nice. I shook my head, not caring about my arm.

"I need to make a statement—for Cheyanne Wrangler's case. I have video evidence of who was the hit-and-run person that killed her. I need someone to hear this." I reached into my pocket, holding my phone up for her to see. "Please, I need to see someone now," I begged. I could see headlights shining through the windows, knowing precisely what would happen. I ignored it. I stayed looking in front. I could hear shuffling behind me. It sounded like Tia and Ben were moving out of the way.

Crap.

"Please, I need someone to hear this now, right now before I get—"

And then, I was hit. At that moment, I did not know where. I just heard glass shatter, and my body went numb. A scream escaped my throat as I dropped to the ground. The front desk lady dropped as well. The pain started to throb in my right hip as well as the arm that was shot at previously. I started looking around, trying to find someone to help me. Leah was approaching me but was taken aback when I heard another gunshot from behind. I then realized that she was hit in the leg.

"Leah!" I called out for her, but she backed into a corner. She watched Ezra enter the doors, eyeing me with every step he took. I found the strength to turn myself around towards him. I could see the twins hiding in the back of the waiting room, Ben trying to break free from Tia's grasp. Ezra looked crazy. His wide brown eyes and gritted teeth were noticeable, not making it any better on his behalf. He got closer to me, eyeing my every move.

"You think—you could get away with this? Nobody knows anything except for you. You will not say a word." He hissed, pointing his gun down at me. I realized now that I had no fear of Ezra. He's already done his damage.

"It's your word against mine. You are in a police station, after all." I grumbled in pain. He was confused by my words. He came closer and suddenly stomped down on my shoulder. I screamed out in pain, hearing the crack of my shoulder blade ringing through my ears. This was the same arm he shot as well. I heard Ben yelling my name as the pain started shooting through my body, causing me to grow weak. I was slowly decaying. Ezra could see it.

At this point, I was looking for Vada. Where was she? I wonder if she will come with him. I saw no sign of her at first. That was when her figure came into view. She stood outside, watching her boyfriend pounce at me. Her lips looked parted from a distance when she saw my wounds.

"Better finish this when I know I'm already going to jail." He grumbled. He got off me and stood his ground over me. My breath was heavy, pain throbbing every bone in my body. My eyes showed it. He pointed his gun up at me. I couldn't help but close my eyes, knowing at that moment I was going to die. I was sweating everywhere.

My thoughts went to Cheyanne. Oh, I wish she was still here so none of this happened. The back of my eyelids showed me the peaceful times. When it was Cheyanne, Vada, and me. We were regular best friends who never had anything mean to say to one another. Our times together were cherished, happy, and surreal.

That was when I heard Ezra yell out, causing my eyes to shoot open. I saw someone jump onto Ezra's back. My vision was blurred; it was hard for me to see. That was when I saw the familiar brown hair and the high-pitched voice yelling. It was Vada—retaliating against Ezra. She used every boost of power she had left against him. She was saving me from him. She started hitting him on the head, screaming at him.

"Leave her alone!" I heard her yell. "Don't hurt her anymore." I watched as Vada attempted to grab the gun from Ezra but couldn't move as fast as him. I was too weak to yell at her. Everything felt as if it was moving in slow motion. My breaths became all I heard for a moment. My head slowly turned to see Leah scooting behind the desk. It looked like the receptionist was pulling her in.

"Get off me, Vada!" I heard Ezra's voice roar through the ringing. When I turned my head back, I saw Ezra reach to grab Vada from the back of her neck. I gasped, knowing what he was about to do. I heard him yell out as he bent down quickly, throwing Vada down next to me on her back. Her body hitting the floor sounded as if it broke into millions of pieces.

"Vada—" I whispered out.

My thoughts were interrupted by multiple gunshots. At first, I thought my life ended when it was Ezra's. He fell back hard on the ground, blood starting to pour all around him, Vada, and me.

I ended up being covered in his blood. This made me nauseous, but the wounds started affecting me.

I had the energy to turn myself in the direction Vada was in. She looked weak, too.

Ezra just took the life out of her, and she knew it. I became scared that he had finally broken her body so severely that she was going to die right here. As much as I had a lot of anger towards her, I still had so much sympathy for her. When I got to her, she slowly opened her eyes, looking at me. Our heads were turned towards one another, shaking as we lay together.

"Thank you," I murmured as she blinked slowly.

"I'm sorry, Emma—for everything. When I saw him—hurt you. I cracked." Vada sounded weak when she spoke. I

Dear Cheyanne

shook my head slowly, slowly reaching my arm out for her. That's when I felt our fingers locked together.

It was forgiveness between us. It warmed my heart, but I knew Vada was about to go to jail. She confessed to being in on it, too. Of course, she needed help first.

"It's okay. I love you." I whispered. I could see Ben running over to me and Tia running to Leah, who was lying on the ground from her wound. He grabbed my phone from the back pocket, handing it to the cops.

"Everything is on here—" I heard Ben speak to the cops. "They both confessed to what they did on it." I wanted to yell out. I didn't wish for Vada to go to jail. After all, she was not the one who killed Cheyanne. It was Ezra; she was just a witness.

Vada knew what she did was wrong. I could tell when I looked into her eyes that she was sorry. She smiled softly at me before cops surrounded her. I then saw the flashing of ambulance lights from behind.

"I love you too," Vada said before we were crowded.

My vision started going fuzzy. I could hear Ben's voice.

"Emma? Emma, can you hear me? Talk to me." Ben called out, cupping his hands against my face to lift my head.

Shortly after that moment, I was gone. I saw nothing but black.

35

All I could see was a white light.
I heard a strange but familiar sound ringing through my ears. I think I am dead. The sound of water crashing against a shore, I was on a beach. The sand was warm on my bare feet. The wind was blowing gently through my hair. The sunset in the distance of the ocean blinded my eyes. It looked like I was on the beach of the Atlantic Ocean on the edge of Oregon. It is beautiful. I sighed at the peace I was in. I enjoyed it. Something was telling me to look to my right. When I did, I saw the one person I'd longed to see. I gasped in excitement. She turned her head towards me, flashing the smile I missed.

"Cheyanne?!" I squealed, tears flooding my eyelids. She looked beautiful. Her hair was wavy, and she wore a white spaghetti-strap dress. She was barefoot, digging her feet into the warm sand. She looked at peace for once.

"Hey, you." She replied. I couldn't help myself. I lunged towards her, hugging her as tightly as I could. I was now sobbing uncontrollably. This was all I wanted in this life was to give her the proper goodbye that I did not get to give her. This is what I needed. I quickly let go of her, looking around at the sights I was seeing.

"Am I—dead?" I asked. She shook her head but gave me the slightest smile. We began to walk towards the beach, sitting down to look over the view.

"No. You are knocked out. I was the first person in your head, so I showed up." She replied, looking back out towards the orange sky in the distance. A small laugh escaped from her lips.

"Well, I've been needing you," I replied as we both gazed towards the sun and the water hitting the shore gently.

"Beautiful, isn't it?" She asked gently. I stayed next to her, looking in the same direction. I couldn't help but smile wide.

"So beautiful. I want to stay here." I spoke, looking towards her.

We sat in the sand together for what seemed like hours. The wind was blowing through our hair. We were silent, but I only enjoyed her company next to me.

"Is this what your world is truly like?" I asked. Cheyanne giggled softly, nodding at my question.

"Yes, it is. Apart from stopping to check on my loved ones." I looked over at Cheyanne. She looked as if she was a pure angel.

"So that was you coming to check on me," I asked. She nodded, looking over at me.

"Of course. I was checking on all of you. Even Vada."

"Vada apologized." I blurted out, causing Cheyanne to snap her neck at me.

"Did she now?"

"Yes. She fought back Ezra when he was hurting me, and – well, she apologized." I said, shrugging my shoulders at the thought. "I forgave her. The last moment I saw her was us holding hands, smiling at each other. I know she's about to go to jail. There was no reason for me to be hard-headed with her."

"You are a good person. I'm surprised she fought Ezra back." Cheyanne spoke. She stayed silent for a moment before letting out a shaky sigh. "I forgive her too. When you wake up and see her again—will you tell her I said that?"

My eyes widened for a moment, almost forgetting I wasn't dead. I wanted to be now. "I don't think I want to go back. I like it here—you could help me go into the—"

"Don't be ridiculous, Emma. You are needed elsewhere. Not here." Cheyanne encouraged, giving me an eyebrow raise like she always used to. That meant she was serious. I scoffed, keeping my eyes on her.

"I've longed to be where I am since you died. My place is by your side. I don't want to go back." I begged. I turned towards her, grabbing her hand so she had her attention on me. "You are alone here."

"I am not alone." She replied. She turned her head as a silhouette formed in the sun's beams. When I saw who it was, I smiled more.

"Thomas!" I squealed, looking up at him. He looked happy. He was thrilled to be back with the person he wanted to be with.

"Hey. Pretty, huh?" He asked, turning towards the sunset. "I sat right there when I got here and saw someone special like you did." He spoke, looking down at Cheyanne. I could see her cheeks turning red from his comment. That meant I did have a chance to stay here with them. I pulled on Cheyanne's hand to get her attention once more.

"Please. Let me stay." I begged. She twisted her lips, shaking her head at my pleading. I sighed, looking down towards the sand. Who needed to live when I had the one person right here? I felt happy, home, and accessible. If this is what heaven is like, I want to live in it forever.

"You will see me when your time comes. But it is not your time yet. Emma O'Connor needs to do more in life before her time is over." Cheyanne explained. "Like Thomas and me. Our times have come, and now we are here In the afterlife, living our best lives. I couldn't imagine it better, but you have more to do."

"I don't want to leave you." I whimpered, tears forming once more in my eyes. Cheyanne frowned, wiping them away and pulling my chin up to look at her.

"Trust me, I will be just fine." She encouraged. "But can you do me a favor and tell Leah something for me?" She asked. I nodded. She leaned down and whispered what she wanted me to say to her, which brought tears to my eyes. "Now, go." She spoke as she stood up. I stood up quickly, too, wanting one more thing before I returned.

"One more hug?" I asked. Cheyanne turned towards me and smiled. She opened her arms wide as I ran into them. I wrapped my arms around her waist as she rested hers on my shoulder. She hugged me tightly, not letting go for a minute. The moment I lived to do again ended quicker than I wanted.

"Goodbye Emma." She whispered. My tears continued to fall, crying at those words.

"Goodbye, Cheyanne. I will miss you so much. I love you," I whispered back. Cheyanne grabbed my cheeks with her soft hands, smiling wide at me.

"I love you too." She whispered, leaning down and kissing my cheeks gently before walking backward. She turned towards Thomas, grabbed his hand, and walked so far that I couldn't see either. Then, they were gone. They were together like they wanted to.

I finally got the goodbye I needed.

Then, everything went white again.

36

When I opened my eyes, I had everyone I loved surrounding me. I saw my parents, Ben, Tia, and even my brother waiting for me. They weren't looking at me, giving me time to process what happened. My hip was sore, as well as my arm. It was wrapped up in a sling. It had to be when Ezra broke it.

I smelled clean. They must have washed me off from the blood that was on my back. My hair was tied up in a braid, which Tia probably did for me. After seeing everything, I decided to clear my throat. Everyone's eyes were on me.

"Hey, honey. You are awake. How are you?" My mom asked. I couldn't say anything. My mouth was so dry. I eye the cup that was sitting on the stand. My dad grabbed it and placed the straw between my lips. I inhaled a small sip before letting out a small sigh and looking at everyone.

"Hi," I mumbled, looking around at everyone. Though I am seeing that one person that should be here too. "Where's Leah?"

"She is in her room. She got shot at as well. I'll tell her parents to wheel her over to you later, okay? Do you need anything? Do I need to get the doctor?" My mom bombarded me with questions. I shook my head to everything. I did not know what to say to either of them. I know I was probably in trouble for everything. I wasn't about to ask things like that.

"What happened?" I asked.

"You were shot at. All because you wanted to hear what he did to Cheyanne from Vada's boyfriend." My dad mumbled.

Oh, Vada.

"What were you thinking? Going into a house willingly, almost getting yourself killed in the process?" My mom started going off on me. I knew it was coming; I just sat there and took it. "You are lucky you weren't too hurt."

"I'm sorry. I just—wanted to hear it from myself. Where's Vada?" I asked. My mom turned towards the twins. It was like they knew more than she did. Ben walked up to me and sat down next to me.

"Ezra was killed when the cops shot at him. Vada was hospitalized for a few days from her injuries, but she was discharged yesterday. The cops came and picked her up. She's in jail now." Ben explained, showing no emotion for either of them.

"How long have I been out?" I asked, looking around. My eyes lingered on the cup of water with a straw in it. Tia saw me and grabbed it. She held it to my lips, taking the drink I've longed for since I woke up.

"You've been out for a week," Ben explained before my dad chimed in.

I sighed at all this information. I wish I could have said goodbye to Vada and told her that Cheyanne forgave her.

I didn't forget about that.

What I saw felt so real.

I groaned; my body started to feel pain. A nurse entered with two kinds of medicine inside a syringe. She started sticking them through my IV to give to me.

"Must be time for medicine." My mom mumbled, turning towards the twins. "Okay, you two. She should get some rest. You can come back and see her soon." My mom commanded. The twin nodded towards her. Tia walked over, grabbed my hand, and smiled down at me. Ben leaned down and kissed my forehead.

"So glad you are okay." He whispered against my skin. Before he could leave, I pulled his arm, making him look me in the eyes.

"Come back and see me in a few hours," I whispered. Ben smirked softly before letting go of my hand and leaving with Tia.

"I'll send Leah in when you wake up." That was when the pain medicine hit through my body, drifting me off into a deep sleep.

* * *

My eyes fluttered open, and when they did. Leah was sitting in her wheelchair next to me. She had a slight smile plastered across her face. When I focused more on her, I could see her entire leg wrapped up in a cast. She had an IV drip hanging from her wheelchair that was stuck into her arm. Her hair was braided up as well.

Tia outdid herself.

"You sleep peacefully but look terrible." She spoke sarcastically with a smirk. I shifted in my bed a bit, sitting more comfortably.

"Don't judge me. These people are pumping me with pain medicine." I grumbled in my sleepish voice.

"Yeah, same here. It feels amazing. I'm due for more medicine in an hour. I just wanted to come see you." Leah replied. She wheeled herself closer to me. As she fixed the blanket, she covered her legs. "How are you?"

"I'm fine. I'm just recovering the best I can. You?" I asked. She shrugged, looking down at her lap.

"I could be better. He shot me in the thigh area. Boy, did it hurt? I heard they killed him. I had blacked out from the pain after the receptionist pulled me back with her." Leah explained.

I tried to return to my memories when I started remembering everything. It made me jump when I heard the gunshots in my thoughts. Leah looked at me concerned, but I gave her a small smile.

"So, he is dead?" I asked with a raspy voice. Leah nodded at my question.

"Yeah. Ben told me they got all the evidence to know what he did. Either way, he was going to be sentenced to life. It was as if they did him a favor." Leah explained more, her eyes wandering down to the ground. It was as if she was feeling the drugs.

"Well, you aren't wrong," I mumbled. That was when I thought about what happened when I was knocked out.

"I saw Cheyanne," I mumbled. I saw Leah look up at me, her facial expressions changing quickly. "She said she loves you; she's watching over you and is proud to be your big sister." I saw Leah's eyes begin to water. She cried as I did, too.

"I love her too. I miss her so much." Leah whimpered, looking up at me. "Will you see her again?" Leah asked. I frowned, shaking my head with the answer I dreaded admitting.

"No. I think she was here to go at peace. Now that Ezra is taken care of. I believe she's where she needs to be. Besides, she's got Thomas." Leah's smile grew wide, loving that her sister was happy where she was. Not to mention, she is safe.

We both heard a knock at the door and saw Ben with flowers. I heard Leah chuckle to herself, turning her head towards me.

"It is about time for medication for me. I better go. I am glad you are okay, Emma." Leah said before wheeling herself out of the room, leaving Ben and me alone. I looked up at him with a small smile.

"Hey." He whispered, slowly walking closer to me.

"Hey," I replied. He placed the flowers before me as I took them in my hands. I inhaled the scent of them, smiling at how good they smelled. "Thank you for the flowers," I said, setting them down in my lap and keeping a grip on them.

"You're welcome. How are you?" He asked, sitting in the chair next to my bed. I shrugged, running my fingers over the petals of the flowers.

"Hm... I'm okay." I replied, still tired after the nap I took. "I'm trying to recover, still in pain," I added. I noticed that Ben had something on his mind and was about to tell me.

"Emma. I hope you never put yourself into a dangerous situation like that again. I felt scared and your family half to death. I thought you died." He spoke gently to me, trying not to yell.

I sighed softly, reaching out for his hand. I twisted my lips at the needle from my IV digging into my skin. I'm not too fond of the needle digging into my arm.

"I'm sorry, Ben. I had to know." I explained. "Cheyanne was my best friend. Nobody tried to help solve this case except for Leah. We did it; now I can continue knowing she has met her peace." I finished. Ben smiled softly.

"I love how caring you are." He complimented, running his thumb over the skin of my hand. His touch caused goosebumps to form on my body.

"It's a good thing I didn't kiss you." I teased while Ben and I exchanged a laugh at my sense of humor.

"Speaking of kiss—" Ben started to speak, but he stopped as a smile grew on my face.

"Are you about to ask if you could kiss me?" I teased more. Ben's cheeks turned red, his smile beaming throughout the room.

"Well, can I?" He asked. We gazed into each other's eyes. I now know what I want.

I wanted him.

He turned my work upside down, making me feel complete after going through a traumatic time. He deserved to be loved like he should.

"Yes, you can," I replied.

Before I knew it, Ben was in my face, and our lips collided with one another; it wasn't a rough kiss. It was gentle, soft, and slow. It was everything I wanted for my first kiss. Our lips moved in sync, his hand touching my cheek to cup it gently. This was the kind of kiss that any girl would dream of having. It wasn't rough or forceful. It was gentle. I loved it. After a minute, our lips disconnected, our eyes looking at one another.

"That was worth the wait—" I whispered as we both exchanged a laugh.

I have felt something for him that I never thought I could feel again. Ben has healed my wounds, which I never thought could happen to me.

I was complete again, and it felt amazing.

Epilogue

6 Months Later

Dear Cheyanne,

I'm okay.

I am okay where I am for the first time in a year.

Everything has gone perfectly since the accident. Though I still have some reoccurring nightmares of getting shot at, those dreams don't define where I am.

The rest of my senior year was a breeze, and I finally lost the name "freak."

I let people into my life finally.

I became acquaintances with Piper Shay and Dylan Summers. For once, they would say hello to me in the hallway, and we didn't hate each other. Piper was thankful for how we made Ezra pay. The two finally considered me a friend.

Though I wouldn't consider them my best friends.

I made my friend group with Tia and Leah. To my surprise, Leah left the popular girls and found out who her true friends were with us.

Ben and I became official right after my accident, and I couldn't be any happier. I got to meet his friend Marissa, and now she and I are talking more than he talks to her.

Bittersweet. She is getting married to her fiancee, Casey, this summer. Ben and I are at their wedding! I can't wait for it!

I am so close to graduating. I have less than a week left. I passed all my finals and can officially brag that I have been accepted to Portland University. I have decided to go to school to become a pediatric nurse. I love kids, which would be an excellent way for me to do so.

I have been going to see Vada at the women's jail once a week. We have been working on rekindling our friendship. I told her about my letters and seeing you. I even told her about you forgiving her. She cried happy tears, thanking you from down below. I hope you saw that side of her. She beats herself up for letting Ezra get in the way of friendship.

I was glad I forgave her and rebuilt our friendship.

Her trial is ongoing, and I have decided to speak out on it. She told me to tell the truth, and I plan on it. By stating she had nothing to do with your death. All of this was on Ezra. I have been telling her everything about my life like I used to with you. She says she is standing her ground with the other prisoners, but the way things go, I believe she will be getting out.

Her parents even come to see her. She apologized to them about everything, and they forgave her, too. She told me her mind feels more open without all the drugs she took. I also told her about Piper's relationship with Ezra, and she felt for her, hoping her life was going better.

I have the old Vada back.

Dear Cheyanne

After our talk on the beach, I finally realized that life is worth living. You must always make the best of it, no matter how bad it is. You made me understand how fragile life is, and it can be taken from you in the blink of an eye. For that, I thank you for everything you've taught me and done for me in the past.

Unfortunately, this is my last letter to you. I must move on with my life and not dwell on my past. This does not mean I will not stop visiting your grave, but now I feel like you are at peace. I can live with that. As I conclude this letter, I miss you deeply, but I know now you are okay where you are. That makes me want to go on.

I will never forget you, Cheyanne Wrangler.

Love and always,

Emma-Jean O'Connor

THE END

What's Coming Up Next ? nm

    Check out my new Vampire Romance series, The Until Series and read an emotional love story of a human, Lorna and a vampire, Devin falling in love in a four-book tetralogy

    For more information about this project, subscribe to my newsletter as I will be talking about this upcoming project more in detail!

Don't forget to sign up for her newsletter down below!

www.aimeelynnauthor.com

Just scroll to the bottom of the home page, fill the box in with your email and you are all set!

About the Author

Aimee Lynn is a 24-year-old who will do anything to get her hands on a good book. Though she did not go to school to become an author, she has had love for writing since she was in 5th grade. She went to college at DeVry University studying Applied Science in Healthcare and graduated in April with an associate degree.

As for writing?

Well, it's a fun thing to do on the side where she can express her ideas and show her love with it while working a full-time job, full-time mother and a girlfriend.

She lives in a cozy home in Ohio with her boyfriend daughter and orange cat Garfield.

Writing has always been a passion for her and throughout the years. She has grown stronger in her English, grammar and word phrases. Why sit and write
these things for herself when she can share her talents with everyone!

Follow Aimee on her social media and keep up with any updates for other projects and more.

Website: www.aimeelynnauthor.com
Facebook: Aimee Lynn Author
Instagram: @aimeelynnauthor
Twitter: @AimeeLynnAuthor
TikTok: @aimeelynn_99

Acknowledgments

I would like to start by saying thank you to my wonderful parents, Mike and Carol, for supporting me through my dreams and pushing me in the right steps of my future. I'd also like to thank my step-parents, David and Maria, for supporting me like I was their own.

I'd also like to add my stepsiblings, Douglas, Kaiden and Gabi for being the best siblings out there and giving me the brothers and sister, I've always wanted.

I'd also like to thank my wonderful boyfriend, Pierce, for supporting me to finish this project. Also, my wonderful daughter Eryn for being my best friend through everything and showing me what love truly is.

I'd also like to thank my grandparents for believing in me as well as my close family for also believing I could do something more with myself.

I'd also like to thank my in-laws for being my second family while also guiding me in the right direction.

I'd also like to thank my wonderful friends for supporting me through all my ups and downs.

Made in the USA
Middletown, DE
13 May 2024